D0842042

PRAISE FOR
COLUMBO: THE GRASSY KNOLL

"Harrington gets every note right and readers will find the action, including the assassination scenes, as vivid as anything on the tube—and without commercials. READERS WILL CLAMOR FOR SEQUELS."

—Publishers Weekly

"A wonderful tale full of spectacular twists and stunning surprises."

—Margaret Truman

"Our greatest detective tackles our greatest unsolved crime—the JFK assassination. A DAZZLING THRILLER YOU WON'T PUT DOWN."

—Jack Anderson, Pulitzer Prize-winning columnist

"William Harrington's first Columbo novel combines the pleasures of the TV series with a serious historical theme—the murder of the President. This is A SMART, FAST AND COMPLETELY CAPTIVATING NOVEL FOR EVERY TASTE."

—Mystery Scene

**Forge Books
also by William Harrington**

COLUMBO: THE GRASSY KNOLL

COLUMBO:
THE HELTER SKELTER MURDERS

WILLIAM HARRINGTON

A TOM DOHERTY ASSOCIATES BOOK
NEW YORK

This is a work of fiction. All characters and events portrayed in this book are fictitious, and any resemblance to real people or events is purely coincidental.

COLUMBO: THE HELTER SKELTER MURDERS

Copyright © 1994 by MCA Publishing Rights, a Division of MCA, Inc.

Cover art by Dan Gonzalez

A Forge Book
Published by Tom Doherty Associates, Inc.
175 Fifth Avenue
New York, N.Y. 10010

Forge® is a registered trademark of Tom Doherty Associates, Inc.

ISBN: 0-812-53026-8
Library of Congress Catalog Card Number: 94-7148

First edition: August 1994
First mass market edition: July 1995

Printed in the United States of America

0 9 8 7 6 5 4 3 2

PROLOGUE

Saturday, August 9, 1969
0914 hours.

> *"Code 2, possible homicide, 10050 Cielo Drive."*
> *"Unit 8L5, roger, responding 10050 Cielo Drive."*
> *"Unit 8L62, will respond 10050 Cielo Drive."*
> *"Columbo, homicide. I'll check out 10050 Cielo Drive."*

0937 hours.

He was not the first homicide detective on the scene. Two other detective lieutenants had also responded to the call and, being closer, had arrived before Columbo did. Four black-and-whites were also there, red and blue lights flashing atop them. As Columbo got out of his car and walked toward an open gate and a driveway, a uniformed officer leveled a sawed-off shotgun at him.

"Take it easy," said Columbo. "I'm on The Job. Lieutenant Columbo. Homicide."

The officer was skeptical. Probably in his judgment this man with the gnawed cigar, uncombed hair, and short raincoat flapping around him could not be an LAPD homicide detective. But he was. He showed the shield.

"What's the story?" Columbo asked.

"It's a goddamned slaughterhouse, Lieutenant," the officer said. "I don't know how many bodies are in there. One in that car over there, too." He nodded in the direction of a white Rambler.

Columbo walked to the car. Inside was the body of a sandy-haired young man. His clothes—a plaid shirt and blue jeans—and the seat of the car were soaked with his blood.

Columbo walked across the parking area, past the garage, and toward the entry to the house.

The house was handsome, not a grand mansion but a comfortable-looking home set in the middle of a clipped lawn. The premises were landscaped with flowers and trees, and a swimming pool was visible beyond one corner of the house.

Not far from the front door stood another uniformed officer, this one cradling a rifle. A second body lay at his feet.

This victim had been savagely beaten and mutilated, his body stabbed repeatedly.

Twenty feet or so beyond this corpse lay another on the lawn: a woman with long, dark hair, wearing a nightgown so bloody it was impossible to tell what color it had been.

Blood spattered the grass and shrubbery. Columbo stepped up on the long, low porch and walked toward the front door. The letters P-I-G were printed in blood on the lower half of the door.

He walked into the living room. A detective he recognized sat on the piano bench but he could not remember his name. The man was in shock. He looked up, stared dumbly at Columbo, and nodded toward the couch in front of the fireplace.

Knowing an experienced homicide detective was not shocked by anything less than horrible, Columbo moved hesitantly toward the couch. He looked over the couch and quickly covered his eyes with his hands.

Lying on the floor was another mutilated corpse, this one of a beautiful young blond woman. She was dressed in a pair of flower-pattern bikini panties and a matching bra, and her blood covered so much of her body it must have been smeared over her. A rope was looped around her throat. The rope hung from a beam in the ceiling, suggesting she had been hanged and stabbed. What was worse, she was hugely pregnant.

A few feet from her lay another blood-drenched body, that of a short man. His head was wrapped in a bloody towel.

One by one, the bodies found at 10050 Cielo Drive were identified.

—The body in the white Rambler was that of Steven Earl Parent, eighteen. He had come to the house the night before to visit a friend who worked there as a caretaker and lived in the guest house beyond the swimming pool. He had come to sell the young caretaker a clock radio. The killers had not intended to murder Steve Parent. He simply had been at the wrong place at the wrong time and had been shot.

—The body near the front door was that of

Voytek Frykowski, thirty-two. He had been shot twice, bludgeoned thirteen times, and stabbed fifty-one times. He was in the house because he was the lover of Abigail Folger, the coffee heiress.

—The body on the lawn was that of Abigail Folger, twenty-five. She had died of multiple knife wounds. She and Frykowski had occupied the house for a few months but were now in the process of moving out. The house had been rented by the film director Roman Polanski.

—The body in front of the fireplace was that of the actress Sharon Tate, twenty-six, the wife of Roman Polanski. She was best known for her role in *Valley of the Dolls*. She had been hanged by the neck before she was stabbed to death. She was eight months pregnant.

—The body lying near that of Sharon Tate was that of Jay Sebring, thirty-five, an internationally known men's hair stylist. He and Sharon Tate had once been lovers but were not anymore, and he was in the house just as a guest.

Sunday, August 10, 1969

Sunday morning two more bodies were found in a home at 3301 Waverly Drive. These two people had been savagely butchered also, in much the same way as the people at 10050 Cielo Drive. They were Leno LaBianca, forty-four, the owner of a string of food stores, and his wife Rosemary La-Bianca, thirty-eight.

Printed in the victims' blood on the walls of the LaBianca home were the words *DEATH TO PIGS   RISE* and *HEALTER SKELTER*.

Monday, January 25, 1971
1127 hours.

Judge Charles H. Older addressed the court. "All jurors and alternates are present. All counsel but Mr. Hughes are present. The defendants are present. Mr. Tubick, has the jury reached a verdict?"

Herman Tubick, foreman of the jury answered, "Yes, Your Honor, we have."

"Please hand the verdict forms to the bailiff."

Columbo watched from the back of the courtroom. He had devoted many hours to solving the mystery of the Tate-LaBianca murders and had become personally acquainted with each of the four defendants.

As he had done several times before, Charles Manson had changed his appearance. He appeared in court today neatly dressed in a white shirt with a blue scarf and with a neatly trimmed goatee. The three young women known as the Manson girls had come to court in their gray jail uniforms. They giggled and whispered. They winked at Manson, and he winked back.

The bailiff handed the verdict forms to the judge, who scanned them and handed them to the clerk. "The clerk will read the verdicts."

Gene Darrow, the clerk, cleared his throat quietly before speaking. "In the Superior Court of the State of California, in and for the County of Los Angeles, the People of the State of California versus Charles Manson, Patricia Krenwinkel, Susan Atkins, and Leslie Van Houten, Case Number A-253,156.

"We the jury in the above-entitled action, find the defendant, Charles Manson, guilty of the crime of murder of Abigail Folger in violation of Section 187, Penal Code of California, a felony as charged in Count I of the Indictment, and we further find it to be murder of the first degree."

The clerk continued to read through the twenty-seven separate verdicts.

—Charles Milles Manson, thirty-six, a.k.a. Jesus Christ, a.k.a. God: guilty of conspiracy to commit murder and seven counts of murder in the first degree.

—Susan Denise Atkins, twenty-one, a.k.a. Sadie Mae Glutz: guilty of conspiracy to commit murder and seven counts of murder in the first degree.

—Leslie Van Houten, twenty, a.k.a. LuLu: guilty of conspiracy to commit murder and two counts of murder in the first degree.

—Patricia Krenwinkel, twenty-one, a.k.a. Katie: guilty of conspiracy to commit murder and seven counts of murder in the first degree.

Manson's hands shook as he heard the verdicts. The girls smiled as though the verdicts had nothing to do with them. When the clerk finished, Patricia Krenwinkel stopped smiling.

"You have just judged yourselves!" she yelled at the jury.

Solving the mystery of the Tate-LaBianca murders, as the case came to be called, had occupied thousands of hours for scores of detectives. One of those was Columbo, who was engaged week after week in the autumn of 1969, checking out leads.

Her autopsy had proved that Sharon Tate had not

been sexually molested before she was killed, but the scantiness of the clothing in which she was found caused some to wonder if she had not at least been stripped. Questioning the housemaid, the caretaker, and Roman Polanski, Columbo learned that matching flowered bras and bikini panties were Ms. Tate's favorite apparel on hot days.

Columbo checked out the suggestion that Leno LaBianca might have been Mafia connected and that his murder was mob related. He learned that LaBianca was known in the Italian community for having no mob connections.

When it began to appear that a ragged collection of assorted misfits that had gathered around a shabby guru named Charlie Manson might have had something to do with the murders, Columbo collared six members of the gang, released four after questioning them, and filed auto-theft charges against two. This brought him into personal contact with Manson, who had been arrested by other officers and was being held. He was present during part of Manson's interrogation, asked him questions himself, and became acquainted with him.

Manson liked to give people nicknames, and he gave one to Columbo: Crisco, meaning Chris(topher) Columbo.

Columbo interviewed the Manson girls. It was a frustrating experience. They had been totally programmed by Manson and, like automata, said only what they thought Manson would want them to say.

Except Susan Atkins, who said many things Manson certainly did not want her to say.

Columbo testified at the Manson trial. His testimony established minor but essential points.

* * *

Manson and the three Manson girls were sentenced
to death, the prosecutor, Vincent Bugliosi, having
remarked that if this case did not deserve the death
penalty, what case ever could? On February 18,
1972, however, the Supreme Court of the State of
California abolished the death penalty in that state.
With their sentences reduced to life imprisonment,
the four became eligible for parole in 1978. Twenty-
five years after the Tate-LaBianca murders, all four
remained in prison.

Why? Why did Charles Manson send these people
to commit such horrible murders?

The most common theory was that he meant to
"bring down Helter Skelter," believing that the
white community would be terrified by these ritual
murders, would turn violently against the blacks,
and generate a race war in the United States. From
the chaos of Helter Skelter, Charles Manson and his
followers would emerge as the new leaders and
rulers of the country.

Most of the members of the one-time Manson
Family are in prison. But not all—

PART ONE

Say, this is some place, isn't it? Khoury . . . Yeah, sure. Khoury, the guy with the great store. No wonder the place looks so beautiful. It comes from Khoury's, it costs money!

ONE

KHOURY'S

The name was on his store on Rodeo Drive, in gleaming stainless-steel block letters—

It was on his license plate—KHOURY. It was on labels securely affixed to ten thousand items of merchandise—IMPORTED BY KHOURY. It was the center of the oval logo fired on the bottom of every plate, saucer, and cup of his line of chinaware—KHOURY & CO. It was engraved on the bottoms of gold and silver cigarette lighters, compacts, pocket flasks, and so on, and on the backs of watches—A KHOURY DESIGN. It was on the labels sewn into his line of lingerie—THE KHOURY COLLECTION. His motion-picture production company was Khoury & Associates.

Discriminating taste was his life: his life's work,

his passion, his chief source of satisfaction. His very name was a synonym for chic. No, for more than that, for elegance.

The name inspired confidence in the people who bought at Khoury's. Since 1946, when his father established the store, the name had connoted urbane and pricey. As they said around town, you couldn't buy tchotchkes at Khoury's. Yussef *père* and now Yussef *fils,* father and son, traveled the world to find merchandise that would honor the name and appeal to their clientèle. They had intuitive eyes for quality. Anything bought at Khoury's was something exquisite, superior for its kind, whatever it was: something simple or something elaborate. A gift might not be what the recipient wanted or had any use for, but the name Khoury's on the box usually made up the deficiency.

The hour was six-thirty, and on an August evening the sun was still high and brilliant. Yussef Khoury could have driven into the store parking lot from the street behind, but he enjoyed driving past, looking at the palm-shaded building and at the stream of customers going in and coming out. His father had had the brick building painted white. The son had had the facade lightly sandblasted, knocking off about half the paint and leaving a dulled white and red surface that was a Beverly Hills landmark. No colored lights shone on the stainless-steel letters that spelled his name. No floodlights shone on the front of the store in the evening. People knew where Khoury's was. They would find it.

His car was a 1954 gull-wing silver Mercedes sports sedan, a classic automobile now worth many times what it had sold for when it was new. Its most distinguishing feature was the doors. Hinged at the center of the roof, they swung up. He drove around the corner and into the parking lot. A uniformed guard and a plainclothesman were always on duty in the lot, and both of them saluted as Khoury drove in. He put the car in the space with his name on it.

"Good evening, Mr. Khoury," said the plainclothesman, as Khoury popped the gull-wing open. "Did you have a good workout?"

"Good evening, Mike. I sure did. With a swim. Best exercise in the world, a swim. Good for the body, good for the mind."

Fifty-four years old, Yussef Khoury was a compact, muscular man of less than average height, with an olive complexion and small dark eyes. He was bald. In past years he had sometimes worn a toupee but hadn't done that for several years. He was dressed as was appropriate for Yussef Khoury —that is, to perfection, in a dark-blue suit tailored to fit him exactly, a monogrammed white shirt, a necktie in the regimental stripe of the Third Royal Welch Fusiliers, and black Gucci loafers. He wore a handsome star sapphire ring and a Khoury wristwatch.

Brushed-aluminum plaques affixed to the rear wall of the building marked two reserved parking places: his own and his wife's. Arlene Khoury's Silver Cloud was not there; and, since she allowed no one else to drive it, he could assume she had left for the day.

He entered the store through the rear entrance, which opened directly onto the main merchandising floor, the ground floor. He glanced around and, with his experience, saw that business was brisk. People were buying, not just looking.

The main floor had departments for jewelry, crystal, china, silver, prints, paintings, small sculpture, and bric-a-brac. Some articles were antiques, but most were of contemporary craftsmanship. Many were museum-quality reproductions. Although the store did not sell clothing, occasionally it would offer a Japanese kimono, a Chinese robe, or something of the like. A popular item was the authentic English "brolly," imported from London: an innovation introduced by Khoury *fils* in 1975, after his father died and could no longer pronounce it trivial. A new department, introduced only in 1987, sold a line of small appliances: digital clocks, telephones and digital telephone-answering machines, coffee makers, multiband radios, and tiny portable television sets—all of them outstanding examples of dramatic yet functional modern design, all of them bearing the Khoury name.

As he walked through the store, sales clerks glanced away from their customers for an instant to nod a greeting. Customers left the counters for a moment to speak to him. A few came to shake his hand and exchange pleasantries.

The store had no windows, so the light inside never varied. It had been carefully designed to display merchandise under the best possible tones —cooler light in the appliances section, warmer in the jewelry section, and so on. No music played. That, in Khoury's judgment, distracted customers from what they were here for: to see and buy. On the other hand, they could step into the Khoury Café and enjoy complimentary coffee or tea while they waited for someone or pondered a purchase. For those who wanted to smoke, there was a smoking lounge with quiet, concealed fans that exhausted the stench and did not allow it to escape into the store.

"Hi, Joe!"

Yussef Khoury suggested his friends call him Joe. Damon Christopher strode across the carpet with outstretched hand. His new film, *Iron Man,* was playing to great reviews and big box office; and his equity in it was going to earn him five or six million dollars, minimum. He was of course a big fellow, like the heroes he played, blond and ruddy faced, with a cleft chin and sensual blue eyes.

Christopher pumped Khoury's hand, then tapped the box he was carrying. "From upstairs," he said with a wide, suggestive grin. "Damned good thing it comes from Khoury's, or she'd never even *consider* wearing it."

He had been to the second-floor lingerie shop. His box was wrapped in the distinctive Khoury aluminum-colored paper and tied with the Khoury ribbon: rich metallic blue. Wherever a package like that went, people immediately recognized it as something from Khoury's.

"I'm glad you found something you like," said Khoury, smiling warmly. "I wish you good luck with it."

"Oh, it will do the trick," said Christopher. "A little argument. This will do the trick."

Christopher slapped Khoury's arm and walked on. He would never have come into the store, probably, if not for the lingerie shop opened in 1975; and he was probably correct in guessing that his wife—if in fact the gift was for his wife—would be far more likely to wear the boldly revealing item in that box because it came from Khoury's. It was a fact that women would wear lingerie from Khoury's that they might have considered cheap and demeaning if it had come from anywhere else.

Khoury had wanted to do the lingerie collection for years before his father died. The old man would never allow it, arguing that it would surely offend some of their lady customers. The son understood otherwise. He had given the second floor over to a group of boutiques, some of them operated by concessionaires—for example, the perfume and cosmetics boutique and the chocolate shop. Placed discreetly out of the sight of those who did not want to shop for scanty undies there, the Khoury Collection boutique was a busy profit center.

Khoury could have taken an elevator up, but he preferred to climb the broad stairway to the second floor, then a narrower stairway to the third.

The third floor was the office floor, where he and his wife, Arlene, occupied executive offices: his a suite, hers a simpler office. All the rest of the administrative functions required for a major retail operation were on the third floor also.

As he walked along the long corridor between the stairs and his suite, the door to his wife's office opened. Her secretary—a dark-haired, attractive woman of forty-six—came out. She was intent on using her keys to lock the office and did not notice him until he was upon her.

"Oh—Hello, Joe," she said, a bit startled.

"Hello, Puss," he said. Her name was Cathy Murphy, but she liked the nickname Puss, so that's what he called her. "How's everything?"

She smiled. "It's a little difficult, you know."

"I know," he said. "Hang in there. We'll do something about it."

He had hired her to work in his own office, as a second secretary. His wife hadn't liked it, hadn't liked an attractive woman with an intriguing past working for him. Arlene had first demanded he send her back to the sales floor, where she had worked before, then had agreed to her remaining on the third floor, provided she would be *her* secretary, not one of his. Arlene didn't like her, just the same, and seemed to take every chance she could find to humiliate her. It was a situation that would have to be remedied, sooner or later, óne way or another.

Khoury knew all about Cathy Murphy. She had spent several years of her life in prison. In fact, she had learned her secretarial skills in the women's reformatory at Fontera. Twenty-five years ago, she had been one of the Manson girls, though not one of those involved in the Tate-LaBianca murders. She had gone to prison for something else entirely. Charlie Manson had bestowed a nickname on her, as he did on most of the girls who clung to him as his "Family": Puss Dogood.

She had dark-brown hair which she still wore long and straight, a style she had adopted when she was a . . . well, a hippie: the word that came to Joe Khoury's mind. She was an attractive woman with regular features and a good figure. She wore no makeup, ever. At work she dressed modestly in blouses and skirts, but he had encountered her in a shopping mall one evening and learned that off duty she dressed like an earth child. He also knew that from time to time she slipped out to smoke a cigarette on the loading dock.

"We'll straighten it out, Puss," he said. "Just hang in and be as patient as you can."

"Thank you, Joe. Your assurance is what makes it possible. Otherwise—"

He held up a hand, stopping her.

"No. Don't think of quitting, Puss. Don't worry, we'll straighten things out."

Cathy Murphy—Puss Dogood—nodded and walked toward the stairs. She stopped and turned. "Joe . . ." She grinned. "If you want to help me get even with her again sometime, just say the word."

Khoury smiled but said nothing and went on into his office.

His secretary was not at her desk in the outer office. She had gone home apparently. But Kimberly was waiting for him. She was sitting on the leather-upholstered couch, smoking a cigarette and reading *Vanity Fair*.

The name she used was Kimberly Dana. She was twenty-nine years old, a tall, slender, athletic young woman, strikingly beautiful: a blonde with near-perfect facial features—accented nevertheless with makeup so skillfully applied that even Khoury could not always be entirely sure it was there. She was an archetypal California beach girl, so much so that she played women's beach volleyball on television and had a small following of fans.

"You know, if you didn't smoke those damned cigarettes you would be utterly perfect," he said to her.

She crushed the cigarette in the ashtray on the table in front of the couch and pulled a breath spray from her handbag. "Only the second one today," she said. "I got bored waiting for you."

"Was Arlene still here when you came in?" he asked.

"No, dear. I waited until the Silver Cloud was out of the parking lot before I came upstairs. Eleanor was gone. The flower child was still here, though."

"Yes. I saw her as I came in. It's hard to believe the double life she leads—working here until six-thirty as the loyal, honest secretary, then going out into the mountains and spending the night with her . . . With whatever you call it. Her commune."

"Her tribe," said Kimberly.

"Well, let's not knock it. Her tribe is going to be very useful to us."

"What we need is in the car. Locked in the trunk."

"Not everything," said Yussef.

He went to a Chinese-style lacquered black cabinet and opened it, exposing a large safe. He worked the combination and swung back the heavy steel door. From inside the safe he withdrew two oval steel batons about seven inches long. They were hollow and perforated with a dozen or so half-inch holes that fit fingertips and afforded a secure grip. Hinged at one end, the two halves of the batons could swing apart.

He handed one to Kimberly. Using both hands, she seized the baton at the end opposite the hinge and pulled the two halves apart. The two halves were in fact the halves of a steel sheath for a six-inch blade. It was a singularly deadly weapon, called a Bali-Song. With the handles closed, the Bali-Song was a heavy bludgeon. With them fully open, that is, swung back against each other, it was a conventional knife. With the handles swung out halfway, to a 90° angle with the blade, an attacker could grip a Bali-Song with both hands and thrust forward with the force of two arms.

It was maybe the most expensive knife in the world. Yussef had never considered offering them for sale in the store, but he had bought half a dozen of them because he admired the design, and he had given several to friends. He had explained to Kimberly when he first showed her a Bali-Song that the Philippines, where they originated, had outlawed them; it was a crime to own one there.

She had smiled and commented, "Well, Joe, you always have the best."

"They will lend a certain elegance to a dirty job," he had said.

She dropped both of them into her handbag before they left the office.

TWO

1

Puss drove an old, battered Chevy Vega. It made smoke and noise and leaked oil, and it barely passed the California emissions tests, but it got her where she wanted to go. Only the pigs were obsessed with cars. Joe Khoury was obsessed with cars and drove that Mercedes that must have cost him enough to feed two dozen families for a year. Arlene drove the Rolls, a nauseating squander. The Vega was car enough for anybody—or had been, anyway, years ago when it was newer.

Nothing was good enough for the royal Khourys. Nothing was good enough for the bloated pigs they catered to. Most of what they sold in the store was utterly useless. Even the useful things were disgustingly extravagant. Stuff that cost a fraction of Khoury's prices would have served people's purposes just as well and maybe even better. What good was a gold-handled letter opener? A little paring knife would open letters better. The store *stank* of moronic extravagance. It was enough to make an honest person vomit.

And none of the nauseating pigs gave a thought to what they wasted or to what the money they threw around could do for human beings in need.

She knew she was right about this. She knew because Charlie agreed with her. She wrote Charlie a long letter every week, and once or twice a year Charlie wrote back: a rambling letter full of wisdom. He told her she was right, so she knew she was right.

She begged him to tell her what to do about Arlene Khoury, but he never responded to that. She didn't know if his advice would be to go on tolerating Arlene's abuse, or to quit her job, or to do something else.

She hadn't seen Charlie for twenty-five years. More than that actually, because the night Charlie sent Sadie and Katie and LuLu and Tex up to Cielo Drive she, Puss, had been in jail in Bakersfield, doing six months for relieving a john of his money and his car. She hadn't seen any of them for more than twenty-five years, because by the time she got out of the Bakersfield jail, all of them were locked up in L.A. and charged with the murders of Sharon Tate and those other people: Folger and Frykowski and Sebring and. . . .

Anyway . . . She never had got all the names just right. Not that they didn't make any difference. They did. Because of them she'd been cut off from Charlie and her very best friends in the world for twenty-five years. As LuLu—Leslie Van Houten—had put it, "You couldn't meet a nicer group of people." *She,* Puss, had never met nicer people. They were her family. The Family.

She smoked a cigarette as she drove. When she got home, she'd smoke something better.

Charlie . . . Anyone who had seen the face of Charlie Manson knew they were seeing the face of God, except the ignorant pigs who *couldn't* see it. She remembered every moment she had ever spent with him, every touch he had ever bestowed on her, every word he had spoken just to her. In the Family her name was Puss Dogood. Charlie gave everyone a name—that is, he gave names to people he cared about. Their new names gave them new identities, in which they could be completely free.

In his letters he still called her Puss. The girls didn't answer her letters anymore. They wanted out and pretended they didn't want contacts with the Family. Sadie—Susan Atkins—even denied now that she had anything to do with the murders. She had stabbed Sharon Tate and had explained why: "You have to have a real love in your heart to do this for people." And now she denied it all.

Squeaky, who was doing long federal time for trying to assassinate President Gerry Ford, was about the only one in prison who had kept the faith. Cute little Squeaky had even escaped once. Prison broke people and apparently had broken the other girls, but it had not broken Squeaky.

Or Charlie. Nothing could break Charlie. By definition. They couldn't break Charlie any more than they could break God. Man's Son. Manson.

Nothing could hurt him. But nothing. Even where he was, he was just as powerful as he had ever been. And he was the world's only hope.

She had done everything she could for Charlie. She had become pregnant by him but had lost the baby, which wasn't her fault. She had worked topless, first as a cocktail waitress, then as a black-jack dealer. She had hustled. She had stolen from johns. All to get money for Charlie, for the Family. She had gone to jail for it, but she had never regretted anything. She knew when she came out the Family would be there, welcoming her back into its circle of love.

But it wasn't there. They had locked up Charlie. The others were still the Family, but it wasn't the same. Squeaky had done what she could to keep them together, but Squeaky wasn't Charlie. Without Charlie, the weak ones drifted away. Only a few still called themselves the Family.

Of those few, two lived with Puss: a man her own age, that is forty-six, and a woman of forty-two who had been only seventeen when the pigs took Charlie away from them and had had love from him only once. The man was Warren Douglas, named Bum Rapp by Charlie. The woman was Jenny Schmidt, named Kid. Three others who did not live with Cathy came to the house nearly every evening. Together, they were a branch of the Family, and they acknowledged Puss Dogood as their leader.

She drove north on the San Diego Freeway and northwest on the Golden State Freeway until she turned off onto Balboa Boulevard and eventually onto a half-paved road called Pitillo Road. The place she and the others rented was a ramshackle, unpainted old house with a rusty corrugated-steel roof. Bum's old Chevy pickup sat in front. The Toyota parked beside it belonged to Buddy Drake, a Family member Charlie had not renamed.

She went in. Someone had been smoking grass; she could smell it; but right now they were drinking beer. The guys wore T-shirts and tattered, faded old jeans; Bum's had both knees out. Kid wore a pair of ragged khaki shorts and nothing more. Even if she wasn't a girl anymore, the guys liked to look at her bare breasts, and Kid had always been accommodating. She had probably accommodated them other ways during the afternoon.

"The working girl," said Bum. "Tillie the Toiler."

"Gimme a joint," said Puss.

"Jeez, sorry, Puss. There isn't any left," said Kid.

Puss had begun to strip out of her workaday clothes. She tossed her blouse onto a chair and lifted her skirt over her head. "We're damn well goin' out and get some," she said.

"Like, after we eat somethin'," said Buddy. "We been waitin' for you and gettin' damn hungry."

Puss stripped naked before she picked up and began to put on her other clothes: a white T-shirt with dark-blue stripes, plus a pair of jeans with holes in the knees, like Bum's. She felt no hesitation about changing clothes in front of Bum and Buddy and Kid. They were, after all, her sister and brothers. Besides, privacy had never been important to her. She'd never had any.

"Okay," she said. "But we're goin' out and get some. I feel like a swim, too. Go to the beach maybe."

2

Arlene Khoury and Steve Heck sat beside the swimming pool at Casa Khoury—the name another Khoury affectation—and sipped Scotch while they watched the sun set into the Pacific. The ridgetop house had a view of the city and the ocean on a clear day. Both wore swimsuits styled for people with better-cared-for physiques.

Arlene was her husband's age, fifty-four. Unlike him, she did not work out in a gym, though he encouraged her to, and she had not aged elegantly; she was no longer a Khoury trophy. She smoked heavily, which had thickened her complexion, and she drank heavily, which had thickened her body. Because her cosmetician and hairdresser labored over her, her hair remained jet black and was stylishly cut, but her face spoke age and weariness. Her belly bulged out over the top of her bikini bottom.

Steve was forty-five. He had sandy hair and laughing light-blue eyes. He had a ready, winning smile and made friends easily. The sun was not kind to him; he turned tan on his arms and shoulders, red on his chest and belly and hips, tan again on his legs, and freckled all over. At Arlene's urging, he wore a green bikini bottom as skimpy as hers. It pinched in his paunch and made it spill forward.

"I can't stop feeling odd about this," he said. "I mean, we ought to go out someplace."

"You mean shack up in a motel? That's what *he's* doing."

"Some night he's gonna walk in on us."

"How many times do I have to tell you?" she asked impatiently. "When he drives up to the gate, he uses his radio controller to open it. That activates the GATE-OPEN signal and switches on the driveway camera. We can look up at the screen and see the Mercedes coming. At that point you have three minutes to scram if that's what you want to do, or three minutes to grab a drink and sit down in the living room. It's plenty of time for either."

"I don't like the idea of scramming, like some naughty kid. I don't like the idea of sitting in his living room, drinking his Scotch, and pretending to be his friend, when I'm balling his wife and . . . Well, you know what I mean."

"And stealing him blind," said Arlene.

"I can't believe he doesn't know it," said Steve, shaking his head.

"If he knew it, we'd know he knew it. Joe never could hide his feelings."

"He's got a temper, too," Steve said.

"Not really," said Arlene. "He's more the cool, calm plotter type. Phlegmatic is the word."

"Even so, I wouldn't want him walking in on us some night."

THREE

1

Khoury always made it a point with parking-lot attendants that they should handle the gull-wing Mercedes carefully, park it in front where they could see it, and watch out for someone who might want to make off with an eminently stealable antique automobile. Jorge Mendez did more. As he had time during the evening, he would wipe it down, making sure no trace of dust sullied its waxed surfaces. He knew that Mr. Khoury and his lady friend would not stay overnight but would leave the motel an hour or so after midnight, and to assure his ten-dollar tip he would be sure the car was ready and gleaming. If he had been still in New York, where he had worked at the same kind of job before he came to California, he would have started the car and warmed it up on a cold night.

"Good evening, Mr. Khoury. Welcome," Mendez said, as Khoury pulled into the valet area of the Piscina Linda motel.

"Good evening, Jorge," said Khoury to the attendant. "You'll take care of it as usual?"

"Absolutely, Mr. Khoury. Your car is never out of my sight. I keep it right out here in the light, where I can see it all the time."

As Khoury handed over his keys, Kimberly Dana entered the hotel. The lobby was decorated in a style that might have been called Southern California gothic: a nod, not quite a bow, in the direction of Mexico, with more of a concession to what Americans might suppose they would find in Mexico than anything they would ever find there. Red lights. Dark wood. Dark-red carpet. Cantinas did not look like Piscina Linda, but many Americans thought they did. Ten years ago this motel had been a chic place, visited by chic people. Today it was more often visited by people doing what Joe and Kimberly were doing—and wanted to do it in some style.

"Good evening, Mr. Khoury," said the desk clerk. "Welcome to Piscina Linda."

"Good evening, Frank. Pleasant evening, huh?"

"Yes, sir. Your suite is waiting as usual. Will there be anything?"

"Well, just the coffee service as always," said Khoury. "At midnight."

"Oh, yes, sir. We'll take care of that."

The desk clerk did not ask Khoury for an imprint from his credit card. He did not ask him to sign the register. He simply handed him a key, which he knew Khoury would drop at the desk sometime after midnight. The motel would send a bill to Khoury's. A check would come in a few days.

Frank did not know the name of the beautiful young woman who came to Piscina Linda with Mr. Khoury. He only knew that she was like everything else about Mr. Yussef Khoury—choice, exquisite, and no doubt very expensive. As always, she carried a capacious Louis Vuitton leather-trimmed drawstring bag, and Frank wondered what Khoury Collection lingerie she had inside. He admired what she was wearing, too—though he had no idea what to call it.

She was in fact wearing an ivory-colored longsleeved, high-necked blouse, trimmed on the pockets and cuffs with black stripes and gold buttons. She was also wearing a black carwash skirt: calf-length skirt with multiple slits thigh high, the fabric slipping away from her legs as she walked, the way the felt strips in a carwash slide over a car. Very stylish, Frank thought.

Yussef and Kimberly went to their suite, which he had reserved by a telephone call that morning. There were only two suites in Piscina Linda, both on the top floor, identical. Each consisted of a sitting room furnished with couch, coffee table, chairs, a television set, and a small round table that could serve as a desk or dining table. The bedrooms were furnished with a king-size bed, another desk, chairs, and another television set.

Once inside, they kissed ardently. But they did not stay in the suite. He visited the bathroom for a moment, and then they went downstairs for dinner.

They asked for and always got the same table, overlooking the swimming pool from which the motel took its name. It was an immense pool, set partly in living rock. Other rock had been hauled in and built into grottoes and coves. The water circulated through pumps that lifted it some six feet and released it into a pond that overflowed, making a waterfall. Palms and tropical shrubbery grew in pots all around the pool. The bar and dining room opened onto the pool, though air curtains— streams of air blown upward from a line of nozzles in the floor and drawn into vacuum holes in the ceiling—kept out all but stormy weather.

Piscina Linda employed models to swim in the pool and sit around in bikinis in gaudy flower patterns: absurd simulacra of Polynesian maidens. Otherwise, the pool was the province of children, sent there to amuse themselves while their parents were in the bar or dining room, from where they could see the children clearly through the air curtains.

Yussef drank Glenfiddich Scotch, Kimberly a Bombay gin martini.

"Nervous?" she asked him.

He tossed back the last of his drink and signaled for another. "Yes. Aren't you?"

"Sure. I wish we could get on with it. I wish we didn't have to wait. But everything depends on waiting. We can't go before it's dark. Besides, it's essential that we keep to our routine here. We've been careful enough to establish it, so let's not attract attention by breaking it now."

"We'll have to keep to the routine for a while," said Yussef. "God! To dine in a motel!"

"They do their steaks alright," she said. "It's not what you'd call a sacrifice to eat here."

"I suppose so. The wine list is . . . undistinguished."

"Let's change the subject," said Kimberly. "Have you given any more thought to a property?"

"I've been thinking more about what we're going to do to get the money for a property."

"I want you to read a novel. *Altarpiece,* by Daniel Lake. See if you don't think it's just perfect. What's more, he's been writing a long time and has never sold a book to a producer. You won't have to bid at an auction to get *Altarpiece.*"

"I might, if somebody sees in it what you see."

"That's why we should move quickly. I think it's perfect. It'll need acting ability, but we can expose the bod, too. I know you'll like it."

He reached across the table and put his hand on hers. "We don't have to expose the bod, Kim. You've got star quality without showing skin."

Kimberly grinned. "Insurance," she said.

They ate steaks and drank a bottle of Glen Ellen red. About nine they went up to their suite. With two hours, almost, remaining before they could leave, they went to bed.

In bed too, Kimberly was like everything else in Yussef Khoury's life, to the extent he could control it; she was superb. He was conscious that he was not, not in the sense that she was. She was superb even in maintaining the pretense that he was all she could ever want from a man. He was glad, anyway, that he kept himself in good shape, working out at the gym, taking treatments to keep his face taut and smooth. If he was not in the prime of life, he was not far beyond it. He had good muscle tone. Beyond that he had not lost his courage or his optimism, which was crucial if he were going to do what she had urged him to do tonight.

Not long after eleven they got up. Kimberly opened her bag and took out clothes. She put on a pair of tight blue jeans and a gray T-shirt, lettered UCLA ATHLETIC DEPARTMENT. She pulled on blue Adidas running shoes. Yussef changed into khaki slacks and a dark-blue golf shirt. He had not brought shoes and kept on his Gucci loafers and black socks.

Kimberly left the motel first, going down the back stairs and through the rear parking lot. Being lithe and strong, she nimbly threw herself over the five-foot chain-link fence and dropped into a field of weeds. Yussef followed her a minute later. He needed two tries to clear the fence, but two were enough. They hurried through the weeds and onto the street behind the motel.

Waiting on the street was the green Oldsmobile Cutlass she had rented the day before.

2

Casa Khoury stood on Mulholland Drive, at the crest of a ridge in the Santa Monica Mountains. Wearing white cotton gloves—they had never touched her rented car with their bare hands—Yussef drove slowly along the drive. A hundred yards from his home, he pulled off into the driveway of a house belonging to a neighbor who was in Europe. Leaving the Oldsmobile out of sight from the road, Kimberly and Yussef armed themselves with the Bali-Songs and with two nine-millimeter pistols.

They walked along Mulholland Drive toward Casa Khoury and within minutes were at the gate. Yussef led Kimberly to the right, up a little mound and down the back side, then to a clump of brush where the day before he had hidden a short stepladder. He set it up, climbed it, and jumped down inside the fence. Kimberly did the same, and they pulled the ladder over the fence and laid it down flat.

Inside the fence they paused and listened for a moment. The alarm system in the house was never turned on until the people inside retired for the night. It was not on now, and it was safe to walk directly up the driveway.

The rooms at the front of the house were dimly lighted, only by light shining from the rear rooms.

The kitchen lights burned bright, glowing through the windows and lighting much of the west lawn. Lamps in the master-bedroom suite cast a warmer light.

Yussef used his key to unlock the front door, then turned the knob with his gloved hand. He and Kimberly walked into the marble-floored entry hall.

Kimberly had never been in the house before and stood staring, wide-eyed, at the opulence of Casa Khoury: at paintings on the walls, at tall vases on brass stands, at a palm growing in a huge stone pot. She was struck, too, by the parallel between the house and the store. It was as though Joe had furnished the place from the store—which of course he had.

Yussef beckoned her to follow him. He opened the door and glanced into the living room, which was quiet and almost dark. Then they moved along a hall toward the rear of the house. The hall branched, and they turned right into another hall, this one lushly carpeted.

Yussef stopped before a pair of double doors. He pointed at her handbag, and Kimberly pulled out the two Bali-Songs. They unfolded them, exposing the blades. He turned the knob slowly and opened the doors.

They walked into the master-bedroom suite. The outer room was a small sitting room, cozily furnished in English-country style. The door to the bedroom was ajar.

Yussef and Kimberly paused for a moment, as if they shared a thought: that they could still back off and not do what they had come here to do. She shifted her knife to her left hand and extended her right hand toward him. For a moment they stood, squeezing each other's hands. Then they released each other, and moved toward the bedroom door.

As Yussef reached for the door, they heard an ecstatic moan.

FOUR

They caught Arlene Khoury and Steve Heck in flagrante delicto. They were naked, and he was on top of her. Grotesquely, his foot was in a boxed pizza, which in his passion he did not seem to realize.

Arlene screamed.

Steve rolled off of her and turned to face Yussef, who was on him like a pouncing cat, the handles of the Bali-Song extended at right angles to the blade and gripped in his two hands. Steve raised his arms to deflect the deadly blow he saw coming, but the two-handed thrust of the Bali-Song drove past his arms, and the blade plunged into his chest. Yussef twisted the knife, then withdrew it and shoved it in again. Then again.

Arlene screamed—until she choked on the blood

coming up in her throat. Kimberly's first thrust had
driven the blade under her lowest left rib and
upward into her lung and heart. The second stab
glanced off a rib, and the blade cut through her
heart a second time. Her scream diminished to a
groan.

Arlene and Steve lay quiet, still alive. They
stared at Yussef and Kimberly, uncomprehend-
ing and unbelieving, as they coughed up their life
blood, as it streamed from the wounds in their
chests. They couldn't move. They could do nothing but know death, feel its unstoppable ad-
vance.

Yussef opened Arlene's handbag and dropped a
wadded handkerchief inside.

For a moment Yussef and Kimberly stood paralyzed by the enormity and horror of what they had
done. Then—

"¡Asesinato! ¡Sangre! ¡Socorro! ¡Socorro!"

Kimberly and Yussef swung around. Sergio, the
houseboy, was at the door, staring at them and at
Arlene and Steve. Damn! He wasn't supposed to be
there.

Kimberly leaped toward him as he spun around
to run. Gripping her Bali-Song by one handle, she
swung the other as a bludgeon. It hit him on the
back of his head, and he stumbled and fell. In an
instant she was over him, driving the blade into his
back.

"¡Policía!" he muttered as blood choked off his
breath. *"¡Socorro!"*

Sergio lay in front of the small green-and-white
vine-pattern sofa in the sitting room of the master-

bedroom suite. He choked and moaned. Kimberly stabbed him twice more.

"I thought you said he wouldn't be here," she said to Yussef.

"He should have been in the other wing. He wouldn't have been able to hear us from there."

"Maybe it's just as well. Three are better than two, if you think about it."

Yussef nodded. "We have work to do. Let's get to it. I don't want to leave the Oldsmobile parked any longer than necessary."

Kimberly knelt beside Sergio and drove her knife into him a dozen more times.

Yussef did the same to Steve, punching the blade into his body a score of times, then more.

When Kimberly returned to the bedroom, Yussef was standing over Arlene, staring at her.

"I'll do that one," she said. "You start some of the other stuff."

Yussef nodded. With a gloved finger, he touched one of the wounds on Steve's body and soaked up blood. With the blood he printed on the wall above the bed—

HEALTER SKELTER
POLITICAL PIGGY

Kimberly stabbed and stabbed at Arlene's silent body. Then she turned away from her and walked into the sitting room. Sergio's blood was easiest to soak up, because he was on the floor. She soaked a gloved finger in it and printed on the sitting-room wall—

ALL PIGGYS DIE
DIE!
WHO NEXT?

Now they pulled off the blood-soaked gloves and stuffed them into a Baggie. They put on fresh gloves.

Yussef had other work to do. From Kimberly's bag he took out a burglar tool: a foot-long bar with a flat blade at one end, a round knob on the other. He left the house by way of the hall and the kitchen door and came around to a window on the rear of the house. Lying in the shrubbery where he had left them yesterday were a piece of two-by-four and a heavy rag. He jammed the blade end of the bar into the crack between the window and its sill, wrapped the rag around the knob to muffle the sound, and began to pound.

This was touchy. If a neighbor heard . . . But he pounded steadily, and after half a dozen whacks the blade broke away wood and penetrated. Shoving down on the bar, he pried the window upward. The simple latch broke, and the window slid up, open.

He tossed the two-by-four across the lawn, into some shrubbery near the fence, dropped the rag, and carried the bar back into the house.

In the kitchen he saw why Sergio had been in the main house and had heard Arlene's screams. He had been heating a can of tomato soup, a late-night snack. It was boiling vigorously. Yussef left it alone. It would burn and set off the smoke alarms.

Back in the bedroom suite, he discovered to his disgust that in his hurry to get outside and do his work, he had stepped in Sergio's blood and left footprints on the white carpet of the sitting room of the bedroom suite. Also, dirt from beneath the shrubbery had become stuck to his loafer. He scrubbed his shoe on the carpet, then stared at the soles, to be sure no blood remained on them.

Kimberly sat on the green-and-white couch, looking glum. She shuddered. "Let's get out of here," she said.

2

They used the ladder they had left inside the fence and climbed over again. In minutes they were back at the Oldsmobile, where they hid the Bali-Songs and the burglar tool in the tire well.

Yussef drove the car to a telephone booth. Kimberly got out, went to the booth, and punched in 911.

"Police emergency."

She mimicked a Spanish accent. "I work a party, Mulholland Drive. Just leave. Go past Khoury house. Yussef Khoury house. Something wrong there. Strange peoples there. Running around house. Not kind peoples Khourys invite their house."

"What's your name, ma'am? And where are you calling from?"

"Call from phone boot'. No name. Don't want get mixed up."

She hung up the telephone and returned to the car.

Back in their suite at Piscina Linda they found the coffee service that had been brought up at midnight, filling their standing order. The ten-dollar bill, the tip, was gone.

They poured two cups of coffee, drank a part of each, then poured all but a little of what remained in the Thermos carafe down the bathroom basin.

They changed into the clothes they had worn in the dining room and stuffed the others into Kimberly's bag. They switched off the television set, left the room, and went downstairs. Knowing their habits, Jorge, the parking attendant, had already brought the gull-wing Mercedes to the door. He held the door open for Kimberly and saluted Yussef with a bow and a happy grin.

"Good night, ma'am. Good night, Mr. Khoury. Hope to see you again soon."

"You will, Jorge," said Yussef, handing a ten-dollar tip from the car window. "You will."

3

Kimberly drove the Oldsmobile to Santa Monica, then up the highway to the beach at San Luis Rio. Two fishermen still sat on the pier, and she had to wait until almost three o'clock before she could walk out on the pier alone. At the end of the pier she dropped the two Bali-Songs and the burglar tool into the water. Then she threw in two blood-stained white cotton gloves and finally, the Baggie that had contained the gloves.

As she drove back, she switched on the radio in the car. Breathless reports of the grisly murders at the Khoury home on Mulholland Drive already eclipsed every other story on the news.

FIVE

Columbo pulled up to the gate to the Khoury estate. The officer on duty there recognized his beat-up old Peugeot and the license 044 APD, and he opened the gate, saluted, and pointed to a place where Columbo could park to the right of the driveway.

Emergency equipment filled the long drive: black and white police cars, seven or eight of them, and two emergency-squad ambulances sat nearest the door, their red and blue lights flashing for no particular reason. People hurried in and out of the house, some of them carrying pieces of equipment. Columbo walked up the driveway, his raincoat flapping around him in the wind, which ruffled his dark hair, too. He stopped for a moment to light the stub of cigar he carried between his lips, but the wind blew out his match, and he tossed it aside with manifest impatience and strode on toward the house.

A sergeant stepped out and came toward him. He recognized Columbo. Most men on the force did. "Good morning, sir. We've got a triple homicide here."

"Yeah, I know. They called me. Woke me up." His New York accent still sounded in his voice, even after all the years in California. "I wouldn't know if there's rest for the wicked. Or maybe I would. Maybe I'm wicked. I sure find it hard to get any rest."

"The victims are Mrs. Arlene Khoury, a man identified as Steve Heck, and a houseboy we know so far only as Sergio."

"Where is Mr. Khoury?" asked Columbo.

"In one of the guest rooms in the west wing," said the sergeant. "Sedated. Dr. Amos is with him. He got home about"—he stopped and looked at his notebook—"a little before two o'clock. Our people were already on the scene, and he wasn't taken in to look at the bodies. Even so, he went into shock, and one of the patrolmen called his personal physician."

"You in charge?" Columbo asked.

"No, sir. Detective Sergeant Jackson has been here since three o'clock or so."

"Well, I guess I'd better go in and talk to him."

He found him sitting on a couch in the living room, talking intently to a younger man. "Hi, Jackson."

"Columbo. About time."

Detective Sergeant Ted Jackson was a twenty-year veteran of the force, a handsome man with thick white hair and a ruddy complexion, dapper in a checked dark-blue and white jacket and dark-blue trousers. He had served as a uniformed officer for eleven years, reaching the rank of sergeant before he was assigned to the detective division. He was known as a highly practical man, unimaginative and plodding but street-smart and effective.

He had been the first detective on the scene, arriving about three in the morning. Having viewed the bodies and decided the deaths were not accidental or self-inflicted, he had called headquarters and asked that the homicide division take over the case. The captain had awakened Columbo about six and asked him to go directly to the Khoury house on Mulholland Drive.

"So whatta we got?" Columbo asked.

"We got three victims," said Jackson, reading from the notes he had written with a blunt pencil on the lined pages of a pocket notebook. "Mrs. Arlene Khoury, a guy named Steve Heck, who was apparently a business associate and friend of both Khourys, and the houseboy, for which we've so far only got the name Sergio. The guys found the bodies of Mrs. Khoury and Heck in bed in the master bedroom—nekkid, probably'd been doin' it. They found the body of the houseboy first, on the floor of the sitting room just outside the master bedroom. Each of them had been stabbed a minimum of twenty-five times, says the medical examiner. The words 'Helter Skelter' are written in blood on the bedroom wall. Only misspelled—'H-E-A-L-T-E-R Skelter.'"

"Who's here? SID?"

"Right. And the doc from the coroner's office."
He turned to the young man sitting beside him.
"This is Mulhaney. Mulhaney's the SID man."

Sergeant Timothy Mulhaney commanded the
unit from Scientific Investigation Division. He
knew the celebrated Lieutenant Columbo was coming, and he stared in disbelief at the dishev-
eled figure talking to Jackson. Mulhaney's father,
who had been a police officer for thirty years,
had often spoken of Lieutenant Columbo—and
had sometimes spoken in droll Irish terms, de-
scribing Columbo as an eccentric, to say the
least—but he had not prepared his son to con-
front this odd little man with his tattered raincoat,
flying hair, stub of cigar, and unpressed brown
slacks.

Mulhaney was a product of a special, federally
funded program at Cal State, which would train a
student in criminology if he would agree to serve a
four-year apprenticeship with an urban police
force. He had never served in uniform but had
made an outstanding record in crime-scene investigation and lab work, which had resulted in his
being made a detective at the end of his four years
and a detective sergeant two years later. He was a
tall, solemn young man with neatly trimmed hair,
wearing round, plastic-rimmed glasses and a dark-
gray suit pressed and brushed.

"Sir," said Mulhaney to Columbo, "it's a pleasure to meet you. I've heard your name for many
years."

"Well, thank ya, Mulhaney," said Columbo. He

spoke warmly and nodded, but his attention seemed fixed on the stub of his cigar. "Uh . . . anybody gotta match?" he asked.

Jackson had a lighter. He snapped it, and Columbo pulled flame into the cigar.

"The medical examiner fixed the time of the deaths as about midnight," said Mulhaney. "We're taking pictures. Also blood samples, urine samples, samples of vomit—"

"All that?" asked Columbo.

"Violent death makes the body let go," said Mulhaney. "All the fluids run out. Solids, too."

"Yeah. So I've noticed," said Columbo. With the stub of his cigar afire, he took a puff. He glanced around. "Say, this is some place, isn't it? Khoury . . . Yeah, sure. Khoury, the guy with the great store. No wonder the place looks so beautiful. It comes from Khoury's, it costs money! Hey, I went in there one time to look at a—Well, never mind. So it's Mrs. Khoury, a Mr.—What'd you say? Heck? And the houseboy."

"With printing on the walls, in blood," said Jackson. " 'Helter Skelter.' 'Death to pigs.' Like that. You've seen it before." He turned to Mulhaney. "Lieutenant Columbo was one of the detectives that worked on the Tate-LaBianca murders."

"It's sickening," said Mulhaney. "They dipped their fingers in blood and wrote on the walls."

Still puffing to keep his cigar burning, Columbo shook his head. "I wouldn't put too much emphasis on that," he said. "In the last twenty-five years we've seen several of these cases—people trying to cover up very ordinary murders by writing that kind of stuff in blood on the walls."

"Except we've got somethin' else with this one," said Detective Jackson. "One of the original Manson girls worked for the Khourys, at the store."

"How'd ya know?" asked Columbo.

"Mr. Khoury. One of the boys told him somebody had smeared Helter Skelter on the bedroom wall, and he yelled out a name—Puss Dogood! Then he said Puss Dogood was Cathy Murphy. That was about all he got out before the doctor gave him a shot. I had the woman picked up this morning, with two of her friends. They couldn't account for where they were last night. We've got 'em in custody."

"The bodies?" asked Columbo.

"Still here. You know we never move them until the homicide man gets here."

"Yeah. Which means I gotta look at 'em."

2

The bodies were covered with blood-spotted white sheets, but an officer pulled those off when Columbo came into the bedroom suite. The officers working there stepped out to let the lieutenant see it all as they had found it.

"Boy, is somebody gonna have to redecorate this place," he muttered to Jackson and Mulhaney.

The carpet was white. The walls were white. So much white had highlighted the vivid colors of the upholstery and bedclothes and the paintings and prints on the walls. Now it afforded a ghastly contrast with the bloodstains and the garish lettering in blood, now all dried to a reddish brown.

The blood of the houseboy stained the carpet of the sitting room—a broad asymmetrical stain. He lay facedown. It was difficult to tell what color his shirt might have been; his blood had dyed every square inch of it an ugly reddish brown.

Most of the other two victims' blood had soaked into the sheets and mattress of the king-size bed. The body of the man lay with his head against the headboard, his shoulders on two pillows. The body of the woman lay on her back with a pillow under her hips. The eyes were open. The bodies had been mutilated by repeated stabs to the genitals, but no part of either torso was without a wound.

"Nothing's been moved?" Columbo asked.

"No," said Mulhaney. "The medical examiner estimated the time of death by the condition of the bloodstains. He hasn't touched the bodies."

"Odd . . ." Columbo muttered.

"What's odd, sir?" asked Mulhaney.

"Well, if they haven't been moved, then they died right like that, lying there just the way they are. Wouldn't you think somebody seeing a knife attack coming would have rolled over or somethin', trying to get away from it? I don't see any cuts on the arms. Wouldn't they have put their arms up, trying to stop the knives coming at them?" He pointed at the bodies with the stub of his cigar. "This looks like they were doing it, alright. And he just rolled off her. But . . ." Columbo paused to scratch the top of his head. "People killed with knives don't just lie back and die, like you see on television. The murderer has gotta stab and stab and stab, like in the movie—I mean *Psycho.* This pair— Tell the examiner to look for slugs. Maybe they were shot first. Tell him to check for somethin' in the blood, like they were drugged and couldn't move."

"That could have been," said Mulhaney. "I found four rocks of crack cocaine wrapped up in a handkerchief in Mrs. Khoury's handbag."

Columbo looked up, his curiosity piqued. *"You* found it. Who else knows about it?"

"Just Sergeant Jackson," said Mulhaney.

"Just the three of us know about it?"

"Right," said Mulhaney. "Just the three of us."

"Don't talk about it," said Columbo. "You'll have to put it in the inventory and hand it over at the property room. But don't tell the news guys, and don't tell anybody else—except maybe Captain Sczciegel. Our little secret. Might be very handy down the road."

"Gotcha," said Jackson.

"When was that pizza delivered, you suppose?" Columbo asked, pointing at the pizza smeared across the bed.

"I called to find out," said Jackson. "Ordered at eleven-oh-seven. Guaranteed delivery within half an hour."

"Who delivered it?"

"They don't know. They're checking."

"Fixes a time when they were alive, probably," said Columbo.

"Right. Anyway, whoever killed them broke in through a window on the back of the house."

"Let's see."

The three men went through the kitchen.

"The smoke alarms were howling when the first units arrived," said Jackson. "Somebody had been cooking tomato soup, and it burned."

Outside, Jackson showed Columbo where the window had been pried open with a burglar tool.

"Not good work, Jackson," Columbo said, shaking his head. He pointed at the ground, at footprints on the soft earth between the foundation shrubbery and the wall. "Wonderful footprints—"

"I'm afraid—" Mulhaney started to say.

"Yeah," said Columbo. "Those are the footprints of the big brogans of the uniformed cops that checked all this out. Tell 'em to stand back next time, Jackson."

"They did better over by the fence," said Jackson. "Lemme show you."

Columbo and Mulhaney followed Jackson to the chainlink fence. There, inside and outside the fence, plaster was drying in footprints in the soft earth. SID had been at work.

"And look at the ladder," said Jackson, pointing at the short stepladder lying just outside the fence. "They're going to try to lift prints off it, though I don't think we've got much chance getting them off wood."

"Scenario," said Mulhaney. "The perps brought the ladder with them, used it to climb the fence, and used it to climb back out. Two sets of footprints are deep, suggesting they jumped down from the ladder."

"How many, y' figure?" Columbo asked.

"Not sure," said Mulhaney. "There are two kinds of prints: leather-soled shoes and the distinctive imprint of some brand of running shoes. All running shoes have special patterns in the soles. So—two people? Could be. Yeah, probably. Maybe three, two wearing the same kind of shoes. We'll know better when we get exact measurements."

"Any prints between the fence and the road?"

"Possibles. Pressure places. Nothing distinct."

"Well, there's a footprint in blood in the sitting room," said Columbo. "Be sure you get a trace."

"Yes, sir," said Mulhaney. "And we'll match the trace to the plaster casts."

"Now y' talkin'," said Columbo, slapping Mulhaney lightly on the arm.

They went back inside the house, to the utility room inside the broken-open window.

"Now, that's odd, too," said Columbo, again scratching his head. "Now, that's very strange."

"I'm beginning to feel like a straight man, Lieutenant," said Mulhaney, "but I'd appreciate knowing what's strange."

"Well, look here, Mulhaney. When the pry bar was pounded in, it splintered the wood of the sill. See? Splinters. Now, to climb in that window, you'd have to put your body down on the sill and kind of crawl over the sill and in. Right? So, how is it that those splinters still stick up? Wouldn't somebody crawlin' across that sill—putting his belly down on it or putting his backside down on it—have pressed the splinters flat?"

Mulhaney glanced at Jackson. He nodded. "And maybe the splinters would have caught on the perp's clothes and left a thread or two."

"There y' are," said Columbo. "Good thinkin'. That's the way you figure things out." He pulled a small spiral notebook from a pocket of his raincoat and began to pat his pockets. "Anybody have a pencil?" he asked. "Mrs. Columbo puts a nice new yellow pencil in my pocket every morning and—I bet it's on the floor of the car. I ought to make a note here."

"You're not buying the idea it was done by the last Manson girl," said Jackson. "Her and her friends."

"Well, you never know about these things," said Columbo. "We gotta get it all straight."

"You know what yesterday's date was?" asked Jackson.

"Uh . . . August ninth. That special?"

Jackson nodded. "It's the twenty-fifth anniversary of the Tate-LaBianca murders. To the day."

"Really? Twenty-fifth . . . anniversary. To the day. Well, they say time flies, and that makes it for sure. It does fly. Twenty—Are you sure?"

"If I wasn't, the news guys would have made me sure. They're already saying this was a Tate-LaBianca copycat crime."

Columbo shook his head. "When they get the name of this young woman, uh . . . What's her name?"

"Cathy Murphy, also known as Puss Dogood. When the news boys get their hands on the name Puss Dogood—"

"Yeah," said Columbo, smiling grimly. "They'll think they've died and gone to heaven."

SIX

Having authorized the removal of the bodies, Columbo moved into the living room, where he lit a fresh cigar and listened to the reports of several members of the Scientific Investigation Division.

Detective Madge Wilson was in charge of a team of three that was lifting fingerprints. "We've made matches," she said. "The house is full of fingerprints, naturally, but we haven't found any that belong to anybody but people who had reason to be here: the Khourys themselves, Mr. Heck, the houseboy, the cook . . . and so on. Unfortunately, we've also found some prints that belong to some of the patrolmen who first entered the house last night."

"The murderers wore gloves," said Columbo.

"I'd guess so, but what makes you sure?"

"Look at the writing on the walls," said Columbo. "Look at it close. That wasn't done with fingers. That was done with fabric, with the fingers of cloth gloves, or maybe with fingers inside handkerchiefs or somethin'."

"That matches something else," she said. "The knob on the front door has only one clear set of prints: the prints of Officer Cambridge, the man who responded to the nine-one-one call. The rest are smudged."

"Wiped off?" Columbo asked.

"I wouldn't say that. Just smudged. The same thing is true of the door to the master-bedroom suite and of the kitchen door, inside and out."

"Figures," said Columbo.

"Think so?"

"Yeah. Figures."

Columbo used his borrowed pencil to make a note. Mulhaney beside him, watched him write, *Sr crm.* Another note, just above it, said, *Hd caulif.* Damn! Sour cream and a head of cauliflower. The lieutenant was writing his grocery list!

"Mulhaney," said Columbo. "Come on. I want to look at somethin'."

He led Mulhaney back to the bedroom suite.

There, just inside the door and short of the big bloodstain, Columbo dropped to his knees and put his head close to the floor to stare at marks on the white carpet. The marks were not dark footprints but three almost parallel lines.

"Mud," said Columbo.

Mulhaney squatted and looked at the marks. He put his finger on the darkest of the three marks and with finger and thumb pinched a tuft of the carpet. He nodded. "Mud," he said. "From the backyard, I'd guess."

Columbo crawled a pace across the floor and stared at the bloody footprint. He looked at the carpet around the footprint. "Look here," he said. He pointed to a small trace of blood about four feet away. "He stepped in the blood. His next step made a footprint. His second step left a little less blood, not enough to make a footprint."

Mulhaney moved over to the second, faint footprint and laid a pencil on it, so no one would step on it.

"The mud, that's somethin' else," said Columbo. "Just a guess, but the way it looks—Okay, the guy got mud on his shoe. He wiped it off on the grass. But some was left on the edge of his sole. He turned his foot over on edge and wiped three times before he cleaned it all off."

"Three lines. Makes sense," said Mulhaney.

Columbo got up from the floor and dusted his hands on his raincoat. "Somethin' about it doesn't make sense," he said.

"What's that, Lieutenant?"

Columbo stuck out his arms and turned up his palms. "Why would a guy who'd made a mess like this be obsessed with gettin' a little mud off his shoe?"

"Maybe he wiped it off before he made the mess."

Columbo shrugged. "Think so? A guy on his way through this sitting room, on his way to kill people with a knife, stops to clean mud off his shoe?"

"I don't know."

"Tell ya what. Have your guys look for other traces of that mud. All over."

"From the utility room to this bedroom," said Mulhaney.

"No. Not just from the utility room to this bedroom," said Columbo. "All over. Kitchen especially."

"You don't think they came in through the utility-room window?"

"Do you, Mulhaney? Do you?"

"I supposed I did," the young man said.

"Well, there's a point, Mulhaney," said Columbo. "Sometimes things look like somebody wants you to think they look like. See? Does that make sense?"

Mulhaney nodded.

Columbo held his hands in front of him—one with his cigar in it—and shook them as he gestured. "I mean . . . somebody didn't climb in that utility-room window. If they had, the splinters wouldn't be standin' up. And I bet you don't find any mud on the utility-room floor. Huh-uh. Whoever came into this house last night, came in through the front door, wearin' gloves that smudged the fingerprints on the front door and the prints on the door to the bedroom suite. They killed Mrs. Khoury and this fellow Heck, then the houseboy. And *then* one of them went out and used a burglar tool to pry open the utility-room window—to make it look like that's how they got in."

"Which lets off the Manson girl?" Mulhaney asked.

"No, no. I wouldn't say nothin' like that," said Columbo. "She worked for the Khourys. She coulda had a key to this house. Maybe she used it to get in but didn't want to leave the place looking like somebody'd used a key to get in."

"I'd worry about her motive," said Mulhaney. "Why would she want to kill Arlene Khoury? Or Steven Heck?"

"Right. Why would she? What good would that do her?"

Columbo tried to puff on his cigar but found it had gone out while he was crawling around on the floor and talking. He looked at it for a moment, felt it to see if any heat remained, then dropped it into the pocket of his raincoat.

Jackson came into the bedroom suite. "A Mrs. Takeshi just came up the driveway. She's the cook and housekeeper."

2

Mrs. Nagako Takeshi sat in the rear of an emergency-squad wagon, holding a clear plastic mask to her mouth and nose, taking oxygen. A woman paramedic was listening to her heart.

"We don't have to talk with her right now," said Columbo.

"It's all right. It's all right," said Mrs. Takeshi. She took a final drag on the oxygen and laid the mask aside. "Are you a detective? I want to do anything I can to help."

Mrs. Nagako Takeshi looked to be about fifty

years old. She was a plump woman, with the glossy, yellow-toned complexion of her Japanese ancestry. She wore her black hair in long bangs over her forehead, and bright red lipstick. Her dress was gray with a white starched collar and white cuffs: the uniform of a domestic in a wealthy home. Her English was without accent—unless Southern Californian was an accent.

"This has gotta be a shock for you, ma'am," said Columbo. "I'm sorry to have to ask you any questions right now."

Mrs. Takeshi shook her head. "I just can't believe it," she murmured. "Sergio, too . . ."

"That raises a point. Sergio is all the name we have for the young man. Can you—?"

"Flores," she said. "Sergio Flores. And I may as well tell you, since you're going to find out anyway, that Sergio was not legal. That is, he didn't have a green card. Mrs. Khoury didn't care."

Columbo retrieved the half-smoked cigar from his pocket and brought it back to life, taking care to stand outside the ambulance so his cigar smoke wouldn't accumulate inside. "Question," he said. "This place has a sophisticated alarm system. It didn't go off. It looks like the murderers came in over the fence, then got into the house by forcing a back window. Why wouldn't the alarm have gone off?"

"The system wasn't turned on till they went to bed," said Mrs. Takeshi. "And it was turned off again at sunrise. Whoever got up to go to the bathroom . . . if the sun was up, they turned it off. The last one to bed turned it on. The first one up in the morning turned it off. Mrs. Khoury didn't want to give anybody a key to the alarm system. I didn't have one. Sergio didn't have one. If Sergio went out to a movie or something and came home late, he could get in without setting off the alarm, provided the Khourys hadn't gone to bed. He could open the door with his door key, but if the alarm was armed he would set it off. Once or twice when he came home and saw the house was dark, he slept in the garage. When I came in the morning, the alarm would already be turned off. I set it off one morning when I came to work. I opened the door with a key, but the alarm was still on. Mrs. Khoury was furious —not at me, at Mr. Khoury for getting up to use the bathroom after sunup and forgetting to turn it off."

"Do you know who the third victim was?" Columbo asked.

"Mr. Heck. They said Mr. Heck."

"What would he have been doin' here at midnight or after?"

"I really wouldn't know, Lieutenant," she said crisply.

"Was he here when you left?"

"Yes. I left a little before seven. Dinner was ready. Sergio would serve it. Mrs. Khoury and Mr. Heck were sitting beside the pool."

"Was seven your usual time for leaving? Did Sergio usually serve dinner?"

"Yes, sir. I worked ten or eleven hours a day. I was paid for that many hours."

"Was Mr. Khoury usually home when you left?"

"Sometimes he was, sometimes he wasn't."

"What was the relationship between Mr. Heck and Mr. and Mrs. Khoury?"

"I really wouldn't know, Lieutenant. Mr. Heck

was in the motion-picture business. So were Mr. and Mrs. Khoury. I believe Mr. Heck worked on one or two of the Khoury pictures."

Columbo nodded. "Are you feeling alright, Mrs. Takeshi?"

"No, I'm not, Lieutenant. Not at all. This is a terrible shock to me."

"I understand, ma'am. So I won't bother you any more for now. You can go home as soon as you want to. The doctor's got Mr. Khoury sleeping under sedation, so he probably won't need anything for quite a while."

"I'll have some breakfast or lunch ready for him," said Mrs. Takeshi.

"Thank ya, then, ma'am. Thank ya."

Columbo walked back toward the entrance to the house. Then suddenly he turned, "Oh. One thing, ma'am."

He walked back to the ambulance, where Mrs. Takeshi was taking another breath of oxygen.

"I'm sorry, but y' know, in this business you gotta catch every little thing. And there's one thing that does bother me."

"Yes, Lieutenant?"

"Well—They didn't turn the alarm system on until they went to bed, and they turned it off early in the morning. And you and Sergio didn't have keys to that system. If he came home too late or you came too early, you'd set off the alarm even if you opened the door with a key. Is that right?"

"Yes," said Mrs. Takeshi. "Sergio had a key to the front door. Actually, it's a key to all the doors. And I had a key. When I came in, about eight in the morning, I could enter the house with my key. The alarm system would be off. Except the one time when it wasn't."

"How did you get through the gate?" Columbo asked.

"A radio controller," she said. "When I pressed the button on it—just like a garage-door controller —the gate would swing back. Inside the house, a bell chimed, saying the gate was open, and a closed-circuit television system showed who was on the driveway. There was a chime and monitor in the kitchen and the same in the master bedroom."

"Let me get this straight, ma'am," said Columbo, pointing from the direction of the gate back to the house. "When you opened the gate, people in the bedroom or kitchen would know it. At any time of day or night. But if the alarm system was off, they wouldn't know you'd opened a door to the house. Right?"

"That's right, Lieutenant. The Khourys had very specific ideas about how they wanted things to work."

"Interesting . . . Sort of unusual. I guess only a few people knew how it worked. Right?"

"Apparently somebody else did too, Lieutenant," said Mrs. Takeshi.

"Right," said Columbo. "It looks like somebody knew how it all worked."

SEVEN

1

Columbo walked along the narrow corridor, with its line of six holding cells, where female prisoners waited pending a court appearance or transfer to the main jail. No matter what was done to keep this corridor and these cells clean, the place always stank of stale cigarette smoke and of urine and sweat. Maybe what they needed was better ventilation in here. Each holding cell was tiny, only about seven feet long by four wide. It had a stainless-steel toilet without wooden seat and a little basin. The bunk was only a steel shelf, on which the prisoner could sit or lie down, without pillow or blanket. The steel walls and heavy bars were painted with shiny gray enamel, some of it chipped off.

A prisoner did not ordinarily sit in a holding cell for more than an hour or so, but Cathy Murphy had been in this one for about six hours. She wore an

orange jump suit with a white T-shirt: the uniform
of the temporary jail. She rose from the shelf,
leaned against the thick, narrow-set bars, and regarded Columbo with conspicuous hostility. She
was smoking a cigarette, and she blew smoke in his
face.

"I'm Lieutenant Columbo, LAPD homicide,
Miss Murphy," he said. "I understand you've been
advised of your rights. Like, you don't have to
answer any questions."

She shrugged. "What's the difference whether I
answer questions or not?"

"Well, if you told us where you were last night, we
might be able to let you outa here."

"Sure," she sneered. "I bet. I never got anything
out of a cop, especially not the truth or a fair
break." She tossed her head to one side to flip her
long dark hair off her face.

Columbo fished a half-smoked cigar out of his
pocket. "Y' wouldn't happen to have a match
handy, would ya, ma'am?" he asked.

"Anything I've got, it's handy," she said, glancing
from side to side at the dimensions of the cell. She
pulled a book of paper matches from the pocket of
her orange jump suit and handed it to him.
"Where'm I going? Sybil Brand?"

She had named the Los Angeles County women's
jail, Sybil Brand Institute, and Columbo nodded.

"Well . . . I've been there before."

"You've got quite a record, Miss Murphy. Never
anything serious up to now."

"I figured three years in Fontera was serious," she
said. "I did two years in Arizona. Also, a year in

Sybil Brand one time, six months another time. Six months in the Orange County jail. That's serious time, Lieutenant. Try doing a year, then you'll know."

"Plus assorted short stretches," said Columbo. "You don't seem to be able to keep your hands off other people's things, their cars especially. You know why you're in here now?"

"I had a stash in my car. Which is my car, incidentally. I have good title to it."

"Four lids," he said. "That's the formal charge they're holding you and your friends on— possession of four lids."

"Yeah, right," she said. "A thousand dollars bail, which of course we can't raise. That's big bail for possession of four lids. You got something else in mind."

"Yes, miss, we got something else in mind," said Columbo. "Three murders."

"That's what they told me. I make the perfect suspect, don't I? I suppose somebody's already told you Arlene Khoury didn't like me and gave me a hard time. You've got me where you want me, don't you? Me, the girl with the criminal record, back on the inside lookin' out. But let me tell you something, Lieutenant Columbo," she said. She gripped the bars so tightly her knuckles turned white. Holding her cigarette between her lips, she muttered, "You can't make it stick. We didn't do it."

"Why don't you help us make your alibi, then?"

"By doing what? What could I say that you'd believe?"

"To start with, you could tell me where you got

the Acapulco gold," said Columbo. "Maybe people saw you. Maybe somebody can testify that you were someplace else but Mulholland Drive at the hour when the crimes were committed."

"Yeah, and maybe the tooth fairy will come and put a quarter under my pillow. I bought the stash on Pershing Square."

"From who?"

She shook her head. "Are you serious? How'm I supposed to know? There are always guys there. You can always get a lid. You can get other stuff, too. I can see it now. The guy that sold it to me comes to police headquarters and says, 'Hey, I hear Puss Dogood's in trouble. Well, I sold her four lids Tuesday night, so she had to be on Pershing Square when those murders came down.' C'mon, Lieutenant . . ."

"'Puss Dogood.' That's the name Charlie gave you, I bet," said Columbo.

"That's right. That's the name Charlie gave me. That's what he still calls me, when he writes. It means I did good whatever he wanted me to do. It doesn't mean I'm a do-gooder. It means I did good for Charlie. Whatever he wanted, I did good."

"What time were you at Pershing Square?"

She shrugged. "Maybe ten, ten-thirty."

"Then where'd you go?"

"Santa Monica Beach. We went swimming."

"You say Mrs. Khoury didn't like you? Why not?"

"She didn't like it when Mr. Khoury hired me. She knew about my record, about who I am. He's a nice man, a kind man. She's somethin' else again.

She drank—I mean drank a hell of a lot. And she whored around. She was sleeping with that guy Heck. Everybody knew it."

"Something about that bothers me," said Columbo. "How could they have been confident Mr. Khoury wouldn't come home, walk in on them?"

"Well . . . He was probably busy. He had a little something goin' on the side himself. One of the store's models, Kim Dana. Model . . . executive assistant. Whatever. She started out as a model, anyway. A real looker. As a matter of fact, she was waiting for him in his office last night when he came back from his workout at the health club. I bet he was going to do something else for his health before the night was over."

She took a final drag on her cigarette and tossed it toward the toilet. It missed the toilet and landed on the concrete floor. She pulled another one from a pack that was almost empty and lit it with a paper match. She leaned against the bars. "You gonna charge me with murder?" she asked.

"Not yet," he said. "We're gonna hold you on the marijuana charge. They'll move you out to Sybil Brand in an hour or so."

"What about Kid? Jenny Schmidt? She's so damned innocent she doesn't know left from right. She's never been in jail before. And you know they'll separate us, put us in different dorms—like she's right now in the cell all the way down at the other end. I kinda feel responsible for her."

"Well, maybe you won't be there long," said Columbo.

"Yeah. Are you serious about—? You mean you're really gonna keep us locked up over *four lids?*"

"That way I'll know where you are when I want to ask you more questions."

She stepped away from the bars and sat down on the shelf. "You think I care? Kid's gonna care. She's probably scared to death right now, and she's gonna stay scared. Bum won't be scared. I mean Warren Douglas. He's been in before. But me? When I'm in a place like this, I'm closer to Charlie. I mean, we're spiritually closer. I mean, Charlie's locked in a cage, and I'm locked in a cage, and that makes us closer. Which is all I want to be, Lieutenant. Closer to Charlie. That's all I want to be."

Columbo puffed on his cigar. "Some guy, Charlie Manson," he muttered.

"Lieutenant . . . You don't understand. If you never met Charlie you can't understand."

"I did meet Charlie," said Columbo. "I was one of the detectives that worked on the Tate-LaBianca murders. Yeah, I met Charlie. And the rest of them."

"Then you should know that locking Charlie up in a prison—or me, for that matter—doesn't make any difference. Charlie will one day lead his people into the wilderness, to protect them from what's going to happen; and when all that's over, we'll come back and govern the world. You think I'm nuts. But that's because you don't really know Charlie. Listen—Manson. Man's Son. Can't you get it? When Charlie is ready, all this kind of thing, bars and locks, will fall away and won't make any difference. If Charlie called me now, I could just walk out of here. You couldn't stop me." She stood again and gripped the bars. "I can't get out of here right now. But when Charlie calls I'll get out. I don't know how, but I will. Because Charlie is love, and there's nothing stronger than love."

Columbo scratched his head and nodded. "Well, that's very interesting, Miss Murphy. I hope I can be here to see it when you walk out. That'll be very interesting."

2

The receptionist at the store had told Columbo he would find Kimberly Dana at a restaurant called Hammond's. "She'll be there at lunchtime, Lieutenant. At twelve-thirty. Doing a fashion show." He had hoped to spend his lunch hour at Burt's, over a bowl of chili and a game of pool, but the newspeople were going nuts over the Mulholland Drive murders, and he figured he had to give up what he'd rather do and keep working.

The parking attendant at the restaurant frowned and shook his head over the wheezing old Peugeot and asked if the gears were in the usual positions.

"Well, in the usual positions for a French car," Columbo told him. "Y' see, my car's a French car."

"You don't see very many like this still running," said the young man.

"No, you don't. But I take very good care of it. One of these days the speedometer is gonna roll over two hundred thousand miles. You take the right kind of care with a car, you can get that kinda mileage."

"I'll take good care of it, sir."

Columbo stood on the sidewalk in front of the restaurant, looking skeptically at the redwood facade. It was going to cost money to eat lunch in this place. Well . . . There was no escaping it. He shrugged and walked in.

A maître d' approached him immediately. "Can I be of assistance to you, sir?" he asked. He was a bald man with a pinched little face, and wore a tropical-weight light-blue jacket, a red bow tie, and white slacks.

"Well, uh, yeah. I'm Lieutenant Columbo, LAPD homicide. I was told I'd find a Miss Kimberly Dana here."

"You will indeed, Lieutenant. She's doing the Khoury show today."

"Show? Oh, yeah. A fashion show, the receptionist at the store told me."

"Yes, sir. On Wednesdays at lunchtime, we show items from the Khoury Collection. Miss Dana is here with the other models. At first I suggested maybe it wasn't appropriate, considering what happened to Mrs. Khoury last night, but Miss Dana said she was sure Mr. Khoury would want the show to go on as usual. So—"

"Well . . . Maybe I should see her some other time, if she's busy."

"Why don't we let *her* decide?" asked the maître d'. "That is she, coming from the dining room now. Miss Dana!"

Columbo couldn't remember ever before having

seen so beautiful a woman. She was statuesque and perfect in every way: she wore a dress of vivid, iridescent green that clung to her figure and showed it off to advantage. She was taller than he was, and he felt halfway foolish looking up into her lovely face.

"This is Lieutenant Columbo, Kim," said the maître d'. "He is a homicide detective."

Her model's smile, which was maybe a little *too* perfect, faded. She frowned. "Yes, of course," she said quietly, then sighed. "We're all in shock."

"Maybe I don't have to bother you now, ma'am," said Columbo. "I wanted to ask a couple or three questions, but—"

"It will be no bother at all, Lieutenant," she said. "In fact, I'd like to talk with you. I'd like to know what progress you're making. Have you talked to Joe?"

"Joe?"

"Mr. Khoury. Yussef Khoury. He likes for his friends to call him Joe."

"No, I haven't talked to him yet. He was sleeping when I was at the house. Under a sedative his doctor gave him. I hope he's still asleep."

"He's awake," she said. "He called about an hour ago and said we should go on with the show. Why don't we sit down?" She turned to the maître d'. "I could use a drink, Emory."

The maître d' nodded. "Let me have your rain-coat, Lieutenant Columbo. What would you like to drink?"

"I don't usually drink when I'm on duty, sir, but maybe a bourbon and water wouldn't be out of line."

Kimberly led Columbo to her table, where she had a Khoury catalog and a Khoury calendar lying open on the tablecloth. "You sit on the banquette, Lieutenant," she said. "Otherwise, you'll have your back to the show."

He looked around the room. Men sat around most of the tables, drinking, eating their lunches— some of them a little too animated, as if excited in anticipation of the show they were about to see. It looked as if few women were interested in the Khoury Collection show.

"This show, ma'am. Just what—?"

"We show things from the Khoury Collection," she said. "Do you know what the Khoury Collection is?"

"Yes, ma'am. I've seen the calendar."

"We'll be showing one of the outfits pictured in the calendar," she said. "The March one."

She flipped over the pages and showed him a picture of a young woman wearing not very much: a pair of black string bikini panties, a black bra, a garter belt of black lace, and stockings.

"That's, uh, very attractive," said Columbo.

"She won't be modeling, but we are showing the outfit," said Kimberly. "Anyway . . . What can I do for you, Lieutenant?"

"It's just a little awkward, ma'am. But I have to ask. It's not that Mr. Khoury is a suspect, but when a wife is murdered and we don't know who did it, we have to try to find out where the husband was at the time. And, uh . . . And somebody says he may have been with you."

Kimberly smiled. "It's no secret, Lieutenant. And it's not awkward. Joe Khoury and I have a relationship and have had for some time. If you want to know where we were last night, we were at a place where we often go. It's a motel called Piscina Linda. In Beverly Hills. We take a suite there, have dinner. We arrived there last evening about . . . oh, say, seven-thirty. We left at—I'm not sure. It was later than we usually stay. We usually leave a little after midnight. But this time it may have been one-thirty."

Columbo nodded. "I'm glad to hear it, ma'am. That means I can put the question of where Mr. Khoury was out of my mind. You can vouch for his whereabouts for hours before and after the murders. And I bet people at the motel can, too. That's very helpful."

"What else do we need to talk about?" she asked.

"Nothin' really," he said. "I—"

He paused as a waitress put a martini in front of Kimberly and a bourbon and water in front of him.

"I guess you maybe know somethin' about Mr. Heck. I hate to have to tell Mr. Khoury this, but, you see, Mrs. Khoury and Mr. Heck were in bed together when they were murdered."

"That doesn't surprise me," she said, "but I can see why you'd want to know if Joe had an alibi for last night. I can see what you'd think: that he caught them in the act and took a husband's revenge."

"Well, no, not really," said Columbo. "He couldn't have done that. Y' see, they were killed with knives. It couldn't have been done by one person, because certainly one or the other of them would have rolled out of bed and tried to get away while the other one was being stabbed. So it had to be at least two people."

"He told me there was writing in blood on the walls."

"Yeah. Stuff like 'Helter Skelter.' You remember where we saw that before."

"Lieutenant, I may be able to give you some information about that, but right now I've got to go back and get my show started. Have some lunch. I'll rejoin you as soon as I'm finished."

She left the table. As he sipped his drink he glanced through the Khoury Collection catalog. The pictures gave him an idea of why some of the men at the nearby tables were so animated. If models came out wearing some of this stuff—Well . . . It was all expensive. Some of it was *very* expensive.

He looked at his menu. Lunch was expensive. The waitress came.

"You don't, by any chance, serve a bowl of chili?" he asked.

"I'm afraid not, sir."

"Ah, well . . . then this seafood salad. I'll have that."

The show began. Emory, the maître d', announced it and then switched on a recorder. Kim herself announced the show, from a tape. "Our first model is Karin, and she is showing the items you see on page twenty-eight of the Khoury Collection catalog."

Few of the onlookers flipped the pages of the catalogs that lay at every place on every table. Most of them stared at the slender blonde model who was walking through the room in a turquoise satin bra-and-panties set. The panties consisted only of a trifle of satin held in place by elastic string, accentuating the model's long, slender, tanned legs. Columbo checked page 28. The bra sold for $63, the tiny panties for $28.

The model walked around the room, stopping briefly at each table to give the people a close look.

Okay. He wasn't going to say, even to himself, that he *wasn't* interested, though he couldn't imagine Mrs. Columbo wearing what the model was now showing or what Miss March was wearing in the calendar. No. Mrs. Columbo was a huskier woman than these models, more athletic. She was a first-class bowler. She was just as sexy as the model, in her way. But . . . in her way.

Another one came out in a fine-weave fishnet body suit. It covered everything, sort of—but nothing, really. That appeared on page 61 and cost $94.

Kimberly Dana came third. She wore a white cotton outfit. It was like a man's ribbed-cotton vest undershirt, except that it was cut short and came to an end six inches above her navel. The panties were bikini style. You couldn't see through the cotton, exactly, but what was inside it wasn't exactly hidden, either. She spent a long moment standing in front of Columbo. "You like?" she whispered.

He nodded, and after she was gone he checked the catalog and saw that the outfit cost $65.

The seafood salad tasted strange to Columbo. They'd put some sort of spice in the dressing, something he wasn't used to. It tasted good, he supposed, but he liked familiar things best, and right now he would have liked the taste of shrimp and crab and lobster, with just mayonnaise. This mayonnaise had something odd in it.

Each of five models showed two outfits. Kimberly

was the last model. She appeared in a bra, bikini
panties, and garter belt, all sheer black and all
trimmed with black lace, with dark thigh-high
stockings and high-heeled black shoes. A big glittering rhinestone was sewed to the center of the bra, in
the V-dipping waistline of the panties, and just
below her navel on the garter belt. After she had
stood and displayed the outfit to him, he looked in
the catalog and saw the three items were priced at
$112—which did not include the stockings or
shoes. She paused before him an extraordinarily
long time, he thought, and he was embarrassed,
unsure of whether he should look up into her face
or glance up and down her body.

Five minutes later she sat down again at the table
with him.

"Here you go, Lieutenant," she said, handing
him a package in the distinctive aluminum-and-
blue Khoury wrapping. "The first outfit I modeled.
Take it home to your wife."

"I . . . appreciate the thought, Miss Dana, but
Mrs. Columbo is a . . . a different-style figure from
you."

"Stretch fabric," she said. "One size fits all."

"Well, that's very kind of you. Mr. Khoury sure
does sell elegant things. I've only been in his store
once, but I saw when I was there that he sells an
elegant line."

"That's his whole life," she said. "Elegance.
Taste. Nothing but the best . . . within reason, that
is. Khoury merchandise is not overpriced, Lieutenant. It's all good value for the money paid. The
lingerie, for example, is all well made, nothing

flimsy. Joe has a very definite pride in what he sells, and a sense of ethics."

Columbo nodded. "Well, he's got deluxe taste, that's for sure. Uh, you said you could tell me something more."

"Yes," she said. "You said someone had written 'Helter Skelter' on the walls. You might be interested to know that Arlene Khoury's secretary is one of the original Manson girls. She was in jail at the time of the Tate-LaBianca murders, but she still considers herself one of Charles Manson's disciples."

"Really?"

"Yes. Cathy Murphy. Joe hired her because he felt sorry for her. She's been in and out of prisons most of her life, so she couldn't get the kind of job she wanted, that is, as a secretary. She was working behind a counter in the store, and he brought her up to the executive suite as *his* secretary. Arlene didn't like it and wanted Joe to get rid of her. She agreed to have the woman stay on, only if she worked as *her* secretary."

"That's very interesting," said Columbo. "The Tate-LaBianca murders were twenty-five years ago. How old does that make this Cathy Murphy?"

"Forty-six," said Kimberly. "But she still thinks she's a—What would you call it? A hippie?"

"It was nice of Mr. Khoury to give her a chance," said Columbo.

"Joe's a nice guy, Lieutenant. I wish I could say as much for Arlene. It's tactless to speak ill of the dead, but Arlene was spiteful and treated Cathy cruelly. Cruel. There's no lesser word to use for it.

She kept Cathy working late. She tore up letters she typed and made her type them over, when there was really nothing wrong with them. One day she'd tell Cathy the margins on letters had to be an inch and three-quarters on each side; the next day, after Cathy had typed a dozen letters that way, she'd scream at her that the margins had to be an inch and a half—and swear that's what she'd told her."

"Aww, that's too bad," he said.

"Lots of people will confirm it. Joe was thinking of transferring Cathy Murphy to some other office, where she wouldn't have to put up with Arlene."

"Are you suggestin' Cathy disliked Mrs. Khoury?"

Kimberly shook her head. "I never heard her say anything like that. Joe didn't either. But how could the woman help but despise Arlene?"

"What do you suppose made her act like that?"

"She was on the bottle," said Kimberly. "Half the time she was in the office, she was drunk. You can find a dozen witnesses to that. The only part of the business she was interested in was Khoury Productions—I mean, Joe's motion-picture investments. She'd go to the studio; she'd come to the office—always full of ideas about pictures."

"What was Mr. Heck's relationship with Mr. Khoury, with the business?"

"Steve Heck is—*Was*. It's hard to get used to speaking of these people in the past tense. He was a production designer. He worked on two of Joe's pictures. He gave them a certain style. Joe's fabled exquisite taste didn't exactly hold up in the picture business, and Steve did a lot to make the last two Khoury pictures successful."

"You said everybody knew Mrs. Khoury had an intimate relationship with Mr. Heck. Did that include Mr. Khoury? I mean, did *he* know?"

"Absolutely. To speak the truth, Lieutenant, I don't think he cared much. Arlene had gotten old and fat. To say it better, she'd *let* herself get old and fat. And he . . ."

Columbo had finished his seafood salad and drunk about half his coffee. "Well, ma'am," he said. "I've taken too much of your time. I'll be getting along. I'll, uh, need to get my check."

Kimberly shook her head. "It's taken care of, Lieutenant."

"Oh, no, ma'am. I couldn't let you—"

"It's on the house," she said. "Part of the deal for the show. Don't worry about it. And please don't call me ma'am. I'm Kim."

"That's kind of you . . . Kim," he said. "I hope I'm not rude in rushing off before you have *your* lunch, but I've got things to do."

"Not at all," she said. "I don't eat lunch. One of the sacrifices I have to make to keep my figure."

"Uh . . . you've been very successful at that, if I'm not outa line in saying so."

"Thank you," she said with a smile.

He slid to one side and stood. "I hope I'll see you again," he said.

"I hope so, too."

"Well, uh—Oh, uh, there is one little thing I guess I oughta ask you. Nothing important. But in my line of work I have to get every little fact straight in my mind. Anything unusual, if I don't get it explained, keeps me awake nights. And you said you did something unusual last night. I was running some of this over in my mind during the show said you usually left the motel not long after midnight, but last night you were there till maybe one-thirty. Was there any particular reason for that?"

Kimberly smiled mischievously. "It's a rather personal question, Lieutenant Columbo."

"Oh. Yeah, I suppose it is. I don't mean to—"

"Even so, I'll answer it," she said, still smiling. "The unhappy fact is, Joe and I went to sleep. I don't know what time. Sometime after our coffee was brought up by room service, which always delivers it to our suite about midnight. We had some coffee, and I suppose about twelve-twenty, twelve-thirty, we went to sleep."

"Coffee doesn't keep you awake, I guess."

"It never did me."

"Well, all right then. Do you do this show every Wednesday?"

"Every Wednesday."

"Maybe I'll come again sometime."

"Let us know. Usually Joe is here. I'm sure you'll be talking with him, so you and Joe will be old friends the next time you come in to see the show."

"Right. I've gotta talk to Mr. Khoury."

PART TWO

I'm no genius, sir. All I can do is get every fact I can find, put 'em together, and when I come across little inconsistencies I have to find the explanation.

EIGHT

1

Yussef Khoury strode into the surf at the San Luis Rio pier. The fishermen on the pier regarded him with hostility. They didn't like scuba divers fooling around in the water near the pier. Sometimes one of them would get tangled up in a fishing line. Sometimes one of them would hook himself and then would complain. Khoury had gone into the water here only once before and was not aware of how the fishermen felt. He wouldn't have cared anyway.

The wind blew warm and gentle on this Wednesday afternoon, August 10, and the surf was not running hard. Swimming out, he was soon beyond where the waves churned up sand. Through his mask he could see the sandy bottom, and he could see five or ten yards ahead. He was aware of the fishing lines and avoided them. He swam between

two of them and then between two piles and
beneath the pier. Under the pier, visibility was
more restricted, but he could see where he was
going.

He swam along, working his flippers smoothly,
heading for the end of the pier.

Reaching the end, he went to the bottom and was
in some twenty feet of water. He had told Kim not
to throw the Bali-Songs and the pry bar but only to
drop them. If waves and current had not moved
them, they should be lying on the sand and gravel
just below the end of the pier. The fishermen cast
their lines out, but he hoped to find what he was
looking for closer in.

Finding the knives was easy. Kim had used good
sense and had opened them, so they would move
less readily and would be more visible when he
came for them. He found one lying within six feet
or so of a fisherman's hook, with only a little sand
drifted over it. The other one was no more than
four feet distant from the first. The pry bar was a
little more difficult. It was half buried in sand and
might in fact have stayed there unfound indefi-
nitely.

He closed the Bali-Songs with gloved hands and
stuck them in his weighted belt. Carrying the
burglar tool in his left hand, he swam slowly
forward, watching intently for the lines dropped by
the men on the dock.

He held back while a fish investigated some bait,
seized it, and thrashed in its struggle against the
upward tug on the line. Joe Khoury ate fish with
much pleasure, but he had always scorned the
simpletons who threw their lines into the water and

dragged the creatures out one at a time to flop and suffocate on the dock or in a boat. His sympathy was with the fish, and he was for an instant tempted to swim forward and cut the line.

But it was essential that he draw no attention to himself, so he swam past the fishing lines and out to sea.

He stayed close to the bottom as he swam out into deeper water. Scuba diving had been his sport for a decade, and he swam confidently. He had the best of equipment, years of experience, and knew his own limitations. As he swam farther out, where the water was fifty feet deep and more, the water became clearer. He saw seals hunting. He spotted a huge turtle. He saw one six-foot shark, but it did not frighten him. He knew the shark would see him as a smoothly moving creature, obviously one not sick or injured, and too big to attack. He could not be certain that the shark actually saw him, but he judged it had, and it went past and on, taking no apparent interest in him.

Two hundred yards or so off the beach he came upon a landmark that he had heard about and then located during his first swim here. It was a twin-engine airplane that had landed on the water in 1968. The pilot and passenger had escaped and were rescued. The plane still lay on the bottom, corroded and slowly collapsing, festooned with weed that acted as camouflage, yet entirely recognizable for what it had been. It told him how far out he was and how far he had to go.

A hundred yards beyond the airplane he came to what he wanted. It was the edge of a steep slope down to deeper water. The slope by no means marked the edge of the continental shelf, but it marked the end of water less than a hundred feet deep and the beginning of water two and three hundred feet deep. The bottom here was a forest of gently undulating kelp, alive like a tropical forest with ten thousand species of underwater creatures, very few of which the scuba diver could ever see.

Khoury swam just beyond the edge of the slope and let go of the burglar tool. It dropped slowly down and disappeared in the kelp. He disliked having to surrender the Bali-Songs to the sea. They were beautiful objects, but he could not risk keeping them. Reluctantly he dropped one, then the other, and they followed the pry bar, down and out of sight, never to be seen again.

Yussef Khoury surfaced, just to orient himself, to see if current had carried him north or south of the pier at San Luis Rio. He adjusted his return course a little to the north and went down again about twenty feet, to be beneath the chopping propellers of boats that might come speeding by. Satisfied with what he had accomplished, and grateful to be in the challenging yet forgiving water, he swam toward the beach.

2

Columbo sat on a wooden bench on the sand some distance from the pier. He knew Yussef Khoury was out in the water somewhere. Mrs. Takeshi had told him Mr. Khoury had gone out scuba diving, to soothe his spirits, to be away for a little while from the agony of the murders committed in his house. He had told her he was going to San Luis Rio; and, sure enough, parked a little distance from the pier was the distinctive gull-wing Mercedes.

"Yeah," one of the fishermen on the pier had said, "some damn dummy is out there someplace, if he ain't drownded. Went wobblin' down the beach like a half-wit turtle and into the water. Maybe half an hour ago."

Columbo squinted into the sunlight on the water. Now and again he thought he saw a head bob up, enveloped in black rubber, but it was his imagination, apparently, because he never spotted the black lump a second time anywhere near the same place.

He had finished the cigar he'd begun just before he went into Hammond's and had decided not to light another one. Even if he'd wanted to, he couldn't, because he had tried his every pocket and couldn't find a match. Maybe it was good luck. A man could smoke too many cigars.

On the other hand, he'd found the yellow pencil his wife had put in his inside jacket pocket this morning. She'd sharpened it but had put it in point down, and it had poked a little hole for itself and slipped down inside the jacket's lining. So he had a pencil for once—just when he didn't have anything to write.

Something was going through his mind while he waited for Khoury. He enjoyed limericks, but he was having trouble with this one. It started—

> There was a young man from New York
> Who feasted on cabbage and pork.
> It made him quite ill
> So they gave him a pill—

And then what? He was tempted to go up to the telephone at the bait shack and call his wife to ask her if she knew. But then Khoury might come out and he might miss him. So. . . .

Anyway, here he came!

A man stumbled out of the surf fifty yards north of the pier and stood for a moment shaking his head while the surf rolled in around him. Then he pulled the mouthpiece out of his mouth and lifted his mask. He shook his head again and began to plod up the beach, his flippers impeding his walk.

Columbo trotted toward him, raincoat flapping. "Sir! Sir! Are you Mr. Khoury?"

The man stopped and stared at him, as if the man in the bizarre raincoat were as idiosyncratic a figure as he himself was in his black rubber with his tanks on his back. He nodded, and the man kept trotting toward him. He covered only fifty yards or so but was winded as he reached him.

"Sir . . . sir," Columbo puffed. "I'm Lieutenant Columbo, LAPD, homicide."

"Ah-hah," said Khoury. He thrust out his hand. "You're investigating . . ."

"Yes, sir. And my condolences, Mr. Khoury. My sympathy."

"Thank you, Lieutenant. It was kind of you not to insist on seeing me this morning when I was just coming out of what Dr. Amos gave me last night."

"Well, sir, there was no reason to put any more burden on you this morning. When I heard you'd come out for a swim, I figured maybe—"

"Of course," said Khoury. He began to plod on up the beach toward his car. "I hope you won't think it's callous of me to go out in the water the day after my wife is murdered. But getting down there, down into that peaceful other world, is really very therapeutic, Lieutenant. Do you dive, by any chance?"

"Well, no, sir. Actually, I can't swim at all. I come from New York City, and I never learned."

"You ought to join a club like ours," said Khoury. "You can learn to swim and to go down diving at the same time." He tilted his head and regarded Columbo with curiosity. "If I judge right, your age and mine are not too far apart. Scuba diving is the very best thing for men our age. It doesn't take great physical strength or even the stamina of tennis, but you do have to work your heart and lungs, and it's great exercise for them. Besides, to get down there and see what's underneath the ocean—Well, it's fascinating. I'm rambling. You can empathize, maybe."

"I sure can," said Columbo. "Yes, sir. And I don't really have to bother you right now. But you can understand. We'd like to close this case as quick as possible."

"I agree with you one hundred percent. Nothing would bring me more comfort than to have the case successfully closed today or tomorrow. I hear you've already made an arrest. Poor Cathy."

"Actually," said Columbo, "she's being held on something else, a narcotics charge. But she can't— or won't—account for her whereabouts last night."

"I know she has a long criminal record," said Khoury, "and I know she was a member of the original Manson Family. I know she's an eccentric. I know she still thinks Charles Manson is God. But even so . . . I can't believe she'd commit such a horrible crime."

"It is a little hard to believe, sir."

"Think of this, Lieutenant. Whoever came to my house last night had to know a lot about the house and the habits of the people in it. How did they know, for example, that the alarm system wouldn't be on? Cathy couldn't have known that. She was never in the house."

"That's a fact," said Columbo. "I'm glad we agree that she doesn't make a very good suspect."

"Well, I . . . I wouldn't write her off entirely. There was a certain antagonism between her and Arlene."

"Enough to make her kill her?" Columbo asked.

Khoury shook his head. "No, I suppose not."

They had reached the small parking lot. Khoury stopped, leaned against a guardrail post, and pulled off his flippers.

"That's a wonderful car y' got there," said Columbo. "It's a German make, isn't it? My car's a French car. That's it over there. What year is your car, Mr. Khoury?"

"It was manufactured in 1954," said Khoury.

"That old! I thought my car was old. You've kept it in very good shape. I try to take good care of my car, but you can see it does need a coat of paint. Needs some dents hammered out, too. Of course, it was never the elegant car yours is."

Khoury walked on toward the Mercedes.

"I stopped at Hammond's and talked to Miss Dana. Saw the fashion show, too," said Columbo. "She surely is a beautiful woman. I—"

"Then you saw her model some lingerie," said Khoury. "You do know she's a beautiful woman."

"Yes, sir. She told me where you were last night. You understand, I had to ask. I don't want to seem like I'm snooping into a man's private life, but—"

"Lieutenant," said Khoury, "I can't imagine how you could investigate Arlene's murder without snooping into my private life. I haven't the least objection to your doing so."

"Well, thank ya. A lot of people don't understand."

Reaching the car, Khoury began to unstrap his scuba equipment. He reached into the back of the car and pulled out a large yellow nylon bag. Carefully, he packed each item into the bag. The idea was to confine any and all saltwater and sand inside the heavy nylon. Having packed the equipment, he reached for another bag, stripped off his black rubber suit, and packed it inside. Under it he was wearing a pair of red Speedo trunks. They were dry and he put his dark-blue knit pants over them. He slipped a white golf shirt over his head. He sat down on the car seat and pulled on a pair of white running shoes. Finally, he put on a pair of dark airman's sunglasses from the glove box.

"According to Miss Dana, you spent the evening with her at a motel called Piscina Linda. That's an interesting name. That means beautiful swimming pool."

"They have an exceptionally fine swimming pool there," said Khoury.

Columbo pulled out his little notebook, flipped over a couple of pages, and frowned at a note he'd made earlier. "You arrived at Piscina Linda about seven-thirty, had dinner in the dining room, and returned to your room at, say, nine. You didn't leave until almost one-thirty in the morning."

Khoury nodded. "Yes. That's right."

"And it was kinda unusual for you to stay there that late. Usually you left an hour or so earlier. Was there any reason why you stayed so much later than usual?"

Yussef Khoury smiled. "I wish I could tell you it was a romantic reason," he said. "The fact is, we got interested in a late-night television movie."

"Have you had a chance to check to see whether or not anything was stolen from the house?" Columbo asked.

"I haven't. Mrs. Takeshi checked the usual things: the silver, television sets, and so on. My wife kept a considerable amount of jewelry in the bedroom. I haven't been in there. I don't know when I will go in there. The way I feel now, I'll probably sell the house."

"The investigating detectives found a lot of jewelry in drawers in the bedroom," said Columbo. "They wrote down an inventory of it and left it where it was. Maybe you can look at the inventory."

"Yes," said Khoury.

"Well, then. I won't take any more of your time this afternoon. I'm sure you know we'll be doing everything we can to clear this case up as quickly as possible."

"I do understand. And I thank you, Lieutenant."

Khoury extended his hand, and the two men shook hands. Columbo smiled and nodded and walked away toward the Peugeot.

He stopped and turned back to Khoury. "Oh, I should ask you one more thing, sir," he said. "There is a little contradiction between something you said and something Miss Dana said. I'd like to clear that up. Nothin' important, it's just that I'm always uncomfortable having any contradiction not resolved."

"What is it?" asked Khoury.

"Well, sir, you told me you stayed at the motel later than usual because you got interested in a television movie. Miss Dana told me it was because you went to sleep. Y' see that's a sort of . . . inconsistency."

Khoury grinned. "You're sharp, Lieutenant Columbo. You don't miss anything, do you?"

"In my line of work, you can't afford to. I'm no genius, sir. All I can do is get every fact I can find, put 'em together, and when I find little inconsistencies I have to find the explanation. Most of them don't amount to anything, but—" Columbo shrugged. "Y' see how it is."

"It's simple enough," said Khoury. "We stayed late because I was enjoying the TV movie. She went to sleep. When she woke up she may have thought I'd been asleep, too. But I hadn't. I've seen that movie maybe four or five times, and I like it. I'd never go to sleep on it."

Columbo nodded. "Okay. That explains it. Inconsistency explained. I won't worry about it."

"Would you like to know what movie so much interested me?" asked Khoury.

"Oh, no, sir. That won't be necessary."

"*Barry Lyndon,* Lieutenant. One of my favorites. Have you ever seen it?"

"Oh yes, sir. I enjoyed that one myself. Thank ya, sir. And, once again, my sympathy."

Yussef Khoury waited in the gull-wing Mercedes until Columbo had pulled out of the parking lot and was almost out of sight down the highway. Then he picked up his cellular telephone and put in a call to Kimberly. They had agreed on *Barry Lyndon* as the picture they'd been watching, but if Columbo called her—which he just might—it was essential that she say *she* went to sleep during the movie, and he probably hadn't. As he put it to her, "We must sing from the same sheet, baby. We must sing from the same sheet."

NINE

1

Columbo hated the morgue. He was smoking a cigar to overcome its cold and antiseptic smell, but it was a smell that nothing could overcome. The smell was not, of course, the worst of it.

"I know you hate it, Columbo," said Dr. Culp. "You've told me often enough."

Dr. Harold Culp was a man of forty, forty-five maybe, and if he were the former he was prematurely gray, with prematurely thinning hair. The round tanned bare spot on the back of his head was not wide enough for the bald spot of a tonsured monk; it was more like the size of a yarmulke. He looked at Columbo through horn-rimmed bifocals as he pulled on a white knee-length coat and rubber gloves.

The corpses of Steven Heck and Sergio Flores were in drawers. The body of Arlene Khoury lay on the examining table. Dr. Culp whipped off the sheet that covered her. Columbo winced and for a moment turned his face away. But he had to look at her. He couldn't refuse to look at her.

In some odd way—as Columbo saw it—she had not looked as ghastly lying in her blood as she did now, washed clean of blood, pallid and cold. Dr. Culp had not begun the autopsy yet, so he had not yet opened her up. But her wounds, now bloodless, were hideous dark holes, sickening to see.

"Do you see anything odd about those stab wounds?" asked Dr. Culp.

Columbo peered at the wounds. He saw what was odd, but he wanted to know if the doctor was talking about the same thing. "Please point out to me what's odd," he said.

The doctor put a gloved finger on a chest wound. "Look at the bruise," he said. "When a knife is thrust into a person, usually it goes in as far as the guard between the blade and handle will allow it—assuming the point doesn't hit a bone. When the guard strikes the flesh, it can make a bruise. In fact, it usually does. But look at that bruise. It's almost ten inches wide. The guard on a knife is never more than three inches wide. Even that's unusual. Most of them are no more than an inch and a half. This bruise is the best defined, but she has several others."

"What are you saying, Doc?"

Dr. Culp turned up the palms of his hands. "I don't know what to think. The blades that killed these people were attached to something, something that made it possible for the blades to strike with extraordinary force. I'd think of the bayonet attached to the end of a rifle, but again the guard wouldn't be nine or ten inches wide."

" 'Extraordinary force . . .' Like what? Like—?"

The doctor shook his head. "The body of Heck . . . It has a cracked rib. Whatever this thing was that the blade was attached to hit him so hard it cracked a rib."

"A strong man," said Columbo.

"Wielding a vicious weapon," said Dr. Culp.

"They were killed with knives, then? They weren't shot or something else?" Columbo asked.

"No. The Latino houseboy was struck at the base of the skull with something heavy. I'd judge he was knocked down first and only then stabbed. His wounds are in the back, as you saw."

"What bothers me, Doc, is how these people were caught and suddenly killed with knives and don't seem to have tried to get away. That's why I asked if somebody shot them or maybe even drugged them first."

"Let me give you something that's going to bother you even more," said Dr. Culp. "The wounds on all three bodies seem to have been made by one blade, or identical blades. The blade or blades that killed these people are sixteen centimeters long, a little more than six inches. Two and a half centimeters wide—just about an inch. No hunting knife. That's a stiletto."

"Zip knife," Columbo suggested.

"Maybe. Yeah, maybe. But somehow attached to some kind of handle that made it possible to hit damned hard with it, so hard it broke a rib."

"Were all of the stabs done with this same kind of blade?"

Dr. Culp nodded. "That's why I haven't autopsied Mrs. Khoury yet. I've measured every stab wound in all three bodies. I've had all three bodies photographed, and I've numbered the wounds. Not every stab went in sixteen centimeters, but they were all the same width."

Dr. Culp picked up a thin steel measuring rule, calibrated in millimeters. He inserted it in one of the stab wounds in the corpse of Arlene Khoury, to demonstrate that the wound was one hundred sixty millimeters—sixteen centimeters—deep.

Columbo scowled and turned away.

"Most of the wounds on the bodies of Mrs. Khoury and Mr. Heck enter at an angle approximately ninety degrees to the plane of the body. One of the wounds on his body enters at an angle approximately forty degrees above that plane. That suggests to me that he was sitting maybe halfway erect when he was first stabbed. That stab penetrated his heart. He would not have remained halfway erect after that but would have slumped down. Two wounds in Mrs. Khoury's body are about twenty degrees above the plane. I would guess she was lying on her back when somebody lunged at her with the knife. The ninety-degree wounds were made by somebody standing above the two people and repeatedly striking downward. All the wounds to the houseboy are close to the ninety-degree angle. I think he fell after he was struck on the back of the head, then someone stabbed down from above as he lay facedown on the floor."

"Were these people drunk?" asked Columbo.

"The two in bed were. Which may explain why

they did not instantly react to the attack. The houseboy was not."

"How drunk?"

"Well . . . Not pass-out-cold drunk. I wouldn't have wanted to go for a drive with one of them. Point-one-eight. That's pretty damn drunk."

"How about cocaine?" Columbo asked. "We found crack in her handbag."

Dr. Culp shook his head. "Not a trace. If they'd had coke in their blood, with point-one-eight alcohol, it wouldn't have been necessary to stab them."

"Of course, there could be another reason why they didn't jump and run or jump to try to defend themselves," said Columbo. "Maybe they *knew* the people coming at them and didn't expect to be attacked."

Dr. Culp shrugged. "I said the alcohol *might* explain. I didn't say it *did.*"

"How about sex?" Columbo asked. "I guess these two people had been—"

"And how," said Dr. Culp. "That could be another reason why they didn't jump up. They were plain exhausted."

2

Columbo was tired. This was turning into a long day. He stopped at a telephone booth, called home, and talked with Mrs. Columbo.

"Yeah, I know, I know. Every station, every

paper . . . Suspects in custody? We got no suspects in custody. The people they're talking about are in for possession of marijuana . . . Captain says what? Case closed tomorrow? I'll be lucky if I can close it in six weeks . . . Right now, I'm checkin' up on the husband, which I gotta do. *Gotta* do. Y' know? Anyway, I got nothin' else going in the case yet. Listen, I've got to check with some people at a motel called Piscina Linda. So I'll be late . . . No, not *too* late. Hey, I had a spicy seafood salad for lunch, so let's have something good and simple for dinner. Good and simple. Simple and good. And I got a present for you. Y' won't believe! I'll explain it all when I see you. Say an hour."

Fifteen minutes later he reached Piscina Linda and pulled the Peugeot into the parking lot. The attendant, Jorge Mendez, welcomed him and asked him if he was just there for dinner or would be staying the night.

"Neither," said Columbo, showing his shield. "I'll be in and out in fifteen minutes."

"'Kay," said the young man. "I'll keep your car right over there, handy."

"Lemme guess," said Columbo. "You're from N' Yawk, right?"

"Right. I talk like you, man."

"Lower East Side?"

"Naw. Other end of town altogether. Washington Heights. I worked downtown. Maybe some of that got into me."

"You read the papers, watch TV?" Columbo asked.

"Yeah."

"Okay. I'm Lieutenant Columbo, LAPD homicide, and if you read the papers, watch television, you know why I'm here. Your name is?"

"Jorge Mendez. What've *I* got to do with what happened to Mrs. Khoury?"

Jorge was a wiry young man, so thin in fact as to suggest he shot something, but the muscles of his arms were like cords, and he was alert and springy on his feet.

"Nothin'. Nothin' at all. But, y' see, when you're investigating a murder, you gotta check out everything, every little thing. Like, right now I need to know exactly when Mr. Yussef Khoury arrived here last night and when he left. Is that because I think Mr. Khoury might have killed his wife? No. It's because that's what I have to do. Did you take care of his car last night?"

Jorge nodded. "I *always* take care of that car. You got a car like that"—he paused and cast a curious glance at the Peugeot—"you make sure it gets nothin' but first-class treatment."

"I know what ya mean. So you'd remember when Mr. Khoury arrived and when he left, right?"

"Right. It was, like, seven-thirty, man. He drove in like always, bringin' that luscious broad of his."

"And he left—?"

"Like one-thirty. Little before. That Mercedes was the last car I handled last night. Usually he leaves earlier. It'd been anybody else, I'd have checked out at one and let him pick up his car keys at the desk. But not Mr. Khoury. I know he's gonna hand me ten bucks for takin' special care of that car."

"Okay, so he came at seven-thirty and left about one-thirty. And Miss Dana was with him, right?"

Jorge nodded. "Sure. Don't quote me, but this is where he shacks up with that broad. That car and that broad! The guy's got it made!"

"Here's the keys to my car . . . uh—You say you're just gonna move it out of the way?"

"Right. It'll be right over there."

Columbo walked into the lobby of the motel. It was an interesting place, though nothing at all like the Khoury home or the Khoury store. Odd place to be favored by a man who made elegance his life's obsession. So, okay, it was where Yussef Khoury brought Kimberly Dana for a little anonymity and privacy. In that sense it wasn't bad. Men took their girlfriends to cheaper places. Columbo could see through the dining room to the swimming pool that gave the place its name. *That* was nice.

He went to the desk and showed his badge to the clerk. "Lieutenant Columbo, homicide. I'm working on the Khoury murder case. Mr. Khoury says he was here last night. Can you confirm that?"

"Yes, sir," said the clerk. "He was here."

"Your name is?"

"Frank Taylor. Mr. Khoury came in about seven-thirty and left sometime after I went off duty. I work from four to midnight."

Taylor *looked* like the four-to-midnight clerk in a hot-sheet motel. If Columbo had seen him on a bus he would have taken the gray little man in the cheap suit and steel-rimmed eyeglasses for a motel clerk.

"Did he sign a register, sign a card?"

"As a matter of fact, no," said Taylor. "Mr.

Khoury telephones in the morning and reserves his suite. He pays by check, sent when he gets our bill."

"He's a regular customer, then," said Columbo.

"Yes, sir."

"Since how long?"

"Four or five months."

"You know what they're here for, I imagine," said Columbo.

"No, sir, I don't. They do come down for dinner, and about midnight they want coffee brought up by room service. That's a standing order. They always spend two or three hours alone in their suite. I don't speculate about what they do. It's none of my business."

"And somebody took coffee up to them last night?"

"Yes, sir."

"I'd like to talk to the room-service waiter who took their coffee to them."

Taylor nodded. "I'll call for him. He'll be in the kitchen and will come out through the dining room. His name is Eduardo."

"Thank ya," said Columbo.

He walked over to the broad open doors of the dining room and looked in. The menu was posted on a lighted stand, and he glanced it over. This was more his kind of restaurant, offering steaks and chops and roast beef, chicken, and several kinds of fish. It had a salad bar. Honest food, nothing fancy, no surprises. Maybe he'd bring Mrs. Columbo here for dinner some night. She'd enjoy looking at the pool.

Eduardo was a slight, gray-haired man. He approached the detective with conspicuous trepidation, so much that it made Columbo wonder if he was not another illegal like the murdered houseboy.

"Relax, Eduardo," he said to him. "I just want to ask you a question or two."

Eduardo nodded.

"You took coffee up to Mr. Khoury's suite last night. Right?"

"Yes, sir," said Eduardo with a thick accent that turned the word "sir" into "seer."

"Do you always do that? I mean, every time he comes here?"

"Yes, sir."

"Anything different about last night?"

"No, sir."

"Did Mr. Khoury say anything to you?"

"No, sir. I never see Mr. Khoury. Always, I put the coffee service on the table and pick up the big tip he always leaves. Mr. Khoury and his lady are in the privacy of their bedroom. I come back after they leave to pick up the coffee service."

"You don't really know if they were in the bedroom, then," said Columbo.

"I hear the voices," said Eduardo.

"How's that? You heard them talking in the bedroom?"

"I hear the voices," Eduardo said again.

"Could you understand what they were saying?"

"Oh, no, sir. Through the door I hear. I knock once on the door, so they will know the coffee is there. Then I leave."

"Did they say 'Thank you' or something like that?"

"No, sir."

"Do they ever?"

"No, sir."

"So all you ever do is come in, leave the coffee, knock once on the door, pick up your tip, and leave."

"I knock outside in hall and say 'Room service.' I wait a little, then let myself in with my key. Put the coffee service on the table. Pick up my tip. Knock once on bedroom door. Then leave."

"Thank ya, Eduardo. You've been very helpful."

The room-service waiter, obviously relieved, turned to walk away.

"Oh. One more thing," said Columbo, stopping him. "Those voices you heard through the door. Could they have been the television?"

Eduardo frowned and nodded. "Could," he said solemnly.

TEN

On Thursday morning Columbo signed in at his office to begin his daily shift. He had a reputation for an untidy desk and for an ever-growing stack of forms he was overdue in filling out, and when Captain Sczciegel came along and said good morning, Columbo glanced at that stack and wondered which one was urgent now.

Sczciegel, a tall, thin man as bald as Kojak, wore a red-and-blue tie and a blue-and-white striped shirt. He carried his snub-nose service revolver in a holster behind his hip—which made Columbo uncomfortable, because he did not carry his own revolver and the captain sometimes asked about it.

"Are we to understand, Columbo, that you don't think the Manson people are very good suspects?" the captain asked.

"There are too many holes in that, Captain. I'm

not saying Cathy Murphy and her friends didn't do it. I'm saying there are a lot of things unexplained. And I don't see the explanations right now."

"What alternatives are there?" the captain asked.

"I don't have any," said Columbo. "But, for example, it's plain that whoever did it knew something about the house and something about the habits of the people who lived there. That doesn't seem to fit Cathy Murphy and her Manson-type friends. Mr. Khoury himself says Cathy Murphy was never in the house."

"Khoury has a girlfriend. Mrs. Khoury had a boyfriend. What's that have to do with it?"

Columbo shrugged. "No quick answer."

"I'm not asking for a quick answer, Columbo. But you know we're going to be pressed."

"Gotcha," said Columbo.

"You've seen this, I suppose," said Sczciegel, handing Columbo a newspaper.

"Yes, sir. I've seen it," said Columbo, though he glanced over the story again.

MACABRE COINCIDENCE OR SATANIC PLOT IN KHOURY MURDERS?
By Al McCoy

By macabre coincidence, or maybe not by coincidence at all, the triple murder on Tuesday night at the Yussef Khoury mansion on Mulholland Drive occurs on the twenty-fifth anniversary, to the day, of the very similar murders of Sharon Tate and her friends by the notorious Manson Family.

The Tate-LaBianca murders are a dark episode in the history of our city, which most people would like to forget. They cannot forget them, however, when so similar a grisly crime is repeated on their twenty-fifth anniversary.

Police say the Khoury murders are not the first Manson copycat murders they have had to investigate. From time to time over the years, someone has killed with brutality reminiscent of the tragedy on August 9, 1969. What gives these murders a peculiarly haunting aspect is that a suspect now in custody is one of the original Manson girls and was once pregnant by Charles Manson.

While it is premature and would be improper to guess at the guilt or innocence of the suspects now in custody, the similarities and the coincidence of the date are so striking as to lead to a conclusion that either the Manson-type suspects are guilty, or they are the victims of an elaborate frame-up.

Police say they are working on both possibilities.

"Al's just doin' his job," said Columbo, handing the paper back to the captain.

"But he isn't making mine any easier," said the captain, as he walked away.

2

Kimberly Dana welcomed Columbo to the executive floor at Khoury's.

"Joe won't be in until after the funeral," she said. "And maybe not for a few days after. He's very upset. Neither of us has kidded you about the way things were between him and Arlene, but she was, after all, the mother of his children."

This morning Kimberly wore a pair of form-fitting white jeans with leather belt, a white T-shirt, and an oversize coral linen blazer. The blazer hung loosely around her, and she had rolled up the sleeves. Columbo guessed it must be a style, because this woman wouldn't wear anything not in style.

"Mrs. Columbo really appreciated the gift and told me to be sure to thank you," he said to her. "And you were right. One size does fit all."

She smiled. "I'm glad to hear it, Lieutenant. What can I do for you?"

"Well, I thought I ought to interview some of the people who work here. Like Mr. Khoury's secretary. Routine, y' know. It's the way we work. Have to talk to everybody."

"Of course. Let me set you up in Joe's office, and anyone you want can come in."

Khoury had furnished his office in the eclectic style that was typically Khoury, with a huge and elaborately carved Chinese ebony table for a desk, a black leather chair, a leather couch, a carved ivory table, assorted lamps, and Impressionist prints on the walls—all inside closed drapes that did not let sunshine in to interfere with the way he had the room lighted.

"My, this is some beautiful office," said Columbo. "I wouldn't want to smoke a cigar in here."

"Joe would appreciate it if you didn't," said Kimberly. "When occasionally I smoke a cigarette, it annoys him. I'll send in Mrs. Russell. She's his secretary. If there's anyone else you want to see, just tell Mrs. Russell."

While he waited for the secretary, Columbo studied two mounted movie posters that hung on Khoury's walls.

The first of the two pictures advertised was called *Galactic Revolt.* The poster featured paintings of the principal characters—a hero clad in a skintight white knit suit with loose, knee-high brown leather boots, brandishing a pistol-like weapon; a nearly naked heroine, dressed as a slave girl with manacles on her wrists; and a man with white beard and glasses, wearing a long white coat, meant apparently to represent a scientist. (Maybe somebody had followed the comic strip "Buck Rogers in the 21st Century," as Columbo had when he was a boy. The scientist character always wore a long white lab coat, thick, round eyeglasses, and had a white mustache, and in his speech balloons began every utterance with "Heh.") The background behind these characters was a collage of lesser characters. About half of them were reptiles that stood erect, wore clothes, and threatened with weapons, and the other half were all-but-naked slave girls.

Robert Norton played the hero, Fairleigh Richmond the heroine, and Mario Salvatore the scientist.

Dino de Mantova had directed. Co-producers were Yussef Khoury and Antonio Vado. Executive producer was Antonio Vado. Production designer was Steven Heck.

The second poster advertised a picture called *Return to the Galaxy*. The artwork was much the same. Robert Norton again played the hero and Fairleigh Richmond the heroine. The scientist character was gone. The same director and production designer remained. Antonio Vado was again co-producer with Yussef Khoury, but the executive producer was Alan Bennet.

The secretary entered the office. "Hello, Lieutenant Columbo. I'm Eleanor Russell."

A handsome woman of perhaps forty years, Eleanor Russell had an olive complexion, black hair, and dark-brown eyes. She wore a bright-red cotton knit dress just short enough to show that her legs were shapely. She sat down on the end of the couch opposite Columbo.

"Uh, Mrs. Russell, I don't want you to think that Mr. Khoury is a suspect in the death of his wife or anything like that," Columbo said to her. "It's just that in the way we work we have to ask all kinds of questions and get all the information we can. I want you to understand."

"Lieutenant Columbo," she said crisply, "Yussef Khoury is perhaps the finest man I have ever known in all my life, and if I *knew* he'd killed Mrs.

Khoury, I don't think I'd help you to convict him of it."

"That's plain enough," he said. He nodded as he turned down the corners of his mouth. "Plain enough. Does that attitude come from another judgment: that Mrs. Khoury was not a very nice woman?"

"Mrs. Khoury was not a very nice woman, Lieutenant. She was an abusive drunk."

"That's plain enough, too," said Columbo. "How about Mr. Heck?"

"Steven Heck was a Hollywood hustler, Lieutenant. Do you know the meaning of the term?"

"I think so. But how about if you tell me?"

"Steven Heck was a liar, a cheat, and a thief," she said. "To put the matter plainly."

"And if you knew who killed him, you wouldn't tell me."

Mrs. Russell drew a deep breath. "I'm not sure I'd go that far, Lieutenant. Or with Mrs. Khoury either, really. Actually, if I knew who killed them, I *would* tell you. They were despicable people, but nobody deserves to die that way."

Columbo fumbled in his pockets for a pencil—and this time found one. He made a note in his book. "Ma'am, I'd appreciate it if you'd tell me just what Mr. Heck did that makes you call him a liar and a cheat."

"Lieutenant Columbo, I think you should talk to Adam Brinsley. Mr. Brinsley is Mr. Khoury's accountant. I think Mr. Brinsley will confirm what I'm about to tell you, that Steven Heck stole from Mr. Khoury."

"How did he do that?" Columbo asked.

"I'm not sure. I doubt that Mr. Khoury would want me to mention it. But I overheard a telephone conversation between him and Mr. Brinsley, and the talk was about money spent on the motion-picture productions Steven Heck designed for Mr. Khoury."

"Tell me about Mr. Khoury's movie business."

"Others can tell you more than I can."

"But you can get me oriented, so to speak," said Columbo. "Just give me an overview of it, as ya might say."

Mrs. Russell drew a deep breath. "All right. I came to work for Mr. Khoury in 1976. Mr. Khoury, Senior, died in 1973, and the present Mr. Khoury had decided to change the business in several ways. One of the ways was that he built the lingerie shop on the second floor and established for it a line of merchandise he called the Khoury Collection. Then in 1978 he began publishing the Khoury Lingerie Calendar. It's more modest than the *Playboy* Calendar and less modest than the *Sports Illustrated* swimsuit issue. Have you ever seen it?"

"As I matter of fact, I have," said Columbo.

"So what's that got to do with his making pictures? I'll tell you. In 1978 he made a video tape of the calendar. It showed all twelve of the models, parading around in Khoury lingerie. That was a big success. He sold a lot of copies. It even ran on some cable television outlets. It's been an annual thing every year since—the Khoury Collection Video. Gradually he improved the production, added music, dancing, scenery, and of course the models had to have the talent to dance or sing. That got him interested in film production, and he formed

Khoury Productions. His first film continued the theme. The heroine of *Joelle* wore Khoury lingerie as her costume in a good many scenes. Lieutenant, would you like a cup of coffee?"

"That'd be kind of you, ma'am, if it's not inconvenient," said Columbo. "Black, no sugar."

Mrs. Russell got up and left the room, and Columbo walked around, looking. Columbo walked over to the posters again and cocked his head to one side as he studied the garishly drawn characters, particularly the nearly naked slave girl.

"Spaghetti sci-fi," said Mrs. Russell when she returned with their coffee. "They made the first one in Italy, on soundstages outside Rome. They made the second one here. Fairleigh Richmond is Anna Maria Tavernelle. She doesn't speak English. They dubbed her voice for both pictures. They tried as much as possible to have her face turned away from the camera when she spoke lines. Actually, she didn't speak many. She was to look at, not to listen to."

Columbo sat down again on the couch. "Did these pictures make money?"

"Really, you must talk to Mr. Brinsley about that."

"Miss Dana referred to Mr. Khoury's studio. What and where is that?"

Mrs. Russell shook her head. "That's a fancy name for Mr. Khoury's other office. He never calls it a studio. Obviously he doesn't keep a soundstage tied up so he can call it his studio. Like any other independent producer, he rents a soundstage when he needs it. He has only made four pictures: *Joelle* in 1987, *Revolt* in 1989, *Return* in 1990, and

Lingering Melody in 1992. Have you ever seen any of them, Lieutenant?"

Columbo shook his head. "I'm afraid not, ma'am."

"If you can get a video tape of it, you should look at *Lingering,*" she said. "It's a fine picture, got wonderful reviews. It wasn't a spaghetti flick, far from it. It had two Academy Award nominations, for best actress and for production design. But it lost money. A lot of money. It was a succès d'estime. It didn't have a gaudy poster. That's why you don't see one on the wall."

"Did Mr. Heck work on that film?"

"Oh, yes. To give the devil his due, Steven Heck had talent. He imprinted a distinctive style on the pictures he worked on, particularly on those where he had a more or less free hand—which Mr. Khoury gave him. That's why he got an Oscar nomination that year."

"Where will I find Mr. Brinsley, ma'am?"

"At the Khoury Productions office. That's in a building not far from Twentieth Century-Fox. I can write down the address. Mr. Khoury shares the office with Antonio Vado, his co-producer. Mr. Vado is working on other productions now, of course. He has to make a living."

"Well, you've been most helpful, Mrs. Russell," said Columbo. "I guess maybe I'll stop by the production office and see who'll talk to me."

"I can call and tell them to be expecting you," she offered.

"No, thank ya. I'm not sure exactly when I'll go there. So thanks for your help. Very kind of you."

Both of them stood. They left the office, and Mrs.

Russell returned to her desk in the anteroom. Columbo paused, fumbling in his raincoat pocket for a cigar, which he would light, being now out of Khoury's office.

"Oh, say," he said to Mrs. Russell. "I did mean to ask about Miss Murphy. Did you know her?"

"Yes. Yes, of course."

"Tell me about her," said Columbo.

The secretary shrugged and shook her head. "You know all about her, don't you? I mean, you know she was a Manson girl and all that."

"Yes, ma'am. I do know all about that. I'm curious about how she was *here.*"

Mrs. Russell stiffened. "She was working downstairs as a sales clerk. She told Mr. Khoury she had been trained in secretarial work and asked if he could use a secretary up here. He knew I could use help—the amount of work he requires is more than one secretary can handle, really—so he brought her up here. He knew who she was. It was very kind of him, and at the same time very idiosyncratic, to bring her into our executive offices."

"Was she any good as a secretary?" asked Columbo. "Come to work every day and on time, and all like that?"

"Uh . . . Yes, she was reasonably good. She was anxious to please. If Mr. Khoury hadn't told me who she was, I would never have guessed she was a Manson girl called Puss Dogood and had spent several years in prison. *I* assigned her work to her. I had no reason to complain about her."

"Did she ever talk about Charlie?"

"Not until I asked her," said Mrs. Russell. "Then she said enough to demonstrate that she was completely flaky on the subject. I understand she smoked marijuana, but she never showed the least sign of it here."

"But Mrs. Khoury didn't like that she was working here," said Columbo.

"No. She didn't like it a bit."

"Ma'am, I'm going to have to ask you a tough question. I can't help it. I *have* to ask. Do you think it's possible that Mrs. Khoury suspected Mr. Khoury had, uh . . . an intimate relationship with Cathy Murphy?"

Mrs. Russell frowned and lifted her chin. "I don't know, Lieutenant. I really wouldn't know."

"So you don't know why Mrs. Khoury was abusive toward Cathy Murphy?"

"Mrs. Khoury was an abusive woman, Lieutenant," said Mrs. Russell crisply. "She would have been abusive to me, except that I plainly told her to go to hell one day."

"Did she complain to Mr. Khoury about that?"

"I don't know if she did or didn't. He never said anything to me about it."

"Well, thank ya again, ma'am. I appreciate your help."

3

Kimberly Dana was in the reception area as he came out, as if she had been waiting for him. "Did you see everyone you wanted to see, Lieutenant?" she asked.

"Yes, ma'am, I did. Mrs. Russell was very helpful. She, uh, did suggest one thing. She said I should see Mr. Khoury's film *Lingering Melody*. It's not part of the investigation, but I certainly would like to see it. In fact, I'd like to see his other pictures, too. You wouldn't happen to have tapes?"

"I can lend you the tapes," she said. "I'll have to ask you to return them. They're my personal copies."

"Hey, that's very kind of you, Miss Dana. I appreciate it very much."

She led him into her office, which was of modest size but luxuriously furnished, with the same posters on the walls as hung on Khoury's. He noticed the lettering on her door—

KIMBERLY DANA
Executive Assistant

"Here they are," she said. She took them from behind a sliding door in her credenza. *"Lingering Melody* and the two sci-fi's."

"I'll bring them right back," he promised.

"Okay. Anything else?"

"Well, I did happen to notice the way you're listed on the door. Would I be totally outa line to ask just what an executive assistant does?"

"I understand what you are suggesting," she said coolly. "And the answer is yes. That's what I do."

"I wasn't askin'—"

"In addition, I have some very specific administrative duties, Lieutenant."

"Oh, I'm sure you do, ma'am. I didn't mean to suggest you didn't."

"There is another element of it. Let's get that straight, Lieutenant. Joe loves me, and I love him. What's happened is a terrible tragedy, beyond what's obvious. I'm trying to protect the man I love, as much as I can. That's why I'm in the office, which is certainly not where I want to be. If I could be where I want to be, I'd be with *him*. You can understand, can't you?"

Columbo suddenly realized that he had been backing away from her. He stopped. "Oh, absolutely," he said. "So thank ya again, Miss Dana. I'll bring your tapes back tomorrow."

ELEVEN

The gull-wing Mercedes was of course a conspicuous, memorable car. Driving it, a man had no
anonymity whatever. Leaving the house late on
Thursday morning, Yussef Khoury drove his second car, an inconspicuous red Toyota that offended
him for its lack of elegance but served him when he
wanted to go somewhere without being instantly
recognized—and without risking the theft of a
classic automobile.

Apart from the car, he was also making a point of
anonymity. He wore golfing clothes: bright-red
slacks, a lemon-yellow shirt, and even a plastic
mesh cap lettered with the words BEL AIRE.

Le Cirque was a restaurant in Pasadena. He
drove into the parking lot, parked his own car, and
went inside. Kimberly was waiting in a booth,

sipping from a Bombay gin martini and nibbling on a sesame breadstick.

"I half expected to see the cop in the raincoat sitting here with you," said Khoury as he sat down. "When I came out of the water yesterday afternoon, there he was, sitting on the beach, waiting for me. That was spooky, let me tell you."

"The man is no dummy," she said. "He's playing dummy. It's an act."

"He hasn't bought the Puss Dogood, Helter Skelter deal at all," said Khoury. "We might as well not have bothered to do that part of it."

"We haven't dealt the Boobs card yet," said Kim.

Khoury nodded. "Deal it. Deal it tonight. It's not going to do much for us, but we went to enough trouble to set it up, we might as well use it." He shook his head. "We need something to reinforce the case against Puss."

"I've been thinking about that," she said. "I've got an idea about what might reinforce it good."

"Like what?"

"Like reporting a piece of Arlene's jewelry missing," Kimberly suggested. "A valuable piece."

"It would have to be a piece of jewelry she never really had," said Khoury. "They inventoried what was in the room yesterday morning."

"I hate to suggest this, Joe, but what about the jeweled gold choker you gave me?"

"Why *that,* for heaven's sake?"

"Listen to me, Joe," she said. "There has to be a record that you bought it, that you paid for it. I've never worn it in public, only when you and I were alone. If it were missing—"

"At least it offers a motive—"

"Exactly. I won't ask what you paid for it."

"You'll have to know. I bought it from Harry Winston's for $48,350."

She seized his hand. "Oh, Joe! I knew it was a very generous gift. But I didn't dream it was that much!"

"If I report it stolen, we'll have to dispose of it. The risk that somebody might someday find it. . . ." He shook his head. "You'll have to throw it off the pier, like the Bali-Songs."

"Oh, my *god!*"

He shrugged and turned down the corners of his mouth. "There's no option, Kim. No option. If we decide to do it. Anyway, I insured it."

"Which brings in an insurance investigator."

"Well, what's he going to do—argue no one was murdered? You know, this may be a very good idea. *I* would hardly have murdered my wife for forty-eight thousand dollars. The Manson crowd might. Somebody else might."

"Columbo is going to ask why the murderers stole that piece alone."

"I can answer that question. The last time I saw it, it was lying on the dresser, in a tray where she kept her wristwatch and other things of the kind when she went to bed. Her regular jewelry was in drawers. The murderers were in a panic and grabbed what they saw."

Kimberly shook her head. "But then why did they come in the first place? I mean, if they knew she had valuable jewelry—and I suppose she had other things—why didn't they take the time to—"

"Two reasons," he interrupted. "Puss Dogood came to murder Arlene because she hated her and had good reason to hate her. She's a member of a group that has demonstrated its willingness to commit murder, for a reason or without a reason. Maybe they came just to kill. Maybe they came to kill *and* to steal. They killed, anyway. Then— Sergio interrupted them and probably screamed. That scared them. They grabbed what they saw and ran."

Kimberly shook her head. "Well, let's think about it a little," she said.

"I can't think about it too long," said Khoury. "I have to pretend I discovered the loss the first time I reviewed the police inventory—which I must have done this morning."

2

Columbo liked Detective Sergeant Ted Jackson. Other people liked Ted because he was a handsome, white-haired, ruddy-faced guy. Columbo liked him as a good, street-smart cop. He liked him also because Jackson shared his fondness for the pool table—also because he was willing to eat bowls of Burt's fiery chili.

Jackson watched Columbo take aim on the nine

ball. It was a tough shot, but he'd make it and win the game. Columbo might clown around on the one ball and two and so on, but he was deadly when it came to the nine ball. He didn't even take off his raincoat, and it was smeared with blue cue chalk.

"Am I wasting my time checking out Cathy Murphy and her buddies?" he asked Columbo.

With his cigar clamped between his teeth, Columbo took his shot, pocketed the nine ball, then pulled out the cigar and said, "Huh-uh. It's never a waste of time to get more facts in the record. The more facts, the better."

"But you're focusing on Khoury."

"That's because I know *you're* handling the Manson Family idea. Find out anything interesting?"

"Yeah. There were four of them out Tuesday night. Not just three. The fourth man is one Buddy Drake. He drove them. His Toyota is the only really operational vehicle the group has. Cathy drives a Chevy Vega and Douglas a Chevy pickup, but only the Toyota is reliable. Drake doesn't live with them. He dropped them off at the shack and went home. That's why he wasn't there when the black-and-whites responded to the shack."

"You arrest him?"

"No. He's a little more of a solid citizen than the others, and since he doesn't know we know about him, we can pick him up any time. He's sweating, I figure, but he hasn't lammed."

"How'd you find out about him?"

"Jenny Schmidt told me. Being in jail has got her

totally discombobulated. All she wants is out, and she'll tell anything to get out."

"She's the one Cathy calls Kid," said Columbo.

Jackson nodded. "I really like the names Charlie gave them," he said. "Puss Dogood, Kid, and Bum Rapp. Buddy Drake doesn't have a nickname. That makes him a kind of lesser member of the tribe. It means Charlie Manson didn't favor him as much—according to Kid. The names are a problem, though. Kid says two or three others came to the shack pretty often. Buddy Drake she knew as Buddy Drake. But two other girls she knows only as Squatty and Boobs. She describes them as looking like what their nicknames suggest, but she has no idea what their real names are or where they live."

"What does Puss Dogood say about that?"

"She says there are no other real Manson people in the L.A. area. She says anybody else who comes around the house is just a curiosity seeker: kids who want to attach themselves to what she calls The Charlie Legend but are too young ever to have met him."

"What about Squatty and Boobs?"

"She says there may have been girls by that name around the house but she doesn't know them. She says she was working all day, and Kid wasn't, so Kid may know people she, Puss, doesn't know. Which makes sense."

"I suppose you searched the shack pretty thoroughly," said Columbo.

"Right. We found their stash, the marijuana Puss says she bought Tuesday night. Three hunting knives, but not ones that could have made the wounds in the victims. A Winchester lever-action rifle. And a Glock nine-millimeter automatic. With ammunition for both. No bloody clothes. Not much money. Nothing that looked like loot from the Khoury house. Mostly junk, nothing Khoury would have owned."

Columbo racked the balls. They were playing for a dollar a rack, and he turned and marked his latest victory on the blackboard. Jackson had won three games, Columbo six. As winner, he broke the next rack. He put the nicely balanced jointed cue in the frame and took down a crude, heavy cue. He clenched his cigar in his teeth, and with that heavier cue he slammed the cue ball into the rack. The balls scattered, and two sank: seven and five. The cue ball hit two rails and wound up behind the seven, blocking any possible shot on the one ball. He shot the cue ball against the right rail and brought it up the table to kiss the one. Good enough. He hadn't scratched. The cue ball wound up against the top rail, leaving Jackson a difficult shot on the one.

"Might be worthwhile locating Squatty and Boobs," said Columbo. "Y' never know what's next."

"Workin' on it," said Jackson.

"And one more little thing. Did you ever find out when that pizza was delivered? The one smeared all over the bed?"

Jackson nodded. "Delivered by a girl named Molly Ridley. At a little after eleven-forty. She was a little worried she hadn't made the thirty-minute delivery and that the guy'd ask for it free. But he didn't. She describes the guy that took delivery and paid her. It was Heck."

"Alive at eleven-forty," said Columbo, nodding.

3

Before leaving Burt's, Columbo checked headquarters to see what telephone calls he had, if any.

"Mr. Yussef Khoury called," said the dispatcher. "He will be at home this afternoon and would appreciate it if you called him or stopped by."

Shortly Columbo drove up the driveway at the Khoury house on Mulholland Drive. An LAPD black-and-white still blocked the driveway, keeping away the news people and the curious. The officer cleared the way for Lieutenant Columbo.

Mrs. Nagako Takeshi met him at the door and led him out to the swimming pool, where Yussef Khoury sat on a chaise longue, dressed in a dark-blue golf shirt and dark-blue slacks and reading a loose-bound script.

"Lieutenant . . ." he said. "Sit down. Can I offer something cooling? Personally, I find Scotch cooling. But it can be Coca-Cola or—"

"I'll take a light Scotch," said Columbo. "And, hey, I want to tell you, I find this a most elegant place. Your home is . . . elegant."

Khoury nodded at Mrs. Takeshi, who went off to the kitchen.

"Well, thank you. I have always tried to live well. It's too warm for the raincoat, Lieutenant, if you don't mind my saying so. Would you care to—"

"Oh, sure," said Columbo. "Y'see, sir, I carry so

much of my junk in the pockets, I'm lost without the thing. Anyway—" He shrugged out of the raincoat and laid it over a chair. His light-gray suit was more rumpled than the raincoat. "Anyway, I got your message."

"You came because I called," said Khoury. "Let me tell you why. You asked me to review the inventory of my wife's jewelry, as found by the officers who investigated the scene. I really wasn't quite up to doing that until this morning. And then—Something is missing, Lieutenant. I still can't bring myself to enter those rooms, but Mrs. Takeshi went in and looked for me. Something is missing."

"Yes, sir?"

"In June, I think it was, I bought my wife a gold choker from Harry Winston's. I paid $48,350 for it. It is not on the police inventory. Frankly, I have not yet been able to bring myself to enter the rooms. Mrs. Takeshi has and tells me the item is missing."

"That's curious, isn't it, Mr. Khoury?" asked Columbo. "I mean, isn't it curious that somebody would steal one item of jewelry and leave all the rest?"

"I can think of two reasons why, Lieutenant," said Khoury. "In the first place, the choker, gold with diamonds and emeralds, from Harry Winston's, was the most valuable item Arlene owned. In the second place, the last time I saw it, it was lying in a tray on top of the dresser. In other words, it was in sight. My theory is that Sergio heard screams and came into the bedroom suite while the killers were writing on the walls. They'd grabbed the choker but hadn't gotten into the dresser drawers. They killed him, but they couldn't be sure he hadn't called 911. Or maybe he screamed so loud they were afraid the neighbors had heard him. So they figured they had no more time, and they ran. Does that make sense?"

"Oh, yes, sir. That makes a lot of sense," said Columbo.

"Well . . . Figuring it out is your business. That's just *my* best idea."

"I'm not sure I'll come up with a better idea."

Khoury turned away from Columbo and looked out over the mountainside, at the Pacific visible in the distance. "We bought this house . . . I don't know why, to tell you the truth. She never really liked it. The kids never lived here. We couldn't afford the place when the kids were at home. If we'd stayed in the old, smaller place . . . Well, who knows?"

Mrs. Takeshi arrived with Columbo's Scotch. He tasted it and knew he'd been given something fine. This was no ordinary Scotch. He'd said light. Mrs. Takeshi had not offended this whisky by putting water or soda in it. She had, in fact, put only one ice cube in the glass. Something more representing the famed Khoury elegance.

"I don't see how you handle it, Lieutenant Columbo," said Yussef Khoury, still staring into the distance.

"What's that, sir?"

"Murder . . ." said Khoury. "I have to cope with it once. I guess you have to cope with it every day."

"Well, sir," said Columbo, "I do have to cope

with it all the time. To do what I do I have to keep a
kind of detached attitude, you understand. I hope
that doesn't mean I've got callous. I don't want to
ever get to be that. In every one of these cases
there's a person who was once living and now isn't
anymore. Investigating that is my business. It's
what I do. But I've always gotta keep in mind that
some person has been made dead. Dead is permanent. That's the whole thing, isn't it?"

Neither of them had more to say. Columbo drank
the last of his Scotch, rose, picked up his raincoat,
and left. Khoury sat silent, his mind maybe focused
on the detective's last words.

4

Kimberly dialed a telephone number for the tenth
time. Maybe the twelfth or fourteenth, she hadn't
counted. Her impatience had grown to outright
annoyance.

"Hello . . ."

At long last! She whispered hoarsely into the
phone. "Boobs?"

"This is Squatty. Who's this?"

"Kid."

"You sound funny."

"You know what's comin' down?"

"What?"

"We been busted. I'm callin' from the slammer.

You got to go out to the house and get those guns outa there. Hang in an' warn everybody. It's what Charlie'd want ya to do. Got it?"

"Got it. What—"

Kimberly hung up.

TWELVE

The double walnut doors were lettered with gold leaf—

YUSSEF KHOURY PRODUCTIONS
ANTONIO VADO PRODUCTIONS

Below, in smaller letters—

ADAM W. BRINSLEY, C.P.A.

Inside, it was obvious that Yussef Khoury had not decorated this suite of offices. The reception area was a model of impersonal efficiency, not of Khoury elegance. Paneled with walnut that matched the doors that opened onto the several offices, the area was carpeted in blue and lighted by spots recessed in the ceiling. Two small palms grew in black plastic tubs. No movie posters hung here, no photographs of stars, nothing to distinguish this suite from a hundred thousand just like it in this city alone.

The receptionist was as grimly efficient as the office. She spoke to Brinsley on the phone, then pointed to a door. Columbo knocked once and opened the door.

Brinsley's office was almost exactly like the reception area. It had just two modest personal touches: photographs of his three children on the credenza behind his desk—of his children, not of his wife, Columbo noticed—and a single Miró print, in depressing dark colors, on the wall.

Adam Brinsley was a small man, short and trim, with pale-blue eyes behind almost-white lashes, a ruddy complexion, and thin blond hair that he kept down and in place with a shiny hair dressing. His carefully tailored summer-weight dark-blue suit was a little limp and wrinkled by the heat and humidity of Los Angeles in August. He sat behind a desk covered with papers—tax forms, mostly— and a desktop computer.

"Eleanor Russell had an attack of conscience over what she said to you about Steven Heck and called to tell me she had suggested you come to see me," said Brinsley. "Let me ask you something in all frankness, Lieutenant Columbo."

"Yes, sir. And I'll answer in all frankness," said Columbo. He was glad to see an ashtray with cigarette butts on Brinsley's desk, so he took a cigar from his raincoat pocket. "Would you happen to have a match handy, sir?"

Brinsley shoved a lighter across the desk—rather brusquely. "My frank question is this," he said. "If

Manson types or Manson copycats murdered
Arlene Khoury and Steven Heck in a wanton,
vicious, animalistic orgy of violence, what difference does it make if Steve was stealing from Joe? I
mean, it looks to me like you're investigating Joe
Khoury."

"Oh, no, sir. Who I'm investigating is Mr. Heck,"
said Columbo, puffing on his cigar. "When a man is
dead by reason of murder, you can't overlook any
fact you can get about him. Any fact at all. That's in
the nature of my business, y' understand. I have to
find out everything I can."

Brinsley lit a cigarette and leaned back in his
chair. "Eleanor says she accused Steve of stealing
from Joe."

"Let's don't worry too much about what anybody
accused anybody else of doing," said Columbo.
"She told me you could give me the facts."

Brinsley hesitated for a long moment. "Lieutenant LAPD, homicide. . . ." he muttered. "Okay.
Steve *is* the one who's dead. I guess you need some
history. How much do you know about Joe
Khoury?"

"Some," said Columbo. "Why don't you tell me
what you think I need to know?"

"Joe Khoury inherited his business from his
father. His father was a genius. So is Joe, some
ways. The store does better than it used to do. But
I'll tell you something about Joe. He calls himself a
merchant, and he thinks being a merchant is beneath his dignity. He has always wanted to be
something better. People with money and position
come to him because he sells wonderful things, but
he has this sense that he's their merchant—which

means he's not one of them. Living in this town, he wanted to be a movie producer. He's put a lot of money into the idea. Too much."

"I understand he's made four movies," said Columbo.

Brinsley smiled. "Yes. *Joelle,* the first one, was a showcase for the Khoury Collection. Short on plot, short on characterization, short on production values. He got Willa Wood to do it. All she ever was was a sex kitten, and in *Joelle* her chief function was to walk on camera in Khoury lingerie, show herself off, pout a little . . . You know the kind of thing. The picture made money. Hell, he didn't spend much on it. But the community laughed at him. It was just one of the Khoury Collection videotapes expanded. So then he hooked up with Tony Vado to make a couple of sci-fi extravaganzas."

"Those were the ones Mr. Heck designed, right?"

"Right. Listen, Lieutenant. Those pictures carried the *stamp* of Steve Heck. It was what he knew how to do. Color. Mood. Atmosphere. Sex. The first one was R-rated because of the nudity. Joe insisted on toning that down a little for the second one, to get a PG-13. *Star Wars* they weren't. But they did well. Tony Vado worked to get good distribution. The pictures didn't stay long in the theaters, but Joe put them on video tape. The tapes sold damned well. The space movies made money."

Columbo reached forward and tapped his cigar on the edge of Brinsley's big ashtray. "So, did Mr. Heck *steal* from Mr. Khoury, do you think?"

"If you weren't a police detective investigating a triple murder, I'd tell you it's none of your business," said Brinsley. "But you are. So . . . A prosecutor would have had a tough time making a case of grand larceny against Steve Heck. Joe would have had a tough time making a case if he'd sued him. It's complicated, Lieutenant. It has to do with Steve overcharging for products and services he used. Common in the industry. Subcontractors overcharge and pay a kickback. It's illegal, of course, but it's difficult to prove. And Steve Heck was an artist at it—which was known to the smart money. People would underbid on Steve's services, knowing he'd make it up by taking a percentage off his contractors."

"For example, sir," said Columbo. "Give me an example, so I can understand. This kind of thing is outside my line of experience, y' know."

"For example, Lieutenant—in a sci-fi space picture there are always a lot of explosions. Making miniature explosions is a minor art form in motion-picture production. I happen to know that the subcontractor for miniature explosions overcharged by twenty percent on *Return to the Galaxy* —and guess who took most of that. That's just one example."

"Are you saying Mr. Heck cost Mr. Khoury the profits on his two space pictures?"

Brinsley stiffened for a moment and frowned, thinking. Then he said—"Yes. Well, not exactly. This business runs on tight budgets, Lieutenant Columbo. If a picture succeeds big, the budget doesn't make much difference. If it fails, it doesn't make much difference. The great majority of pictures fall in between—that is, between making it big and outright failing. On those, the budget does make a difference. A big difference. Steve Heck skimmed enough off those two films to make them modest winners when they would have been very respectable winners."

"Miniature explosions. . . ." Columbo mused, puffing on his cigar.

"Lieutenant. Miniature explosions is just an example. A space picture requires *models,* expensive models—and they blow a lot of them up in miniature explosions. Animation. Computer animation. Artists. Special effects designers and technicians. Blowing up a model city with miniature explosions can look like blowing up a stack of matchboxes with firecrackers if the special-effects people aren't on the ball. There are a hundred special contractors on pictures like *Galactic Revolt,* each bringing some special skill or talent to make a scene look the way it's supposed to look. Steve Heck knew them all, every last one of them, and knew which ones would kick back how much. That was his business."

"Then Mr. Khoury made a picture that lost a lot of money," said Columbo. "Was that Mr. Heck's fault?"

"No. Of course, Steve was up to his tricks on *Lingering Melody,* but that's not why the picture lost so much. To know the reason, you have to understand Joe Khoury. You know the store. You've seen his home. In Los Angeles, Khoury is another name for good taste, style, flair. Maybe it wouldn't be on Fifth Avenue, but in L.A. it is. Joe takes great pride in that. He didn't think his pictures reflected well on the Khoury name and reputation. When some people called *Galactic Revolt* a spaghetti sci-fi, he refused to make the sequel in Italy, even though he could have brought it in a lot cheaper over there. But *Return to the Galaxy* was the same kind of thing, even though he made it in Hollywood. The town didn't like either of the sci-fi's much. They didn't get good notices. And Joe hated that. He had a notion that the industry was laughing at him. He wasn't entirely wrong."

"Miss Dana lent me video tapes of the two sci-fi's and *Lingering Melody*," said Columbo. "I'm planning on watching them this evening, if I can."

"I agree, you should," said Brinsley. "Not because it has anything to do with the murders, just because *Lingering Melody* is a damned fine motion picture. Joe's proud of it—and has every right to be. Of course, he paid Diana Cushing six bloody fortunes to star in it; and her shit—meaning having to hire *her* makeup artist, *her* hairdresser, even *her* cameraman, and so on—cost two fortunes more. It seems like a simple little film, but it cost more to make than either of the big, splashy sci-fi's. The *Times* loved it. *Vanity Fair* loved it. *The New Yorker* loved it. It got two Academy Award nominations. But distributors—" Brinsley turned down the corners of his mouth and shook his head. "It was 'too arty,' they said. 'Too gloomy.' 'Too preachy.' 'Too long.' It ran in only about a third as many theaters as ran the sci-fi's. And, frankly, I have to admit that audiences weren't exactly crazy about it. Joe lost a lot of money on it."

"Then is he out of the movie business?"

"He is until he recoups his fortune. Right now he can't afford to sink money in another picture."

Columbo took a final puff on his cigar, then laid it in the big glass ashtray on Brinsley's desk, to go out. "Mr. Brinsley . . . It's not my business to dig up gossip. I always hate to have to bring up somethin' like I'm going to bring up, but I suppose you know that Mrs. Khoury and Mr. Heck were in bed together at the time of the murders."

"So? What's your question, Lieutenant?" asked Brinsley coldly.

"I guess my question is, does that surprise you? I hope you don't mind my askin'."

"The answer," said Brinsley, shaking his head, "is that it doesn't surprise me." He crushed his cigarette beside Columbo's cigar. "What does that tell you? Anything?"

"It tells me the matter was no secret," said Columbo. "Which means that Mr. Khoury knew about it. Right?"

"And Arlene knew about Kim," said Brinsley. "There was no love lost in that foursome, Lieutenant, but there was no great hostility, either. They simply faced the facts of life. It goes on all the time in this town."

Columbo nodded. "Other towns, too, from what I read."

Brinsley smiled. "Other towns just don't get the publicity," he said.

"You suppose Mrs. Khoury knew Mr. Heck was getting kickbacks on contracts and that way taking money out of her husband's pockets?" Columbo asked.

"Arlene wasn't stupid. She didn't miss much."

"Well . . . tell me. When Mr. Heck made Mr. Khoury poorer, he was making Mrs. Khoury poorer, too, wasn't he? Community property. In California. She owned half of what he owned. Right?"

"Simplifying, yes."

"Which made her an . . . intimate friend of a man who was stealing from her. Am I missing something here? I have trouble picking up on subtle things. What is it I don't understand?"

"You said you didn't want to get into gossip, Lieutenant."

"Right. But it's an inconsistency, sir. That's a big part of my job, resolving inconsistencies."

Brinsley shook another cigarette from a pack of Marlboros, looked at it a moment, apparently thought better of it, and returned it to the pack. "It's a large part of mine, too," he said while still staring at the cigarette. "I've got no explanation for you. I can confirm that Steve Heck skimmed money off Joe's productions, but I didn't know Arlene very well. You should talk to Tony Vado."

THIRTEEN

1

Happily for Columbo, Antonio Vado was in his office. He sent out word that he would talk to the lieutenant this afternoon, if he was willing to wait a few minutes.

Columbo sat down to wait. He picked up a copy of *People* magazine and glanced idly through. He saw an article about Diana Cushing, the star of *Lingering Melody*. The story was about how she and her three children lived happily in an old farmhouse in Connecticut, absent the husbands she had divorced, the fathers of the children. She would make no more than one film a year from now on, the article said.

Photographed in blue jeans and sweatshirt, she "looks like anything but the star-crossed lover of *Lingering Melody* or the glamorous but tragic New York fashion model of *Fifty-Third and Park.*"

Columbo liked the pictures of her on her farm better than the publicity stills from the two pictures. She was a beautiful woman, though, whatever she wore: a blonde with long hair, with a flawless face and figure.

Antonio Vado came out. "Lieutenant Columbo!" he said in a hearty, booming voice. "We've never met, but I know your name."

"And I know yours too, sir," said Columbo, shaking hands with Vado.

"Ah. But you may wonder why I know yours. Not that you aren't famous. I mean, you have quite a name and a reputation for success. But do you remember the murder of Anna Piccolini? She was a second cousin of mine, by marriage."

"I'm glad I was able to clear that up," said Columbo.

"Probably just a routine case for you," Vado suggested.

"No, sir. There's no such thing as a routine case, when somebody's dead."

"Ah. Well . . . Of course. That's true. Come in. What can I do for you?"

Vado was a big handsome man with a strong face and curly graying hair. Voluble, with deceptively ingenuous enthusiasm, he spoke English with a distinct Italian accent. His gray suit was of a shiny fabric Columbo didn't know the name of. His shoes were identical to the ones Yussef Khoury wore: Gucci loafers.

His office was totally unlike Brinsley's. Movie posters hung on the walls—including the space-picture ones Columbo had seen in Khoury's office. Spotlights shining from track fixtures on the ceiling highlighted some of them. Their bright colors gave the office a gaudy ambience—gaudy but also exuberant. Vado also maintained on the walls a gallery of autographed star photos.

"At this time of afternoon," said Vado, "it's not too early to offer a drink. Not too early to have one. What would you like, Lieutenant?"

"Technically, I shouldn't drink on duty," said Columbo. "But I suppose a light Scotch and soda at this time of day wouldn't hurt anything."

Vado lifted the top of one end of his credenza, exposing a bar. He poured Scotch and soda for Columbo, a gin and tonic for himself, then closed the bar. Columbo noticed that the Scotch was Johnnie Walker Black, fine whisky but not the outstanding Scotch Yussef Khoury served. It didn't offend this Scotch to put a little seltzer in it.

Vado sat down, facing Columbo across his desk. "Well . . . I bet you'd like to ask me some questions," he said.

"Yes, sir. I guess you knew Mrs. Khoury and Mr. Heck pretty well."

Vado shrugged. "I suppose so."

"Mr. Heck had a reputation for skimming money off contracts," said Columbo. "He did that to Mr. Khoury, I'm told."

"Did it to me, too. I was co-producer on two films with Joe Khoury. If you want the bare truth, Lieutenant, there was no love lost between me and Steve Heck. I won't deny his talent, but I resented his dishonesty."

"Tell me something, Mr. Vado," said Columbo. "Just what is a production designer?"

"Industry bullshit," said Vado. "The conventional wisdom these days is that pictures are 'created' by directors. In fact, actors, producers, special-effects men, writers, and composers create them. *And* production designers. The production designer has many of the same responsibilities as the director. He gives the film its special . . . flavor. He gives it its *look,* and if he does it well, credit goes to the director."

"Thank you. Mr. Heck stole from others, not just from you and Mr. Khoury, right?"

"Absolutely."

"Then a lot of people might have thought they had reason to kill him," said Columbo.

"You don't buy the idea he was killed by a gang of . . . a gang of two-legged *animals?"* asked Vado.

"Maybe he was," said Columbo. "But I've got to eliminate other possibilities. Everybody I talk to says Mr. Heck was very good at what he did. But everybody also says he was a thief."

Vado sipped from his gin and tonic, frowned, and then asked, "How much time do you have, Lieutenant?"

"My time is your time, sir. I'll take whatever time it takes to clear up some of the inconsistencies."

"I will show you some bits of video tape," said Vado.

He pulled a cord that exposed on the wall to the right of his desk a large video projection screen. Columbo noticed now that a cube-shaped coffee table was in fact a video projector, when it was opened. Vado pulled from a drawer four video tapes.

"I show you," he said, "only snippets. Just to demonstrate."

He shoved a cartridge into the projector. Sound filled the room, and an image appeared on the screen—of a young woman in Khoury lingerie, modeling—the same kind of thing Columbo had seen at Hammond's Restaurant at noon yesterday. She swept back and forth before the camera, pulling off a negligee and showing herself in sheer panties and a sheer bra, a little bolder than what the models had shown in the restaurant.

"You see?" said Vado. "Joe's start in the business. There was money in this."

He stopped the tape, removed it, and inserted another cartridge. This one he rolled forward for a half minute before he stopped it and began to project it. It was the same thing, except that the young woman in the Khoury bra, panties, garter belt, and stockings walked across a luxurious room to a bar and said, "You'll have a drink, surely." Vado let the tape run a minute or so while the young woman poured two drinks and walked back across the room to where a somewhat greasy-looking man sat on a couch.

"Willa Wood," said Vado. "You recognized her, of course. The film was called *Joelle*."

"Yes, sir," said Columbo. "I've seen one or two of her other pictures. On television. Cut a lot, I imagine."

"All right," said Vado. He stopped this tape, too, and replaced it with another one. *"Galactic Revolt,"* he said as he shoved another cartridge in and set it on fast-forward to roll to the scene he wanted to show.

The difference between this picture and the others was striking. It did not take a connoisseur of motion pictures to see the difference. The scene was dark and brooding. It was of a swamp, with alien foliage not to be found anywhere on earth. Bubbles popped to the surface in pools of turbid water, emitting wisps of smoke. A young woman ran as if in terror through the swamp. She was stark naked and only partly obscured either by foliage or mist. Though she was running, the sound of her breath, indeed even the sound of her splashing through the water, was not heard on the screen. She ran in eerie silence, until a blast of music overwhelmed any sound she might have made.

Vado let it run but turned off the sound. "Anna Maria Tavernelle," said Vado. "In the screen credits, Fairleigh Richmond."

She ran and ran, until a grotesque monster overtook her and leaped to crush her to the ground. But as the monster leaped, a red laserlike beam stopped it in midair and blew it to bits. The hero, in spotless white leotards, stepped calmly forward and lifted the frightened girl from the ground.

Light filled the screen. Like sunrise. The appearance of the rescuing hero had inspired a complete change of mood. What had been murky gray-green now turned gradually yellow and white, though the scene was the same swamp.

Vado stopped the tape. "Steve Heck," he said. "A little crude, but effective. Now look. *Lingering Melody—*"

The final tape rolled forward to the scene Vado wanted to show. It seemed at first to be of an Edwardian dining room, a scene from a gaslight movie. The dim, yellowish light suggested as much. Looking closer, Columbo saw that the men and women on the screen were not in Edwardian dress but very modern dress: the men in business suits, not tuxedos or tails, the women in short cocktail dresses. Music overcame most conversation, though a few words here and there could be heard: conversation about money, also gossip. The scene was not of an Edwardian dining room but of a contemporary urban dinner club. Waitresses appeared: young women in satin corselets and net stockings, carrying trays and serving drinks.

"Now watch," said Vado. "Diana Cushing."

The actress Columbo had seen in blue jeans and a sweatshirt in the magazine a few minutes ago came toward the camera carrying a tray of drinks. She passed by the camera, which turned and followed her as she approached a table.

The waitress served the drinks, placing each one before one of the men and women at the table. The camera switched back and forth between the waitress and a woman her own age, sitting at the table with cigarette in hand and gossiping with the man beside her. At first she hardly noticed the waitress, but when she took a sip from her glass she raised her head and snapped, "Oh, *please,* dear! I *emphatically* said Tanqueray." Again the camera switched back and forth, as the woman shook her head over her drink and the waitress at first panicked, then mumbled an apology, saying she would bring a Tanqueray martini immediately. "Before everyone else's ice melts, if you can manage it," said the customer.

"You see?" said Vado as he switched off the projector. "Steve Heck? He did the set, the lights, the costumes, the music. The director . . . Well, the director of *Lingering Melody* was Ben Willsberger. He controlled the acting, the camera work, and so on. But you see the mood, the emotions? If I had shown you a few minutes more, you would have seen that the woman did *not* order Tanqueray. Diana Cushing's reaction, her fear at first, her humiliation, is brilliant acting. The director called for that and caught it on film. But Steve Heck designed it all. He gave Diana a setting . . . a box in which to act. Diana couldn't have achieved the power of that scene in the *Joelle* set. The club, incidentally, was his idea; it was a very different place in the script. That was Steve Heck. He was a genius."

"Then why did he have to skim off money?" Columbo asked.

Vado shrugged. "The industry," he said. "It has its own peculiar way of placing value on things. A script writer, for example, may get $80,000 for making a far bigger contribution to the success of a film than its $400,000 director. Why? I don't know why. The reviewers always give endless 'scholarly analysis' to what directors do—ignoring the fact that most of what they get credit for doing was done by others. I don't know why."

Columbo turned down the corners of his mouth and nodded.

"Mr. Vado, I guess you know Mrs. Khoury and Mr. Heck were in bed together when they died. That doesn't seem to surprise anybody, including Mr. Khoury. Just what contribution did she make to Mr. Khoury's films?"

"I'd say she made no contribution whatever,"

said Vado bluntly. "Maybe I'm not the one to ask. She was a meddling bitch."

"I haven't yet found anybody who liked her much," said Columbo.

"You haven't even found anybody who's sorry she's dead."

"But I don't think I've found anybody with motive to murder her," said Columbo. He accepted his second drink from Vado. "Also, I've got another question. You'll have to excuse me. Asking questions is my business. Meddling, prying into other people's business. That's my business. It's what I have to do."

"Understood, Lieutenant. No problem."

"Well, y' see, people talk about Mrs. Khoury different ways—as a meddler, as a drunk, as aggressive, as unkind . . . What do you suppose Mr. Heck saw in her? I mean, they must have been pretty close. He was ten years younger than she was, kind of a good-lookin' guy. It's an awful personal question. . . ."

Vado looked thoughtful for a moment. "For years and years," he began, "before I knew the Khourys, Arlene was a quiet, dutiful housewife. She brought up their kids. That's what she wanted in life, what she thought was natural, maybe inevitable. Then the kids grew up and went out on their own, and there wasn't anything left for her. She hung around the country club. She tried golf, but mostly she played cards, and she was bored out of her skull. She got to drinking too much. She knew Joe saw younger women, so she decided to see younger men. Problem was, what did she have that would

attract them? Well, she attracted the tennis pro at
the club. What she had that attracted him was a lot
of money and a sex drive bigger than all outdoors.
So I heard. I figure that is what attracted Steve
Heck."

"Did she really meddle in Mr. Khoury's business?"

"In the picture business, yes. She was around this
office more than I wanted to see her—and she
would come around the soundstage when we were
shooting. She was full of ideas. Finally, even Steve
Heck joined the rest of us in telling her to get lost."

"When do you suppose Mr. Khoury will make
another picture?" Columbo asked.

Vado shook his head. "Not until he comes up
with the money. His losses on *Lingering Melody*
effectively put him out of the picture business.
That's particularly galling to him, because he wants
to find a vehicle for Kimberly Dana and do a film
starring her."

"Is she an actress?"

Vado nodded. "Some kind of an actress. No
Diana Cushing. But good enough. We tested her.
Ever see her on television?"

"No, sir, I never did. What's she on?"

"Beach volleyball," said Vado with a grin. "Look
at it on Sports Channel sometime. She plays volleyball in the sand with a team of other girls, all
wearing bikinis. It really is sort of a sport. Not like
TV wrestling. She *sweats,* Lieutenant. They all do.
Caps with visors to keep the sun out of their eyes.
And bikinis. They play hard. Kim is something of
an athlete."

Columbo frowned thoughtfully. "Athlete . . ." he

muttered. "Okay. Well, sir, I've taken too much of your time. I thank ya. Very interesting, all you said."

"Any time, Lieutenant. I didn't like Arlene at all and Steve not much, but I'd like to see the people who killed them brought to justice. There is one thing I'd like to say, though."

"Okay. What is it?"

"Your line of questions seems to me to suggest you might suspect Joe Khoury. Let me tell you for sure, Lieutenant: Joe Khoury is no murderer. Even if the bitch deserved it—which I don't say—Joe couldn't have done it. It's just not in the guy. He's not the kind."

"Well, I appreciate what you just said, Mr. Vado," said Columbo. "I've got an awful good impression of Mr. Khoury myself. It's hard to think he could have had anything to do with—Anyway . . . Thanks again." Columbo moved toward the door and reached for the knob.

"Oh. Let me give you a couple of tapes, Lieutenant Columbo. Here's *Galactic Revolt* and *Lingering Melody.*"

"Oh, sir, I—"

"No problem," said Vado. "I copy them, make as many copies as I want."

"Well, thank you again, then," said Columbo. He stopped, took his hand off the doorknob. "Oh. There was one other little thing I meant to ask. Something was stolen from the Khoury home. Just one item, it seems like. An expensive necklace. Worth over forty-eight thousand dollars. A choker actually. Are you familiar with that item, sir? Can you give me a description of it?"

Vado shook his head. "I'm not aware of it, Lieutenant."

"You never noticed it on her," said Columbo. "Never saw her wearing it?"

"Never," said Vado.

"Not something you'd forget, is it?" Columbo asked.

"I think if I saw a choker worth forty-eight thousand around Arlene Khoury's neck, I'd remember it," said Vado.

2

Kimberly Dana parked her green MG in the small parking lot near the pier at San Luis Rio. She was wearing a pair of frayed denim shorts, purple-and-white striped, with a rib-knit white cotton top. Her hair was tied back, and she wore wraparound sunglasses. She got out of the car, then reached back in and pulled out a big straw handbag.

She walked a little distance out on the beach and sat down on a wooden bench. It was in fact the same bench where Columbo had sat yesterday afternoon when he was waiting for Yussef Khoury to come up from scuba diving.

From her bag she took a mayonnaise jar. Running the lip of the jar across the sand, she scooped up enough sand to about half fill it. She glanced around to see if anyone was watching. Seeing no one, she reached into the bag again and pulled out the Harry Winston choker. She dropped it into the jar. She scooped in more sand, covering the choker and filling the jar. Finally she screwed the lid on tight and returned the jar to her bag.

This was what Joe had told her to do. Filled with sand, the jar would sink to the bottom. Because it was a smooth object, a fisherman would not snag it on a hook. Tomorrow he would come out and dive for it, as he had done for the Bali-Songs. If he could find it, he would carry it out to deeper water and drop it in the kelp forest.

It seemed to her like an uncertain and over-elaborate way to give up the beautiful gold choker. But Joe had said he wanted it disposed of *today*. However remote the chance might be, he did not want to risk it being found in a search of her apartment. Why, then, didn't he bring it out here himself and take it to the deep water this afternoon? He said he couldn't come out scuba diving this afternoon; he was meeting with his lawyers about Arlene's will.

She walked slowly out on the pier, conscious of the stares of the fishermen—of *some* of the fishermen, actually; nothing could distract most of them from their concentration on their lines.

At the end of the pier she sat down and let her legs dangle over the end. Two fishermen, feeling apparently that she had intruded on their territory, edged away and put a little distance between her and them. That was fine with her. Maybe she could drop the jar without any of them noticing.

She looked down into the straw bag. The beautiful choker lay in the sand in one side of the jar, and the gold glinted through the glass. It was a lovely thing. She hadn't guessed how much he had paid for it. To throw it—

Suddenly she formed a resolution. She closed the bag and stood up. She walked back along the pier. To give up an exquisite thing like this was foolishness. With all that was at stake, it should be invested, not squandered. And she knew how she would invest it.

FOURTEEN

1

Yussef Khoury had entered the water a hundred yards north of the pier. There was no point in letting the fishermen see him again. They thought him an annoyance at best, and it would be just as well if they did not remember him. He swam out, then turned south and approached the pier.

That was when an unhappy accident happened. Suddenly he felt a jerk against the rubber of his suit, in his left armpit, and in a moment he realized a hook had pierced the rubber. A fisherman had snagged him.

Annoyed and at the same time struck by the preposterous nature of the situation, Khoury turned and grabbed the line in his gloved hands, to prevent the hook from tearing the rubber even more, maybe even tearing his skin. A hundred-seventy-five-pound man and a strong swimmer, he should have been able to overcome any effort by the fisherman to land him. He could have, too, but the man on the pier made it very quickly apparent that he was not going to surrender this big catch without a fight. He let his big fish run out line, then stopped him and began to try to haul him back.

Khoury understood the fisherman's strategy, which was to tire his fish, ultimately to exhaust him. And it *was* tiring, or would be very quickly. Khoury could not use his arms to swim because his hands gripped the line. He could only use his flippers. He did not gain much distance while the fisherman was giving him line, and shortly he felt the relentless tugs that were meant to land him.

Impatient and a little frightened, he wrapped the line around his left hand and drew the knife from his belt with his right. With a slash he cut the line.

2

Columbo checked in for the day at Parker Center, Los Angeles police headquarters. On his way out, he came on Ted Jackson in a corridor.

"Hey, Columbo! You're not the easiest man in the world to find. I need to talk to you. Got somethin' to tell you."

They stood under glaring fluorescent tubes: Jackson turned out as usual in a handsome checked jacket and knife-creased slacks; Columbo with necktie loose, raincoat covering his wrinkled light-gray suit. He carried a fresh cigar in his right hand.

"Listen, Columbo, I made a collar this morning. It's maybe gonna change your mind about something."

"I'm all ears," said Columbo.

"All right. Remember I told you that Kid named two other girls who came to the house on Pitillo Road. House? Shack is more what it is. Anyway, two other girls called Boobs and Squatty. Dispatcher had a call last night, said the Manson crowd was gettin' together in the house and raising a lot of hell. I heard the call go to the black-and-white, so I went out, too. Guess who was there? Boobs and Squatty. And you won't believe this, but they claimed they didn't know where Puss, Kid, and Bum were. They didn't know they're in jail! They'd heard of the Khoury murders but didn't make any connection between that and Puss Dogood."

Columbo shook his head. "How could anybody not know, livin' in this town, looking at the newspapers, looking at TV? How could anybody not know?"

"They knew about the murders," Jackson said again. "But they made no connection between that and Puss Dogood. Believe it or not. That's what they said."

"Yeah," said Columbo. "Believe it or not. How you figure? You believe it?"

Without waiting for an answer to a question he had not expected to be answered, Columbo started walking again, and Jackson walked beside him. "Anyway," Jackson went on, "they'd come out there in an old car, so both of them had driver's licenses. I got an ID on them. Came in the office this morning and, guess what?"

Columbo stopped to light his cigar. Jackson, without being asked, offered a lighter.

Jackson went on. "Boobs is Melissa Mead. Squatty is Patricia Finch, a.k.a. Trish Smith. Couple of girls from Greenwich, Connecticut. We've got rap sheets on both of them. Possession. Vagrancy. Prostitution. A little time locked up. Not much. All of which doesn't have much to do with anything, except that—"

"I was wonderin' if you'd come to it," said Columbo, who had resumed walking toward the exit.

"Okay. Okay, man," said Jackson. "Let a guy have a little fun. So okay, one big weakness in the Manson and Helter Skelter connection to the Khoury murders is—*was*—that Puss and her friends had never been inside the Khoury mansion. Not to worry any more. Boobs worked in the house for about two weeks, as a maid, until she was fired for stealing. It's on her rap sheet. Mrs. Takeshi, the housekeeper, reported the thefts, and in June of this year Boobs was arrested and booked for grand theft. But Khoury didn't want to press it, didn't want the publicity, and we dropped it. But Boobs knows the house inside and out. Huh?"

" 'Huh' means I've gotta go talk to the girl. Where you got her? On what?"

"Possession. She had a stash. It was in her purse. Squatty didn't have any. I couldn't hold her."

3

Columbo drove out to visit to Puss Dogood at Sybil Brand Institute. An officer asked him to check his sidearm before entering the big jail. He raised his eyebrows, smiled, and shrugged. She led him to an interview room. As a police officer he did not interview suspects in the visitors' room but in a private interview cubicle, a spare little room furnished with two aluminum and vinyl chairs and a small table.

While he waited for the prisoner to be brought in, he sniffed an unlighted cigar. A sign on the wall was inelegantly lettered with a stencil—

NO SMOKING

An officer brought her to the cubicle. Puss Dogood. She wore the shapeless gray cotton dress that was the uniform at Sybil Brand. Her dark-brown hair, which usually she let fall to her shoulders, was tied back.

"We've got Boobs locked up," he said. "You know—Melissa Mead."

She shrugged. "So?"

"It doesn't do you any good . . . Uh, listen, what would you rather I'd call you, Cathy Murphy or Puss Dogood?"

She sneered. "On my rap sheet and fingerprint

record I'm Catherine A. Murphy. But of course I like best the name that Charlie gave me. I'd like that best, no matter what it was."

"Charlie didn't give Boobs her name, did he?"

"Boobs never met Charlie. Charlie doesn't even know she exists."

"She's totally devoted to the guy, just the same," said Columbo, shaking his head.

Puss sneered. "What could she know? She's a dumb rich kid that came to L.A. looking for kicks."

"I thought you didn't know her."

"I don't. She was around. I never paid any attention to her. She was a friend of Kid, I guess. She and Squatty wanted to be called by the kind of names Charlie gave people. But if Charlie didn't give them, what good are they?"

"Charlie's one hell of a man, huh? He's put a lot of your friends in jail for life."

Puss pressed her hands flat together and put them before her face, as if praying. She sighed. "I don't know . . ." she said quietly. "Maybe I'd be better off if you sent me to Fontera for life. Looking back on the time I did there, it . . . it wasn't so bad. What do I get on the street that I didn't have there? Grass. Beer. Maybe a man now and then . . . And he, likely as not, gives me a fat lip. What's so good about the street? Tell you what, Columbo. You get the powers that be to promise me I can write Charlie and get letters from him, and I'll plead guilty. Well . . . Maybe. I'll think about it. What's the difference? When Charlie is ready and says the time has come, we all get out anyway."

Columbo frowned and shook his head. "You'd plead guilty to three murders?"

Puss shrugged. "Why not? Being back in here has reminded me of something. Inside, you got nothing to worry about. Oh, hell, most of them worry themselves sick about getting out. But if you don't worry about that, you got nothing else to worry about. I could just relax and wait for Charlie to call down the day."

"Lieutenant . . . Sorry to interrupt." An officer of the jail was at the door and beckoned Columbo to step outside.

"What's up?" he asked.

"Call from headquarters," she said. "Detective Jackson said to tell you a man identifying himself as Yussef Khoury is under arrest for assault and battery. The officers who have him are waiting to hear from you."

"Where? Do you know?"

"At the pier at San Luis Rio."

Columbo stuck his head back in the interview room. "Sorry. Gotta go. I'll be back."

Puss Dogood shrugged.

4

Columbo called the dispatcher and asked her to radio the officers at San Luis Rio to do nothing until he got there. It took him forty minutes to make the drive.

"Hi-ya," he said to the uniformed corporal standing beside the black-and-white as he walked across the parking lot, puffing on a cigar. "Columbo. Homicide. Where's Mr. Khoury?"

"I'm Corporal Schneider, Lieutenant," said the beefy, blond, red-faced officer. "Mr. Khoury went in the bait shack to use the phone. This is the damnedest thing I've ever seen."

"Yeah?"

"Yeah. What happened is that Mr. Khoury was scuba diving close to the pier where guys fish. Mr. Delmonico snagged him on his hook and tried to land him like a fish. Mr. Khoury cut his fishing line. When Mr. Khoury came out on the beach, Mr. Delmonico ran down the beach after him, madder'n hell. There were words, and Mr. Khoury decked him. There's some antagonism all the time between the scuba divers and the guys who fish off the pier. Most of the scuba divers keep a distance from the pier, but Mr. Khoury didn't today and—"

"Where's Delmonico?" Columbo asked.

"In the back of the car," said the corporal. "My partner put a bandage on his nose. He wants us to haul Khoury in. I recognized the name and called headquarters. They said hold everything till you get here."

"I'll talk to Delmonico," said Columbo.

John Delmonico was a lean, wiry man in his late sixties, as Columbo judged. He looked like a retired plumber or electrician. Drops of blood stained his ribbed vest undershirt, and he held his right hand on the thick bandage the second officer had taped over his nose. He had a cigar going, even so.

"His nose is not broken, just bloody," the second officer said to Columbo.

Columbo put his hands on the car door and stuck

his head in the window. "Mr. Delmonico," he said, "I'm Lieutenant Columbo, LAPD homicide. How ya doin'?"

"Homicide! What's homicide got to do with that smart-aleck bastard bloodyin' my nose?"

"Mr. Delmonico, the man that bloodied your nose is Mr. Yussef Khoury. Know the name?"

"Never heard of him. And what's the difference, anyway? Is this Curry or whatever his name is so important he can go around bustin' people's chops?"

"Sir . . . Mr. Khoury's wife was murdered Tuesday night. I thought you might have seen some word of it in the papers or on television."

"Murdered? That guy's wife?"

"Plus a friend of his. Plus a young man that worked at his house. Three brutal murders. You can see how he might be upset and short-tempered."

"Got ya," said Delmonico. "You're sayin' don't press charges, 'cause the guy's got enough troubles."

"Well, that's up to you, sir. But I thought you might give it a thought."

"What the hell. Live and let live. If I say I'll drop it, can I get back to my fishin'?"

"Why not?" said Columbo, glancing at Corporal Schneider, who nodded agreement.

"What the hell," said Delmonico again. "Give the guy my sympathy about his wife. He is some kinda nut, y' know. That's what he is: some kinda nut."

"Yes, sir. And, uh—There is a question I'd like to ask you. Do you get bothered much by scuba divers here?"

"Only once in a while. It's no great place to dive. There's nothin' out there, no shipwreck or nothin'. One of them comes along just once in a while. Y' know, they don't have to dive here. There's plenty of places for them, only just a few for us guys that like to wet a hook. These scuba divers are guys with money, y' know. And their broads. I'm afraid the place is gettin' popular with those kind."

"Like how, sir?"

"Like, yesterday afternoon the most beautiful girl you ever saw in this world came out here. Dressed like a princess. Walked out to the end of the pier and sat down and stared at the water like there was somethin' out there she was interested in. Then she got up and left, sorta spanking her own backside as she walked. She'd got the bottom of her pretty purple-and-white shorts dirty."

"It takes all kinds of people to make a world," said Columbo.

5

Columbo was waiting beside the gull-wing Mercedes when Khoury came out of the bait shop. "You get around, don't you, Lieutenant? What's the story?" he asked.

"Mr. Delmonico has gone back out on the pier to fish some more," said Columbo. "He asked me to give you his sympathy about Mrs. Khoury."

Yussef Khoury squinted in the sunshine, looking

at the pier. He was still wearing his rubber suit. Carrying his flippers, he was barefoot. His tanks and valves were in his car. "The funeral is Sunday," he said. "Well . . . I mean Arlene's. Steve's is this afternoon. I'm not going. I don't think it would be appropriate, all things considered. The time I lost here means I'm missing Sergio's. Arlene's sister is flying in all the way from Beirut. Her mother's still living, but she can't come. I'm paying the air fare, but it's a matter of the old woman's health, not the money."

Columbo nodded. "Getting in a little therapeutic relaxation here this morning?" he asked.

"That was what I had in mind."

Columbo looked out at the Pacific. "Maybe I oughta try it," he said. "First thing, I'd have to learn to swim. Is it hard to learn?"

Khoury shook his head. "No. Not at all. We have a club. You learn in a pool."

"What about dangerous?" Columbo asked. "I mean, here you got caught on a fisherman's hook, but what if somethin' bad happened, like one of your hoses came loose?"

"Usually we swim on the buddy system," said Khoury. "That is, you go with another swimmer, and the two of you watch out for each other."

"Well . . . That's interestin'. That's very interestin'. I'll have to really think about it. It must be beautiful down there."

"It is, Lieutenant, it is."

"I won't take any more of your time, sir. I'm glad I could help straighten out this little deal here this morning."

"I'm grateful."

"It's okay," said Columbo. "So I'll . . . see you later."

"Fine. And if there is anything at all I can do to help, let me know."

Columbo turned and took three steps toward his Peugeot, then stopped and turned back toward Khoury. "Oh," he said. "There is one more little thing. You usually swim with other members of your club, you say?"

"Right, Lieutenant. You'd be perfectly safe."

"Good. But you—Wednesday afternoon and today you were swimming alone."

"I'm an experienced diver, Lieutenant Columbo," said Khoury. "I can handle myself."

"Oh, sure. I get ya. It's okay for you. Suppose I took lessons and got so I could do it. Could I swim with you?"

Khoury smiled. "Of course. I'd be happy to swim on the buddy system with you."

"Here?" Columbo asked. "Is San Luis Rio a particularly interestin' place to dive?"

"No, not very," said Khoury. "I came here because I wanted to be alone."

"Okay. I'll have to think about it. I sure wouldn't want to get hooked and mistaken for a fish. What's the name of your club? I'd want to have some lessons before I bothered you, askin' you to swim with me."

"The Topanga Diving Club," said Khoury. "Tell them I sent you."

6

Columbo grabbed a slice of pizza and a bottle of root beer for lunch, then went to see Melissa Mead. She was in the same cell block where Columbo had interviewed Puss Dogood on Wednesday.

"'Possession,'" she taunted Columbo in a soft voice and with a big innocent smile. "You're not holding me on possession. You think Puss killed Mrs. Khoury and those others, and you're getting ready to charge me with it, too. Well, make it stick, Lieutenant. I've got witnesses that'll put me miles from there that night."

"Yes, ma'am," said Columbo. "I bet you do. Did you give Sergeant Jackson the names of those witnesses?"

"I'll give them to my lawyer."

"You got one? A lawyer?"

"I called my father, back in Connecticut. I'll have one pretty quick."

Melissa Mead—Boobs—deserved her nickname. She was a dishwater blonde, broad of face, broad of shoulders, broad of hips. Her rap sheet said she was thirty-four years old, which meant she was too young ever to have met Charles Manson. She was a graduate of Greenwich Country Day School and of Radcliffe. Confinement behind the heavy bars of a holding cell, dressed in an orange jump suit, had made no apparent impact on her aplomb, which was that of a young woman accustomed to deference for her name. She had spent just enough time in jail that the mere fact of being locked up held no terror for her; and, in her judgment, she was a Greenwich Mead, entitled to a certain deference, in jail or out.

"None of my business exactly why a girl of your background came to California and got to be a hooker, among other things—" Columbo began.

"Right," she interrupted, still smiling as though the conversation were entirely social and in no sense confrontational. "None of your business."

"On the other hand," he continued, "it is my business that you worked in the Khoury house and were also a good friend of Puss Dogood. That's some of my business, Miss Mead. You say you can prove you were miles away when Mrs. Khoury and the others were killed. Maybe you can, but your lawyer will advise you that's not gonna help you much if we find out you told Puss the layout of the house. That'd make you—"

"An accessory," she said softly, nodding.

"Somethin' like that."

"You figure Puss couldn't have found her way around the house unless I told her the layout."

"Somethin' like that," said Columbo. "Maybe you did it, huh? You'd do anything for Charlie, wouldn't you?"

"Let me explain something to you, Lieutenant. Saint Paul never saw Jesus, except maybe once in a vision, and he never heard him preach, wasn't there for the Sermon on the Mount, but that didn't prevent him from becoming the second most important man in Christianity. There are the things you see, and there are the things you know. Like, I never met Charlie Manson, but I know who he is. Maybe you *have* met him, but you *don't* know."

"How long have you known Puss Dogood?" Columbo asked.

Boobs shrugged. "Maybe ten years. Maybe twelve. Squatty and I came to California looking for truth. Most of the people who knew some had chickened out by the time we got here. Charlie was in the slammer. So were most of the good people. But we found Kid, and she introduced us to Puss. That was good luck. Puss has told Charlie about us. He'll be looking for us when he comes out, and we'll be ready for him."

"Of course, you never told any of the people about the layout of the Khoury mansion."

Boobs shook her head. Holding one bar in her left hand, she began to pirouette and to sing in a childlike falsetto voice—"Tra-la *la* la-la-la, tra-la *la* la-la-la. Tra-la-la-la-la-la-la-la-la-la." It was Carmen's song to Don José. *"Pres de la porte de Seville, chez mon ami Lillas Pastia . . .* Are you going to keep me in prison for a long time, my brave policeman?"

"Only as long as it takes to straighten this case out," said Columbo.

"I can straighten it out for you right now," she said in innocence too simple to be mocking. "You see, Puss wouldn't hurt anybody. Puss is a *good* person. Like me. Like me, that incidentally didn't steal from the Khoury house. A good person. That's all you need to know. Go talk to Charlie. He'll tell you, and Charlie is incapable of speaking anything but the truth."

Captain Sczciegel authorized travel, and in the middle of the afternoon Columbo flew to Sacramento and went out to Folsom. It was going to make a long day. By the time he got back it would be late in the evening.

Folsom Prison and especially its "adjustment center," designated 4-A, is the toughest lockup in California. It confines typically about thirty men, regarded as the state's most dangerous prisoners.

Charles Manson did not look like an exceptionally dangerous prisoner. He was a small man, anything but prepossessing. His hair and beard were long and unkempt. His eyes, once widely described as "hypnotic," showed nothing now, not even resignation or defeat—just nothing. His prison uniform, heavy blue denims, hung on whatever his body was, like canvas on tent poles.

Even so, his custodians thought he was dangerous, and he shuffled into the interview room in leg irons and handcuffs fastened to a belly chain.

"Remember me, Charlie?" Columbo asked.

"Lieutenant Crisco," said Manson, grinning. "I don't forget anybody. I remember *everybody.* Every*thing* . . . It's gonna make a difference to you someday whether I remember you as a friend or enemy. The day comes, you know. It comes. For sure."

"Someday," said Columbo. "You know they're layin' one on you in L.A. Again."

Manson turned to the two officers standing behind him and jerked on his handcuffs and belly chain. "You gonna unhook me, or are you not?" he asked angrily.

One of the officers shook his head. "No, Charlie. Talk to your visitor."

Manson snapped his head around. "What they layin' on me in L.A.?" he asked.

"You heard of the Khoury murders?" Columbo asked.

Manson shrugged. "What would I know from murders in Los Angeles? We got stabbings inside here. *That* I know about. Who's Curry?"

"Puss Dogood is in Sybil Brand, charged with possession but really held on suspicion in the Khoury killings."

"Puss Dogood . . . ?"

"You had her pregnant one time."

Manson sneered. "Lieutenant Crisco, I don't have fingers and toes enough to count the girls I've got pregnant."

"You must have kids," said Columbo.

"Does any of them send me a box of cookies?" asked Manson.

"Puss Dogood," said Columbo. "The Kid. Bum Rapp. Squatty. Boobs. Your Family, Charlie. You care?"

"Look," said Manson. "Lots of people have always wanted to associate their name with mine. Some people call me Jesus Christ, and some call me God, so naturally they'd want to call themselves apostles. Jesus had trouble like that. Apostles that ain't apostles. Y' know, there's a great line from *Jesus Christ Superstar*. My git-fiddle is back in the cell, besides which they won't unhook me, but if I had it and if they would, I'd sing you a great song. Best I can do, it goes:

> Always wanted to be an apostle.
> Always knew I'd make it if I tried.
> Now I'm gonna retire and write a gospel,
> So people will remember when we've die-ied.

Manson grinned. "Always lots of people want to call themselves disciples. But they can't do it. 'Cause I got no disciples. They go out and do shit, and they wanta lay it on me. I won't let 'em. I been in this joint almost twenty-five years, locked up, chained up, and put down. But when twenty-five years is up, they've gotta let me go. You know why? I've got a perfect record, is why. Perfect." He laughed. "They fucked themselves. How can a man chained up and locked up make anything else but a perfect record? I got a perfect record, and they gotta let me go. Twenty-five years, they gotta let me go."

"What do you want me to tell Puss Dogood?"

Manson's face twisted into an insane leer. "Tell her to go fuck herself. Tell her not to talk about me. Not to use my name! If I call her, she can come. Don't come unless Charlie calls!"

Columbo stared at Manson for a moment. Then he said, "I'm glad they didn't unhook you, Charlie. I hope they never do."

PART THREE

"Well, you see there wouldn't be any gunpowder residue in there. That pistol has never been fired. I mean, that pistol has been well taken care of. I keep it wrapped in an old scarf and—"

"You mean you don't carry this weapon, sir? Regulations require—"

"Don't wanna risk shooting myself in the foot."

FIFTEEN

1

Columbo signed in at headquarters. He would not have been on duty Saturday and Sunday, but he knew the pressures on the Department would not allow him to take days off while the Khoury murders remained unsolved.

On his way out to the garage he met Captain Sczciegel, who was going to the garage.

"The Khoury funeral is tomorrow," said the captain. "It would be great if we could announce we've closed the case. Any chance of that, Columbo?"

"We can do it," said Columbo.

"Hey! That's great! What do we say?"

"We say that Cathy Murphy, also known as Puss Dogood, has agreed to plead guilty to all three murders. I talked to her out at Sybil Brand, and that's what she's thinkin'. I think we've gotta let the

Public Defender talk to her first, but if he doesn't talk her out of it, she'll plead. Anyway, that's what she told me a while ago."

Captain Sczciegel stopped in the middle of the hallway. "And you're tellin' me you don't like it," he said. "I can hear it in your voice, Columbo. You don't like it."

Columbo shook his head. "Well . . . That's right, Captain. I don't like it."

"Well, why in hell would the woman plead guilty to three murders if—"

"Because she's nuts," said Columbo curtly.

"What about the arrest of this woman called Boobs? Doesn't that nail it? The only thing we didn't know was how Puss and Kid and Bum knew their way around the premises so well. Now we know how they knew it. And we know the motive. It was to steal a $48,000 necklace."

"No way," said Columbo. "Sorry, Captain, but Boobs—Melissa Mead—was fired in June, and Mr. Khoury bought the $48,350 choker in July."

"Okay. Puss worked for Khoury. Maybe she knew he'd bought the—What did you call it? Choker?"

"Gold, diamonds, and emeralds," said Columbo. "A strange thing about it: no one I've talked to so far ever saw her wearing it. It was the kind of thing you'd wear at a fancy-dress ball. Suppose Puss did know she had it. Wouldn't you think she'd figure a thing that valuable would be kept in a safe? Or something? According to Mr. Khoury, it was lying out on the bureau top. I don't think whoever stole it came there to steal it. I think whoever stole it came there for another reason, saw it and snatched it."

"It's not much good to anybody," said Captain Sczciegel. "A thing like that's one of a kind. You couldn't fence it. Of course the insurance company—"

"Will pay half its value at least, to get it back and not have to pay Mr. Khoury the other half," said Columbo.

"Was Khoury short of money?" asked the captain.

"Not short anything like $48,350," said Columbo. "Short two or three million, which is what he needs to buy into another movie, which is what he wants to do. That kinda money—$48,350—wouldn't help him."

Sczciegel turned down the corners of his mouth. "Some people live by different standards from you and me, Columbo."

Columbo nodded. "Ain't it the truth."

"Are you serious in telling me that Puss Dogood will plead guilty to three murders?"

"That's what she said about an hour ago."

"But you still don't buy it?"

Columbo shook his head.

"Tell you what, Columbo," said the captain. "I want you to do something. To start with, take Sunday off. I'm not gonna announce the case is closed, even if Puss does try to confess. So nothing's gonna happen between now and Monday."

"Appreciate the suggestion, Captain," said Columbo. "I could use some rest."

"Not altogether charitable," said Captain Sczciegel. "Columbo, I want you to take your service revolver out to the range this afternoon and practice until you can hit something, then qualify.

Do you know you've got the longest-running record in the whole police force for not qualifying with your service revolver? That gets noticed. I get heat about it. Do me a favor and qualify."

"Uh . . . Well, I do have a problem, Captain."

"What? What, besides the fact you swear you can't hit anything?"

"Well . . . The problem is, I'm not sure I can find the thing. Last time I saw it, it—"

"Columbo! I'm gonna pretend I didn't hear you say you've *lost* your service revolver."

"Oh, it's not lost," said Columbo. "More like . . . mislaid. Misplaced. I prob'ly can find it. It's in the house someplace. I think I know where it is."

Captain Sczciegel swelled indignantly. *"You find it, Lieutenant!* Find it and qualify! Don't report for duty until you do!"

"Yes, sir."

2

Columbo picked up his revolver and drove to the police pistol range. He walked up to the firing line. A dozen men were firing pistols at paper targets fifty feet away.

"I gotta be quick about this," he said. "I got an appointment with a young lady."

"Won't she wait for you?" asked Sergeant Dan Brittigan, the range officer.

"Yeah, she will, come to think of it. She's not goin' anywhere. She's in Sybil Brand."

Sergeant Dan Brittigan was a big, ruddy-faced man who carried himself with the obsessively stiff bearing of the marine drill sergeant he had once been. Wounded in the line of duty as a police officer, he was serving out the remaining years till his retirement as range officer at the police pistol range.

"Have you brought your pistol this time?"

Columbo stood on the hillside with the ocean behind him, his raincoat billowing in the wind, his cigar smoke whipped away to his right, eyeing the ranks of paper targets with pronounced skepticism. "Yeah," he said. "I found it." He reached into a raincoat pocket and pulled out the .38 revolver. "I, uh . . . I suppose you got some ammunition."

Sergeant Brittigan reached for the pistol, took it, and frowned over it. "Did you clean this, sir?" he asked.

"Right. There was dust in the barrel, so I wrapped a paper towel around a fondue fork and ran it through."

"That wouldn't clean out gunpowder residue, sir," said the sergeant.

"Well, you see there wouldn't be any gunpowder residue in there. That pistol has never been fired. I mean, that pistol has been well taken care of. I keep it wrapped in an old scarf and—"

"You mean you don't carry this weapon, sir? Regulations require—"

"Don't wanna risk shooting myself in the foot," said Columbo.

"When did you last qualify, Lieutenant? Don't I remember your being out here and firing my Beretta about a year ago?"

"Right. I didn't really try to qualify that time, 'cause I supposed I oughta qualify with my own gun. You got any bullets for this pistol?"

"Yes, sir."

Brittigan reached into his pants pocket and pulled out a handful of .38 cartridges. He rolled out the cylinder and loaded Columbo's service revolver.

"I'm supposed to shoot at one of those targets out there, huh?" said Columbo.

The sergeant handed the pistol to Columbo. "Yes, sir," he said. "Target number five. Station five shoots target five."

Columbo drew a deep breath, blew it out, and leveled the sights of the revolver on the target.

"You can pull the hammer back, Lieutenant."

Columbo lowered the muzzle and used his thumb to pull back the hammer. He sighted again. And fired.

Sergeant Brittigan pulled a small spotting scope from a leather case on his belt and squinted through it at the target. "Good work, sir," he said. "An eight."

Columbo stared skeptically at the revolver. "Eight . . ." he muttered. He shook his head, took aim again, and fired a second shot.

Brittigan raised the scope and took a look. "Right in the X-ring," he said. "Bull's-eye!"

Columbo tossed his cigar on the ground. A small smile came to his face.

"Borrow your scope a sec', Sarge?" asked a

uniformed officer standing behind the next shooter down the line, at station six.

Brittigan handed the man the scope and waited impatiently for it to be returned. The man checked the target belonging to his shooter and shook his head.

Columbo fired again.

"Seven," said Sergeant Brittigan.

Columbo's next two shots were an eight and a nine.

"Damned good," said the sergeant. "Come over here, and I'll fill out your qualifying report."

Columbo shook the empty cartridges out of the cylinder as he walked with Sergeant Brittigan to the range table and signed the report that would go to Captain Sczciegel on Monday.

As Columbo walked away to his Peugeot, the officer behind the shooter at station six took another look through Sergeant Brittigan's scope. "Goddammit, Murphy," he said. "This is station six. You been shootin' at target five."

"Uh-oh. Brittigan will—"

"Never mind. What Dan Brittigan don't know won't hurt him. Only thing is, I wonder where the shots from the guy in the raincoat went."

3

Columbo returned to Sybil Brand Institute to resume his interrupted talk with Puss Dogood.

"Is Charlie God?" he asked. "I flew up to Folsom to see him yesterday afternoon, and I didn't quite get the answer."

She grinned and shook her head. "That's a dumb question. You only ask a question like that because you don't understand the thing about Charlie. C'mon, Columbo! Was Jesus God? The answer is yes, and the answer is no. To understand about Charlie you'd have to spend a lot of time listening to him. I mean, listening respectfully, listening attentively. He makes everything clear. Everything."

"Boobs says Saint Paul never met Jesus, never heard him preach, but was still the second-most-important man in Christianity."

"Meaning she's important even without ever meeting Charlie? No one's important that never met Charlie."

"She's important for a very different reason," said Columbo. "You know what's on her rap sheet?"

"You tell me," said Puss derisively. "Let's see. She shot Kennedy. No, she shot Martin Luther King. No, she was one of the Watergate burglars!"

"She was arrested for grand theft, for stealing from the Khoury place on Mulholland Drive," said Columbo. "She'd worked there about two weeks."

"So?"

"One of the weak points in the case against you is that nobody can remember when you were ever inside the Khoury house. So how could you have known how to find the different rooms? How'd you pick the window to break open? How'd you know they didn't turn on the alarm system until they went to bed? Well . . . Boobs worked there, so maybe she told you."

"Yeah, maybe she did. What the hell? Maybe I oughta plead guilty and not have to worry about it anymore."

Before he left Sybil Brand Institute, Columbo stopped in to see the resident psychologist.

"Cults, Lieutenant," the woman said. "We get quite a few of them here: cultists of one stripe and another. Once a person falls under the spell of a charismatic, it's all but impossible to reach her. They give their money, in the easiest case. They give their lives. At worst, they commit crimes the leader orders. Puss and Kid are the only two Manson girls I've ever talked to. They're thoroughly programmed. I can't get through to them."

"Off the record," said Columbo, "if Puss does talk to you, try to discourage her from pleading guilty. That'll close the case, and I'm not at all sure it oughta be closed."

4

Columbo knew where he was going Saturday afternoon, but he had time first to take a look at the Topanga Diving Club.

He leaned on the Peugeot and studied the little building. On the edge of a state beach, it seemed to have been designed to have a modest appearance, neither to attract nor to offend the users of the public beach. It was a one-story cinder-block building, painted pale green and shaded by half a dozen palms. The parking lot would hold no more than twenty cars. It had anything but the appearance of the sophisticated and expensive and exclusive kind of club Mr. Yussef Khoury would be likely to join.

He had parked his car along the edge of the road when he spotted a hot dog vendor with an umbrella-shaded cart. A fellow selling hot dogs from a cart like that could be depended on, he knew from experience, to sell a tasty hot dog. And he'd been right. He liked the first one so well, he had bought a second: a boiled hot dog, not grilled, in a nice bun with relish and yellow mustard. On a grilled hot dog he liked darker mustard, but this yellow stuff was just right for the classic boiled wiener. With a bottle of orange soda, it made the kind of lunch a man could really enjoy.

"Sell here every day?" he asked the vendor when he walked back to his cart to deposit his used napkins and paper cup in the man's litter bag.

"Every day but Friday," the man said. "That's my sabbath."

"Friday?"

"For the followers of Allah, the beneficent, the merciful," said the man. "You can be sure, too, that hot dog's all beef. A man of the faith will not poison the guts even of the unbelievers with unclean meat."

"I appreciate that, sir," said Columbo. "I really do. A man can't be too careful about what kind of meat he eats. I wanted to ask ya. Do you ever see an unusual car parked down there by that building? I mean a car that"—he paused to put his hands on his hips and run his elbows up and down "—opens and closes like that."

"A 1954 Mercedes gull-wing sports coupe," said the Muslim hotdog vendor.

"Right."

"It parks there from time to time. It is the property of Mr. Yussef Khoury. He is of the faithful. Or was, once. His father was faithful. The son"—The man paused to spit on the ground—"The son and his wife became heretics."

"Yeah, right. Well, I'm Lieutenant Columbo, a homicide detective with the Los Angeles Police Department. Anyway, you say Mr. Khoury comes here from time to time—"

"He parks the car there," said the hot dog vendor. "And he goes out into the sea, wearing a rubber suit and air tanks and all that. The devil fish don't eat him. Limitless is the mercy of Allah."

Columbo nodded. "I see. Well, thank ya, sir. You serve a good hot dog."

"Thank *you,* sir. I shall see you again, I hope."

5

The man behind the counter in the diving club was a mass of hard muscle and contradicted Khoury's argument that scuba diving was for the older and flabbier man, not for the athlete. His muscles bulged inside a yellow T-shirt, and he wore black swimming trunks. "What can I do for ya, buddy?" he asked.

"I'm Lieutenant Columbo, homicide, LAPD. I'm investigating the murder of Mrs. Yussef Khoury. In the course of talking with Mr. Khoury, I got a suggestion from him that I oughta stop by and talk about joinin' your club and learning to dive."

"Bill McGinnis," said the man behind the desk, extending his hand. "Lemme show you around the place and give you an idea of what we got."

He led Columbo through a door and into a locker room, then through another door and into a room that housed a surprisingly small swimming pool. After a moment, Columbo understood what he was looking at: a small round pool that was as much as fifty feet deep. Thirty at the very least. It was not a pool; it was a tank. Diving equipment hung from hooks around the walls.

"How good a swimmer are you, Lieutenant?"

"Well . . . the truth is, I can't swim at all."

"I can teach you that in twenty minutes," said McGinnis, not in the least taken aback. "The problem a lot of people have is, they think they've gotta have some way to stay afloat. Once you get that idea outa your head, you can dive. You aren't gonna drown, 'cause you *can't* drown. You can't. You're carrying your own air with you, on your back. You got a few bucks for a first lesson, I can take you down to twenty feet right now."

"Well, I just ate a couple hot dogs," said Columbo.

McGinnis laughed. "And mother said never swim right after you eat." He clapped Columbo on the shoulder. "Okay, buddy. You really wanta dive? Or did you come about something else? Is Joe Khoury a suspect in his wife's murder?"

"No," said Columbo. "Of course, y'understand that whenever a woman is murdered, we have to do a little checking on the husband. I mean, I couldn't file my report if I didn't eliminate the possibility that the husband killed his wife."

"I thought it was plain enough that some Manson types did it," said McGinnis. "That's what all the newspapers and television guys say."

Columbo nodded. "That's probably who did it, all right. But we haven't got the proof of that, so we gotta look into everything. Gotta close all possibilities. Y' know what I mean?"

McGinnis shrugged. He walked away from the pool, back into the office and behind the counter.

"Joe Khoury's a real gentleman," he said.

"Oh, I certainly agree with that," said Columbo. "Anyway, did he learn to dive here?"

"Right. He's in good shape, a strong swimmer. He picked it right up."

"Where does he usually dive?" Columbo asked.

"Two places," said McGinnis. "He can just walk down the beach here and swim out. He'd trail a marker buoy so that boats wouldn't run over him. There's some interesting stuff out there. I mean there are three wrecks on the bottom. Some sharks work around here, just enough to make it interesting, give the divers something to think about. We've never had a problem. The other place he dives is where we take him. We arrange boat trips and take our members out where there are interesting things to see. An old square-rigged sailing ship. A tanker. Some airplanes. Reefs. Joe goes on those trips."

"Is Mr. Khoury a safe swimmer?"

"Meaning what?"

"Well, does he use the buddy system and never go out alone?"

"You got it. He never goes out alone. In fact, a friend of his is almost always his buddy. Ben Willsberger. Ben's a movie director: a good one, too, I'm told. He's Joe's age, and he's a good swimmer. I think Joe and Ben worked on a picture together."

"Do any of your club members ever dive off the beach at San Luis Rio?" Columbo asked.

McGinnis shrugged. "Not that I know of. There's nothing up there."

SIXTEEN

1

Columbo parked the Peugeot along the side of the road and left the card in the windshield that showed it was a police car on police business. Puffing on a cigar, his raincoat flapping around him in the stiff breeze that had begun to come in off the Pacific, he walked toward the cheering crowd standing around a roped-off section of beach. He squinted into the sunlight and wore a faint, skeptical smile.

Beach volleyball. Columbo had heard of it. More than that, he had watched it on television. The cameras were there now, three of them on platforms raised a little above the sand. A pair of broadcasters with microphones sat on another platform. A van with a dish antenna on top completed the television paraphernalia.

They were taping a show for broadcast later.

Columbo pushed his way through the beach

crowd and up to the rope that separated the playing
area from the rest of the beach. "Hi-ya, Gonzalez,"
he said to the uniformed policeman guarding the
rope, reading the name off the board on the officer's
shirt pocket. "Lieutenant Columbo, homicide.
How's it goin'?"

"I could draw a worse assignment," said Gonzalez, glancing at the bikini-clad young women
playing volleyball. He lifted the rope and gestured
that Columbo should step inside. "The wife'll see
me on TV when they broadcast this. She'll say
that's how I spend my days, watchin' half-naked
broads playin' in the sand."

"Half-naked?" said Columbo. "I'd call that a
good deal more than half."

Gonzalez nodded. "Yeah. And, know somethin'?
Those girls are makin' more money doin' this for
an hour than you and I are going to make for our
eight-hour shift."

"Well, I guess that represents the American people's sense of values."

"Hi, Lieutenant!"

That was Kimberly Dana. Her words were cut
short by her labored breath. Walking up to the
beach, he had seen her working hard at an exchange
of shots over the net. Now, in position to receive a
serve, she was only a few feet from him.

"Hi, Miss Dana," he said. "I stopped by to return
your video tapes."

She nodded and turned quickly toward the net,
to ready herself as a young woman on the opposite
side struck the ball with her fist and sent it flying.

The crowd, held back by the rope, cheered for
nothing more than a serve, then jumped up and

down with excitement as the ball flew. All of them wore beach clothes; many of the spectators' bikinis were far scantier than those worn by the volleyball players. They drank beer from cans and wiped away sweat on the backs of their hands. It was a youthful crowd, fun-loving, watching a fun game.

"You know her?" asked Gonzalez.

"Right. She's a close friend of Yussef Khoury. Mrs. Khoury was murdered Tuesday night."

Gonzalez stared for a moment at Kimberly Dana. She was bouncing around the sand, maneuvering to stop the ball. "She's no Manson girl," said Gonzalez. "Didn't I read in the papers that it was probably Manson girls that killed Mrs. Khoury?"

Columbo grinned. "Kimberly Dana's no Manson girl. That's for sure."

The tall, lithe, and leggy Kimberly Dana wore a red-and-yellow bikini. She had tied her hair back and threaded her ponytail through a Dodgers baseball cap. Dark, wraparound sunglasses completed her outfit. She gleamed with streaming sweat.

Beach volleyball might not be a sanctioned sport, but it was not a rehearsed show like TV wrestling. Because they taped the program and did not broadcast live, there were no interruptions for commercial breaks. The two teams played hard. From time to time a player fell and came up with sand clinging to her sweaty body. Two had angry red knees. The coaches pulled out players and sent in others. Players cooled off with damp towels, sipped Gatorade, and jumped up and down on the sidelines when they were not in.

"They don't kid around," said Gonzalez. "Bein' the best lookin' or wearin' the skimpiest swimsuit doesn't win points. On the other hand, she ugly, she not gonna make the team."

Columbo pursed his lips around his cigar and squinted at the two volleyball teams. "Yeah," he agreed. "No ugly ones. Not an ugly one on either side."

"Which is no coincidence," said Gonzalez.

"How long this game got to go?" Columbo asked.

"Just about over."

It ended a few minutes later. Kimberly Dana scored the winning point and shot a fist at the sky as she took the cheers of the crowd and the congratulatory slaps of her teammates. She took a drink of Gatorade, then walked over to where Columbo was waiting, carrying a towel and wiping sweat off her face as she walked. Her chest heaved as she gasped for breath.

"Hey . . . Lieutenant . . . Columbo. There's . . . no place . . . we may not . . . run into you. Is there?"

"Well, I checked your office, and they said you were playing out here this afternoon, and I wanted to return your tapes. So . . . Congratulations. You play to win."

"Is there another way?" she asked.

Having wiped the sweat from her face, she now used the towel to wipe it off her body.

Columbo grinned and nodded. "Not that I ever heard of," he said. He frowned over his cigar, then dropped it in the sand and stepped on it. "My only game is pool, and I play to win."

"Did you enjoy the tapes?"

"Oh, my, Miss Dana! Mrs. Columbo asked me to add her thanks to mine. Three movies on one night!

We stayed up late last night. Mrs. Columbo said to tell you she thinks *Lingering Melody* is one of the best pictures she ever saw. Me, I liked the space shows better, but . . . they were all fine. They were all fine."

He handed her a brown paper grocery bag containing the three video cartridges.

"You have a few minutes, Lieutenant?" she asked. "I usually pop into a bar down the beach and have a cool drink after a workout like this. It's a place where they don't get excited if somebody comes in a bathing suit. I get cool, I'll get dry."

"I'll *make* a few minutes, uh—"

"You call me 'ma'am,' the invite is off," she said.

"Kim . . ." he said. "Okay. A nice cool drink. I think a beer would go good right now."

It was true that in this dark, cool bar no one noticed women in bikinis or men in slingshot swim trunks. The man in the rumpled raincoat drew the stares.

As he drank a cold, foamy beer and she sipped from a daiquiri, Columbo asked Kimberly Dana a question. "Mr. Khoury is reporting the theft of a valuable piece of jewelry. Do you know anything about that?"

"He bought her a Harry Winston choker early in the summer. I suppose it was worth ten or twenty thousand dollars. Wouldn't be surprised, anyway. I, uh . . . don't know whether she demanded it of him or if he bought it for her as some kind of compensation, if you know what I mean."

"Did you ever see it?"

"No. She never wore it. Actually, I mean, of course she wouldn't. Not where *I* would see her. It was the kind of thing a woman would wear to some kind of fancy affair, not to the office, not to the country club. You'd wear it to the Academy Awards, you know—if you got to go."

"I never saw a piece of jewelry worth that much money," said Columbo.

"Neither have I, Lieutenant, I promise you. If I had that kind of money, you wouldn't find me in a bikini, playing volleyball for television cameras."

When they left the little bar they had to stand just outside for a minute or so, letting their eyes adjust to the bright sunlight. They walked back toward the volleyball court.

"My car," she said, stopping beside her green MG.

"My, that's a nice car," said Columbo. "English, isn't it? I'm very interested in foreign cars. Y' see, my car's a French car."

Kimberly Dana reached into her car and picked up a ribbed-knit white shirt. She pulled it on over her bikini top. Then she stepped into a pair of purple-and-white-striped denim shorts and pulled them up her legs.

"So long, Lieutenant," she said as she sat down behind the wheel of the MG. "Good luck to you."

"And to you, Miss Dana. And to you," said Columbo, reaching up with his left hand to scratch the top of his head as he walked away.

2

Columbo had one more call to make that afternoon. He went back to headquarters and stopped in at the office of Sergeant Fred Beers.

"Hi-ya, Fred. You got that tape for me?"

"I got it," said Beers. "Wanta hear it?"

"Yeah, if it's not too much trouble."

Sergeant Beers was in charge of the 911 system— that is, in charge of the service that received emergency calls. All 911 calls were taped.

"Wednesday, August 6, 12:36 A.M.," he said as he put the reel of tape on a player and rolled it forward. He pressed the PLAY button.

Police emergency.

I work a party, Mulholland Drive. Just leave. Go past Khoury house. Yussef Khoury house. Something wrong there. Strange peoples there. Running around house. Not kind peoples Khourys invite their house.

What's your name, ma'am? And where are you calling from?

Call from phone boot'. No name. Don't want get mixed up.

"Spanish accent," said Columbo.

"Sounds like it," said Beers.

"But maybe not," said Columbo. "Could ya—"

"I'm ahead of you, Lieutenant. Here's two tape cartridges. I had the call copied. There's a little other garbage on there, enough to give you a lead-in."

"I thank ya, Fred. I thank ya kindly."

SEVENTEEN

1

It would have been inappropriate—un-Khouryish, Yussef thought—to hold the reception after the funeral in the house where Arlene had been murdered, found dead indeed in bed with her paramour. To hold it in a hotel would have been unseemly too, as if the occasion were some sort of celebration. Finally, he settled on the store. It was closed for the weekend, in memory of Arlene, and he arranged for a caterer to serve food and wine in the art department toward the rear of the first floor. Limousines brought family and friends from the cemetery to Khoury's, and there in the first floor, among reproductions of statues and paintings, the mourners gathered to nibble and sip and talk about Arlene Khoury and her tragic, untimely death.

Though he was always reluctant to do it and

never failed to feel he was intruding, Columbo had
attended the funeral service and had gone to the
cemetery. More than once he had observed something in the interactions among mourners that
suggested a line of inquiry. Once, a murderer had
shown up at a funeral and was quietly arrested
outside. He had told Columbo he absolutely had to
see the corpse, to make sure the man was really
dead and that he, the murderer, was not going to be
the victim of some complicated deception.

Columbo had not intended to go to the reception,
but the producer Antonio Vado had spotted him
standing at the rear of the crowd and pushed his
way through to him to insist that the lieutenant
come to the reception.

For once, Columbo had left his raincoat in the
car. Even without it, he was self-conscious in his
wrinkled gray suit—in the midst of impeccably
turned-out people in expensive clothes.

Yussef Khoury had shaken his hand and solemnly thanked him for coming.

"My deepest sympathy, sir," was all Columbo
had said.

Eleanor Russell, Khoury's tall, handsome, dark-
haired secretary, had attached herself to Lieutenant
Columbo, maybe because she sensed he was ill at
ease but maybe because someone had suggested she
do it. She and Mrs. Nagako Takeshi, the Khoury
housekeeper, both dressed in mourning black,
seemed to be the only two people genuinely affected
by the death of Arlene Khoury. Even the Khoury
children—a grown man and woman with their
spouses—kept apart in a little cluster, talking quietly to each other and not much to anyone else, and

showed no particular sign of distress.

Adam Brinsley, the accountant, was also there.

"That is Mrs. Khoury's sister," said Eleanor Russell, noticing that Columbo's eyes were on a stocky little woman, dressed in black, her hair wrapped in a white scarf. "She speaks only a little English, but she read the papers and knows what the situation was when Mrs. Khoury was killed. She's very judgmental about it."

"I haven't seen Miss Dana," said Columbo.

Eleanor Russell smiled weakly. "Mr. Khoury has a strong sense of propriety," she said.

Antonio Vado approached, leading by the hand a tall, strikingly beautiful woman. "Lieutenant," he said. "I bet you haven't met Fairleigh Richmond."

"No, I sure haven't. But I'm glad to. I've seen some of your pictures, Miss Richmond."

"Buongiorno, Tenente," she said.

"Sono molto lieto di fare la sua conoscenza," said Columbo.

"Ah! Columbo! Noi siamo Italiani! Io sono Anna Maria Tavernelle. Capisce?"

"Capisco. Un più grazioso nome."

"Hey, you guys!" Vado interrupted with a grin. "It's not polite to talk so Miss Russell can't understand."

The actress smiled at Eleanor Russell. "Forgeeffa you me," she said. "I canna no speak . . . very good."

"Your English is better than my Italian," said Eleanor Russell smoothly.

"Ah . . . Iss eassy learn my language. You try. Learn very fast. Eassy language. Very nice."

Broad smiles, even quiet laughter, came so easily to them that after a moment they fell silent, concerned that smiles and laughter were not quite suitable for the reception following a funeral.

"Over there is someone else you should meet, Lieutenant Columbo," said Antonio Vado. "Let me introduce you."

Columbo took his leave from the Italian actress and Khoury's secretary and accompanied Vado across the store. "Ben! Let me introduce Lieutenant Columbo of the Los Angeles Police Department. Lieutenant, this is Benjamin Willsberger. He was the director of *Lingering Melody,* you'll recall."

"I sure do," said Columbo. "I saw a tape of *Lingering Melody* just two nights ago. I'm pleased to meet you, Mr. Willsberger."

"Ben," said the diminutive man. He was small, gray but nearly bald and wore glasses deeply tinted a brownish-red tone. He wore a black double-breasted suit. "You are investigating the death of Arlene Khoury."

"Yes, sir."

"I would like to talk to you sometime."

"I would like to talk with you, sir. When would that be convenient?"

"Say Monday morning," said Willsberger. "I'm shooting a picture on one of the Culver soundstages. There are lots of breaks. I'll have plenty of time to talk to you. I'd leave a pass for you at the gate, but I suppose that won't be necessary, you being a police lieutenant."

"No, sir. No, it won't. I'll be looking forward to it. I'll be there as early as I can."

Arlene's sister, whom Yussef had met only once before, had arrived from Beirut. A devout Muslim, she did not take wine, and using only her face and not a word she made Yussef understand she did not approve of his drinking it either.

It would have done no good to remind her that he and Arlene had long since abandoned the faith and lived like Americans. So far as the sister was concerned, the world was divided between the believers and the unbelievers, and she knew where she stood.

"In our village, my sister would have been stoned," she said to Yussef.

"How fortunate she did not live in your village," said Yussef coldly.

He had expected the reception to be an ordeal, even more than the funeral and the ceremony at the grave: an impossible mixture of forced cordiality and artificial solemnity. And it was. The situation was irremediable—a wife not just dead but murdered, and scandalously murdered in bed with another man. Their son and daughter were of the new generation of renewed morality, did not accept their parents' lifestyles, and tended to regard their mother's death the way her sister regarded it: as the inevitable consequence of living an immoral and frivolous life. He was the subject of genuine compassion here today, but it did not come from his son or daughter.

He endured it all as long as he could, then slipped away. He had come here in a funeral limousine, so the gull-wing Mercedes was not in the lot. They would suppose the strain had become too much and that he had sneaked out and gone home—maybe home, maybe to a hotel. Those in the know might guess he had gone to Kim's apartment.

In fact, where he went was up to his office. She was there, waiting for him.

She was wearing a pair of shimmery gold nylon stirrup leggings, so tight they might have been painted on, with a sleeveless black cotton-knit top. If she hadn't been smoking and didn't stink of it, she would have been perfect.

"You like?" she asked, parading sensuously around the office to give him the best view of herself and her outfit. "I picked it up out of the shop. It seemed to me that, after what you've gone through this morning, you ought to have something happier to look at. Of course—If you want me to go downstairs and see people, I have a black dress in the closet."

He seized her and kissed her ardently. "I want to sleep in your apartment tonight," he whispered. "That damned detective—"

"It won't make him any more suspicious," she said. "I've already told him I love you . . . and that you love me."

"Damned reporters might—"

"Then Piscina Linda again," she said. "Columbo knows we go there. The news guys don't."

"We can have dinner brought up," he said. "Go in your car."

"Sooner or later we have to go public," said Kimberly.

"Yes, of course. And we will. But not on the night after the funeral."

"Have you filed the insurance claim?"

"I told Brinsley to do it."

Kimberly sat down on the couch beside Khoury. "Baby . . ." she whispered. "Is there anything more we can do to protect ourselves? It would have to be something more to strengthen the case against Cathy, I suppose. But . . ."

"Are you worried?" Khoury asked.

"Aren't you? The news people are saying the Manson gang killed Arlene and Steve, but the police haven't said so yet. Obviously, Columbo doesn't buy it. Even the arrest of this other girl, who worked at your house, hasn't settled the matter for Columbo. I tell you, Joe, he's after us! That sneaky son of a bitch is after *us.*"

Khoury sighed. "Sooner or later, I have to go back downstairs. Look, uh . . . You go on to Piscina Linda tonight. Be there about eight. I'll call right now and reserve our suite. I'll get there some way. Maybe in a cab."

"'Kay," she sighed. "I'll be there. I *need* you, Joe."

"I need *you,* Kim."

3

When Columbo left Khoury's store, he found a man waiting beside his car in the parking lot.

"Lieutenant Columbo," he said, extending his hand. "Remember me? Earl Schob."

Columbo did indeed remember Schob, whose name was pronounced "Schobe." He was one of the most successful criminal lawyers in Los Angeles. A pudgy man who seemed always to be growing out of his suits, he smoked a pipe, which he now knocked on the heel of his shoe, nimbly holding his left foot up against his right leg.

"I have a new client, Lieutenant. Thought I'd check with you. Melissa Mead. I'm afraid she's better known as Boobs. You can see why."

Columbo nodded. "Gotta match?" he asked.

Schob lit Columbo's cigar with the stream of almost invisible blue flame from his pipe lighter. "Her father has retained me to get Melissa out of jail. You're holding her on a charge of possession of marijuana. Right? But you suspect she's some way mixed up in the Khoury murders. Right?"

"It's a possibility," said Columbo noncommittally.

"I'm gonna apply for bail on the marijuana charge. Monday morning. You gonna charge her with murder, or being an accessory to murder? You gonna oppose my bail application?"

"That's not up to me," said Columbo. "Up to the DA."

"Who tosses it back at you," said Schob. "I already asked him. His answer is, it depends on what Columbo wants to do."

"I've got no reason to charge Miss Mead with being an accessory to murder. Is that what you wanted to hear?"

Schob nodded. "Then I can get her out. Her parents will be here Monday. They're gonna take her home."

"I doubt if she'll go," said Columbo, puffing on his cigar and getting into his car. "Anyway, I'd appreciate it if they didn't. I may need her as a witness. I don't want to ask to have her held as a material witness."

4

Mrs. Columbo's bowling team competed for a league championship on Saturday night. Columbo promised her they would go to the beach on Sunday afternoon—after he went over to Sybil Brand Institute and interviewed Boobs again, before Schob got her bailed out Monday morning.

The young woman was brought to an interview cubicle. She wore the gray uniform dress, which draped awkwardly over the ample figure that gave her her nickname. She was of course bare-legged, but for reasons of her own she had kicked off the canvas-and-rubber shoes that were issued to prisoners and was barefoot too.

"Y' gotta understand what kind of guy I am," he said to Boobs–Melissa Mead. "Sometimes I can't get to sleep. Little things keep comin' to mind, and I can't get rid of 'em."

"Try checking into a nice hotel, like Sybil Brand," she sneered. "It's real quiet here at night. Oh, real quiet, and you can sleep like a baby."

"You won't be here tomorrow night," he said.

She shrugged. "So I hear. You don't happen to have any cigarettes with you, do you?"

"Sorry. I only smoke cigars. Anyway—" He pointed at the NO SMOKING sign stenciled on the wall of the interview cubicle.

"Rules, rules, rules. They say they're going to put me in lock because I won't wear their damned stinky shoes."

"Look, uh, Miss Mead . . . I gotta couple of questions I want to ask you."

"The little things that are keeping you awake at night?"

"Right. If you—"

"Why should I help you make a case against Puss?" she asked defiantly.

"Maybe you'd like to help me make a case that would *help* Puss," said Columbo.

"Help her? I just bet!"

"Lemme ask you what I wanta ask you. You figure whether it will help or hurt. I can't *make* you answer."

"No rubber hose, Lieutenant?"

"No rubber hose. First question: Isn't it an

odd coincidence that the cops should come to the house on Pitillo Road just when you and Squatty were there? You weren't there when Puss and Kid and Bum were picked up for murder. There were no cops there Wednesday night. But you go to the house Thursday night, and *bang,* you got a black-and-white. Not only that, you got Detective Jackson, who's working on the Khoury murders. He IDs you, and Friday morning he collars you."

"What you trying to say?" she asked, tipping her head to one side and frowning.

"Maybe somebody set you up," said Columbo.

"Shee! You got a wild imagination. Why would anybody want to set me up? And for what?"

"How'd you come to be on Pitillo Road that night?" Columbo asked bluntly.

Boobs hesitated for a moment, then said, "Squatty got a phone call from Kid. Thursday. Said she was calling from here, from the slammer. Said we should go out to—Well . . . That's why we were there. And you're right. We'd hardly got there when the cops came down on us."

"How come you took a job at the Khoury mansion?" Columbo asked. "You're not the housemaid type."

She sighed. "I needed some bread quick. Real quick. I owed somebody. Puss said she'd ask Mr. Khoury if I could work some way at the store, like in the stockroom or something. Next thing I know, I'm wearing a black dress and a white apron, and I'm a maid in his house. I ran the vacuum cleaner and dusted and polished furniture and washed dishes: all that kinda shit. But I tell you something for sure. *I didn't steal.* I didn't plan on staying long, but I didn't steal anything from that house!"

"Those are the things I've been worrying about," said Columbo. He stood up and rapped on the window in the door. "It'd be a good idea if you didn't take off for Connecticut or anywhere. I may need to ask you some more questions, and I don't want to have to hold you as a material witness."

An officer opened the door, but the young woman ignored her. She shook her head. "I'll admit something, Lieutenant," she said. "Being in jail gets awful tiresome awful quick."

5

Jenny Schmidt, a.k.a. Kid, was forty-two years old. She was a wan, conspicuously unhappy woman, a natural blonde, the kind of woman no one would take a second look at on the street, because she was neither particularly pretty nor particularly homely. If Puss Dogood didn't insist that Kid had never been in jail before, Columbo might have taken her for a woman who had spent much of her life in jails and prisons.

"I didn't have anything to do with it," she said before he could ask her a question.

"Sergeant Jackson says you don't much like it here," said Columbo.

She shook her head. "I've never been in a place like this before. There's *awful* women here!"

"Well, help yourself out," he said. "Did you make a telephone call to Squatty on Thursday?"

Her eyes widened. "Phone call . . . I haven't been near a phone since I was busted!"

"I can check the log."

"Check it! I haven't called anybody!"

He checked. She was telling the truth.

6

When Columbo arrived at headquarters on Monday morning, he was painfully sunburned. His Sunday-afternoon hours on the beach with his wife had cost him a penalty. He hardly got inside the door before three people told him Captain Sczciegel wanted to see him immediately. Three more told him before he reached the captain's office.

"What the hell happened to you?" the captain asked as soon as Columbo walked in.

"I sunburn easy," said Columbo.

"Well . . . Must've spent all day on the firing range. I didn't even get in here this morning before your qualifying certificate, signed by the range officer, was on my desk. Congratulations, Columbo. Now that you know you won't shoot yourself in the foot, I imagine you're carrying your service revolver, as per regulations. Right?"

"I'll, uh, have to check out some bullets," said Columbo. "I couldn't find—"

"Ammunition, Columbo! Cartridges. Not bullets!" The captain turned to Sergeant Jackson, who was also in the office. "Ted, lend the man some . . . bullets, so he'll be equipped like a cop when he leaves here."

"Whadda ya carry, Columbo?" Jackson asked.

"One of those, uh . . . uh—"

"A goddamn *revolver!"* said Captain Sczciegel. "He needs some thirty-eight ammo."

"Sorry. Can't help him," said Jackson. "I carry a nine-millimeter Beretta."

"Anyway," said the captain. "Where were you on your way to this morning, Columbo?"

"Culver Pictures," said Columbo. "Need to talk to a man named Willsberger."

"Got something that takes priority," said Sczciegel. "I want both of you to go look at this one. We had a call from a Mrs. Russell. You know, Yussef Khoury's secretary. Seems like a package arrived in the mail Saturday. It's addressed to Miss Cathy Murphy, better known to us as Puss Dogood. They don't think it's a bomb, but they've taken it out to the parking lot. Two black-and-whites are on the scene. A bomb squad is on its way. I want you guys there. Find out what somebody mailed to Puss Dogood—something that arrived while she's in jail."

"How *did* ya get sunburned, Columbo?" Jackson asked as they drove to Rodeo Drive.

"Once or twice a year, I take Mrs. Columbo to the beach. She loves it. I'm not much for it. So I sit there under an umbrella, smokin' a cigar, and by the by I go to sleep. And the sun moves around, which means I'm not in the shade anymore. Somethin' always happens. One time I gut stung by a jellyfish."

"You can't even swim, as I remember."

"Well, I'm gonna learn. I'm gonna learn to scuba dive. You got those tanks of air on ya, so you can't drown; and you got a rubber suit on, so jellyfish can't eat ya. Also, a guy in a rubber suit doesn't look tasty, so the sharks don't bother him. It's the way to do it."

Two more cars had arrived, and the parking lot behind Khoury's was roped off. A crowd stood back at a respectful distance. The word *bomb* had circulated.

Columbo parked the Peugeot in front of the store, and he and Jackson walked through. They found Yussef Khoury, standing beside his gull-wing Mercedes parked just beside the rear entry. He looked as if maybe his chief concern was protecting the car.

"The package was delivered Saturday morning," he said to Columbo. "Because the store was closed out of respect for Arlene, no one took any notice of what had come in the mail. Eleanor saw it this morning and immediately called the police."

Two men parted the yellow tape that cordoned off the parking lot, and the heavily armored bomb-squad van pulled in.

Columbo walked across the lot. "Hi-ya, Hogan,"

he said to the big detective, so fat he would have been dismissed from the force as overweight except for the known facts of his expertise and courage in a job nobody really wanted.

"Hi, Columbo. Really a bomb?"

"Doubtful," said Columbo. "But ya can't be too careful these days."

The package lay on the pavement, between two LAPD black-and-whites parked to either side, to take as much as possible of the force of the explosion if the package were in fact a bomb. The squad's van pulled up close. A pneumatically controlled arm ran out from the rear of the van, carrying a heavy steel-mesh box, which it lowered over the package. Hogan shoved a wheeled steel shield forward and approached the box and the package.

After Hogan had peered at the box and package for a moment, he signaled for a dog. A uniformed officer led the German shepherd forward, and the animal circled the box, sniffing and wagging its tail. Hogan nodded and began to pull on a heavily padded suit reinforced with teflon panels. He put on a shielded helmet and huge gloves. He ordered the box lifted, and he knelt and photographed the package from several angles. The dog came up closer and sniffed curiously, then wagged its tail. If a dog could shrug, the dog shrugged.

Hogan took a knife from his pocket and cut the paper and tape. He opened the package, a small paperboard box.

"Columbo! My god, look!"

Columbo strode forward and knelt beside Hogan. Lying inside the package, in a wad of crumpled newspaper, was a jeweled gold choker, resplendent with glittering diamonds and emeralds.

"Forty-eight thousand three-hundred fifty dollars," Columbo muttered.

"Guess that settles that," said Jackson, who by now knelt beside Columbo.

Yussef Khoury came near. He stared into the cut-open package. "My *god!*" he croaked.

"Like I said, that settles that," Ted Jackson laughed as they pulled away from the store, carrying the superb piece of jewelry to the police property room, to be impounded as evidence.

"Figure so?" Columbo asked.

"Puss Dogood and her partners murdered Arlene Khoury, Steve Heck, and the houseboy. Figuring the cops would come looking for them, they had to get rid of the choker temporarily. So they mailed it to Puss at the Khoury office."

"Why'd they *figure* the cops would come?"

"A Manson-style murder. They were the only known Manson types still hanging around together in L.A."

"If they figured the cops were coming for them, why didn't they take off?" Columbo asked. "Look at it another way. If they were the only known Manson group in L.A. and they wanted to do a robbery, why'd they write 'Helter Skelter' and all that? Why'd they make it so obviously a Manson-style killing?"

"They didn't figure we'd have enough evidence and would have to let them go—as the guys almost had to let Charlie go, twenty-five years ago, as you'll remember. And if we hadn't come up with Boobs, which gives us the link to the house, and now the choker—"

Columbo shook his head. "Funny . . ." he said thoughtfully.

"What's funny? What's wrong?"

"Odd, the way that package was mailed," said Columbo. "That's a postage-meter imprint."

"Sure. When you mail a package at a post office, they weigh it and imprint the postage on a piece of white paper tape, which they stick on the package."

"Yeah . . ." said Columbo. "I guess that's what they do. I don't know. It, uh . . . But that is exactly what they do."

EIGHTEEN

1

The finding of the choker had so delayed Columbo that he did not arrive at the Culver soundstage for his appointment with Ben Willsberger until nearly eleven o'clock. He identified himself to the guard at the gate, then to another guard at the entrance to the soundstage. Both of them telephoned word of his arrival to someone inside, and a young man hurried out to meet him.

"Good morning, Lieutenant Columbo. I'm Bill Fodor. Mr. Willsberger is expecting you. You've come at a good time. Mr. Willsberger's about to shoot, and after that there will be an interval before the next shot."

Fodor led Columbo into the soundstage, a building as big as an aircraft hangar and in many ways similar. They had built a set in the middle of the

vast open space. It represented a shabby kitchen in
some urban flat, furnished with a kitchen sink that
stood on legs, a glass-front cabinet containing a
modest collection of dishes, an ice box, a table
covered with red-and-white checkered oilcloth, a
bare wooden floor, and buff-colored plaster walls
hung with just one decoration: a 1939 calendar.

Huge hot lights stood on stands facing the set
from all sides. They were arranged to make it
appear that the chief light in the kitchen was from
daylight entering through the window above the
sink. Booms stretched out over the set, putting
microphones in position.

Benjamin Willsberger saw Columbo and saluted.

"Here," said Fodor, handing Columbo a fat
bound script open to page 96. "This is what he's
shooting now: Shots one hundred eight and one
hundred nine. You can follow it on the script."

Columbo sat down on the chair offered him—
not a wood-and-canvas folding chair but an
aluminum-and-vinyl chair—and frowned over the
script.

108   INT. SCHMIDT KITCHEN—DAY

Kurt sits at kitchen table, smoking a cigarette,
a tumbler and whisky bottle at hand, reading a
newspaper. He wears a ribbed vest undershirt
and dark pants.

KURT
So, what the hell? Is it gonna happen or is
it not gonna happen?

Nancy appears in doorway. She too is smoking

a cigarette. She wears a very ordinary bra and pair of panties, obviously cheap and worn.

> NANCY
> What he says. It's what he says. How'm I s'posed to know? It's gonna is what the man says.

> KURT
> (dismayed)
> Not the time for it.

Nancy walks over to him and puts her hand on his shoulder.

> NANCY
> It's God's will, I guess.

> KURT
> God's will? Well. Yeah, I suppose it is. If it's the decision of the Man Upstairs, I suppose we gotta live with it. Maybe we shoulda—

> NANCY
> Too late to think about what we shoulda. Now we have to think about what we gotta. We have to think about makin' some stuff different.

109   KURT and NANCY fill the FRAME as KURT pushes back his chair, rises, embraces, and kisses NANCY.

> KURT
> Anyway, I love you, and that's what counts.

NANCY

More than anything else. Which means we've gotta change some things.

KURT

I promise.

KURT reaches behind NANCY and unhooks her bra. He pushes her back, admires her breasts, then bends forward and kisses each in turn.

CUT TO:

110   INT. HOSPITAL—NIGHT.

Columbo watched fascinated as these two shots were filmed. It was unlike the Hollywood cliché. Willsberger did not cry "Lights, camera, action!" He did not yell "Cut!" to stop the shot. He simply made a few gestures, and the highly professional people of his cast and crew did what they had rehearsed doing. To make the transition between Shots 108 and 109, the two actors just paused briefly, holding their places and expressions, while the camera rolled forward a few feet. When the shots were finished, the whole process stopped, without any command.

"Kids," Willsberger said to the actor and actress when the camera stopped, "I want to do those two shots one more time. What I want you to do is drab it down a mite. You follow me? Drab it down a measure. You're a little too bright yet. You're still yourselves: a couple of bright, handsome people. Bring it down to what Kurt and Nancy are. Take fifteen minutes, and let's try it again."

No one yelled "Fifteen minutes!" Fodor walked around, quietly telling the crews that they would shoot the two scenes again in fifteen minutes.

Benjamin Willsberger beckoned to Columbo to come over beyond the main camera and sit down with him. "Coffee, Lieutenant Columbo?" he asked.

Columbo nodded, and Willsberger nodded at Fodor.

The director did not dress like Cecil B. DeMille. He wore a pair of khaki slacks and a light-blue golf shirt. "Brad Volney and Katherine Boyd," he said, nodding toward the back of the stage, where the dressing rooms were located.

"I recognized them," said Columbo.

"Well, Lieutenant, who killed Arlene and Ted—not to mention the poor houseboy?"

"I wish I knew," said Columbo.

"In other words, it's not as simple as it seems?"

"In my line of work," said Columbo, "you've got to be careful about the easy and simple answers. Not many things are easy and simple. On the other hand, it's foolish to overcomplicate. Y' know? Sometimes the simple and obvious is the answer."

Benjamin Willsberger smiled, whether knowingly or condescendingly, or both, would have been difficult to tell. "I said I wanted to talk to you. You said you wanted to talk to me. Suppose you tell me first what you wanted to ask me," he said.

"Well, sir, I mostly wanted to talk to you about scuba diving."

"Scuba diving?"

"Right. Mr. Khoury suggested I ought to take it

up. I thought maybe you could tell me something about it."

Willsberger's smile turned skeptical. "All right," he said. "Scuba diving. I took it up because golf bores me. That's about it. A man my age and position ought to do something by way of exercise, something in the outdoors."

"Who took it up first, you or Mr. Khoury?"

"He did. Oh, he's been a scuba diver for a long time. He got me interested."

"I understand he follows the rules for safety," said Columbo. "And that's what interests me. Mr. McGinnis over at the Topanga Diving Club told me Mr. Khoury never goes diving without a buddy. In fact, he said you were Mr. Khoury's buddy and that he never goes diving without you. Is that true?"

"That's true," said Willsberger. "Personally, I never go down alone. I doubt if Joe ever does."

"Well, he did twice last week," said Columbo. "Wednesday and Friday, off the beach at San Luis Rio."

Willsberger remained silent while Bill Fodor put down a TV tray between the two men's chairs. On the tray were a coffee pot, cups and saucers, cream and sugar, and spoons. The director poured.

"I think you have to understand something, Lieutenant," said Willsberger. "Joe Khoury has to be in a state of immense emotional distress."

"I'd suppose so," said Columbo. "After all, his wife murdered and—"

"There may be more to it than that," said Willsberger. He drew a deep breath. "I suppose, uh . . . I suppose I can speak to you in confidence. I mean, if what I am about to suggest turns out wildly wrong, can I count on you not to mention it to anyone?"

"Yes, sir. I can keep a confidence. Keepin' confidences is part of my line of work."

"Well . . ." Willsberger began. He glanced around to be sure Fodor could not hear. "The fact is, it's possible, just wildly possible, that Arlene and Steve may have been murdered by Kimberly Dana."

2

This idea was not something Columbo wanted to discuss in what remained of a fifteen-minute break. He stayed in the soundstage and watched the two actors "drab down" their scene. An hour later he and Willsberger sat down in Willsberger's office in Santa Monica. The room was unimaginatively furnished in spun aluminum, stainless steel, black leather, and glass. Over drinks poured from the office bar, they talked about the picture Willsberger had been shooting that morning. It was not until they had box lunches before them—deli sandwiches and salads—that Willsberger returned to the subject of Kim Dana and Joe Khoury.

"You think I'm nuts?" he asked.

Columbo ran a hand over his tousled hair, in a futile effort to smooth it. It was a gesture he consciously used to cover awkward moments and give him time to think of an answer to a difficult question. Willsberger had persuaded him to leave his raincoat in the closet in the reception area and he realized he had neither a pad for notes nor a pencil to write them—and what was more, no cigars, though Willsberger had assured him he would join him in a cigar after lunch. He checked his sandwich—at first skeptically, then appreciatively, eyeing what looked like first-rate salami.

"I mean, to suggest that Kim might have done it," said Willsberger. "Do you think the idea's nuts?"

"Well, sir, I can think of a lot of reasons why it doesn't seem likely, but I'd be more interested in your reasons for thinking it might be."

"Is it impossible?" Willsberger asked. "Tell me it's impossible. Tell me why it's impossible."

Columbo frowned. "Uh . . . We haven't told the news people anything about this. Understand? But, uh . . . Well, you know that Mrs. Khoury was in bed with Mr. Heck when she was murdered. *That's* been in the news. What hasn't been is that at the same time, Mr. Khoury was in bed with Miss Dana."

"How do you know?" Willsberger asked.

"Both of them say so. Besides, the night staff at a motel saw them there."

"Suppose Joe is trying to protect Kim? Suppose she slipped out of the motel, went and did it, and came back—and he's lying for her, to protect her."

"Why would he do that?" asked Columbo.

"Because he's one hundred percent in love with

her. Because he thinks she's the greatest thing that ever happened to him."

"Well . . . Even so, Mr. Willsberger—"

"Ben. Please, Lieutenant. Ben. Even so, what?"

Columbo put the tips of his fingers over his eyes. "Start with somethin'," he said. "There had to be *two* people. At least. One person couldn't have done it."

"Go back to your simple solution, Lieutenant Columbo. The simple solution is that the three Manson types did it. Well, maybe they did. But maybe Kim Dana *procured* them to do it."

"Why? Why would Miss Dana want Mrs. Khoury dead?"

"Maybe it was Steve Heck she wanted dead," said Willsberger. "Maybe it was both of them."

"Start with him," said Columbo. "Why would she want Steve Heck dead?"

"To understand what might have motivated Kim, you have to understand her history. She's a beautiful young woman. Do I have to tell you that? But she hasn't got talent one. She can't sing. She can't dance. And she sure as hell can't act. Give her two great female leads, say, in *The Prime of Miss Jean Brodie* and *Cat on a Hot Tin Roof.* She'd play them so alike you couldn't tell them apart. But she's got delusions and ambition. What she needs is a guy like Joe Khoury to stake her to a part—by which I mean put up the money to make a movie starring his girlfriend."

"I wondered about that," said Columbo. "But what's that got to do with Mr. Steve Heck?"

"A girl like Kim, with her looks, her—She does

have one talent. She's great in bed, Lieutenant. To which I can attest from personal experience. So could Steve Heck." Willsberger took a bite from his sandwich. "Hey, you can't find better salami than this, incidentally."

"I agree, and bein' a New Yorker born and bred, I know something about salami. This is first rate. But . . . You mean Miss Dana. . . . It's that way, huh?"

"That way. With whatever man she thought could make her a star. She settled on Joe Khoury because she saw in him a guy who could finance a picture for her and wouldn't be too discerning or too demanding about talent. After all, Joe had funded pictures for Willa Wood and Fairleigh Richmond. He didn't sleep with those two, incidentally."

"Still, why would Miss Dana want to kill Steve Heck?"

"Revenge. He'd rained on her parade all over town. When she left him, he was jealous and furious and decided he'd kill whatever little chance she had to make it in Hollywood. Whenever her name came up, he put her down. He did it repeatedly. I don't think she had much chance anyway, but—"

"She left Mr. Heck for Mr. Khoury?" Columbo asked.

Willsberger shook his head. "For me. As a director I could have—but . . ." He paused and shook his head. "The only way Kim was going to star in a picture was to find a sugar daddy to fund it. It never occurred to me that would be my old friend Joe Khoury."

"Uh . . . Ben, I don't know exactly how to put this, but—"

"Yeah. You're about to suggest I got some bad feelings about Kim. You're right. I do. About Joe, too. He took her like she was some kind of beautiful object he'd found and wanted to put in his store. And she jumped at the chance. I'd thought I . . . maybe had a little stronger relationship with her. Hell, I'd thought Joe was a better friend than that—though you can't be too hard on a man in his fifties who falls for a girl like Kim. Anyway, it's for sure I wouldn't be talking like I'm talking for any emotional reason. I just don't want to see some innocent people convicted because somebody didn't give you information you should have had. Remember, I said to you from the beginning I was only talking about a remote possibility."

"What about Mrs. Khoury?" Columbo asked. "Was she in the way of Miss Dana's ambitions?"

"You better believe it. In the most fundamental of all possible ways," said Willsberger.

"Meaning?"

"Let me go back a little bit. Did it occur to you to wonder why Steve Heck was having an affair with Arlene Khoury?"

Columbo shrugged. "I wouldn't want to suggest that Mrs. Khoury wasn't the town's most attractive woman."

"Joe Khoury is cash poor," said Willsberger. "He lost a lot of money on *Lingering Melody*—more because Steve was stealing from him. And in that, incidentally, Arlene was helping him. But Joe Khoury is not assets poor. Khoury's is worth . . . god knows how many millions. But Joe would never consider borrowing against the store or, god forbid, cashing out. But suppose you're Steve Heck, and you're flattering Arlene Khoury, who is ten years older than you, and have her emotionally tied to you. Suppose Arlene divorces Joe. Suppose you marry Arlene. Under California community property law, Arlene owns, maybe not half, but a big chunk of Khoury's. Now you are never going to have to worry about money again. What's more, you can stomach it, because Arlene is a Middle Eastern woman, totally complaisant about whatever her man wants her to do—I mean, physically."

"If Mrs. Khoury had divorced Mr. Khoury—"

"It would have been financial disaster for Joe. Oh, he'd have recovered, in time. But time is what Kim Dana doesn't have. She's twenty-nine and has never made a picture. Given a few more years, she'll have to have real *talent* to become a star."

"Did Mrs. Khoury in fact threaten to divorce Mr. Khoury?"

"I don't know. He never told me she did. Not in so many words. But, you know, under the law today, you don't have to have a reason. I mean, you used to have to prove adultery or nonsupport or abandonment—whatever. Not anymore. Anyway, Arlene could have proved Joe slept with Kim, also that he did with the Manson girl."

"Cathy Murphy?"

Willsberger grinned. "Puss Dogood."

"You know her?"

"Oh, Joe allowed me to play around with his cast-off. I'll tell you something, Lieutenant. Puss is *nuts*. She's also the most honest person I've ever met. You know what they said about Heinrich Himmler—that if you could just overlook one little thing, you had a man of principle and honor. Well, it's that way with Puss. If you can overlook the fact that Charlie Manson—or maybe drugs—destroyed her mind, you have a woman of innocence and honor."

"You don't think she and her pals killed Mrs. Khoury and the others, then?"

"Not so far as its being her own idea. If she did it, she was influenced by somebody else. A psychiatrist would call Puss 'an influenceable personality.' Manson influenced her. So could someone else."

Columbo had before him a can of Diet Dr Pepper. He tipped it back and took a sip. "People aren't very complimentary about Mrs. Khoury," he said.

"There was nothing wrong with Arlene except that she grew old," said Willsberger. "Once her children left the nest, she had nothing to do, no purpose in life. She never shared Joe's obsession with elegance. She interfered in his business. She didn't help. She couldn't. It must have been tough for her, being married to Joe Khoury, a man whose whole life centered on beauty, and not *be* beautiful. For example, Joe and Arlene went to the Motion Picture Association awards dinner and ball, about . . . Oh, Jesus, it was just about a week before her death. Monday, August first. I mean, he took her to that affair, and she looked great, in a green dress. She looked good. But you could just see that Joe was disturbed because the woman on his arm wasn't the beautiful Kim Dana."

Columbo shook his head. "That had to be tough on Mrs. Khoury. Mr. Khoury doesn't care about anything but—"

Willsberger interrupted. "The point is, whatever Joe touches, he wants it to be perfect, perfect and exquisite—and he's very unhappy if it isn't. Let me show you something. I'll show you what I mean."

Willsberger picked up from his credenza a lacquered cigarette box. It was inlaid with mother of pearl and overlaid with gold leaf.

"Look at that," he said. "We've seen a thousand of them, right? Cigarette box, what th' hell. But look at that one. Khoury. Somebody gave you that, who'd want to put cigarettes in it? Open it. Silk satin, f' god's sake!"

Lying inside the box was in fact a pair of silver cuff links in the shape of two owl faces.

"Cuff links," said Willsberger. "I don't wear the shirts for them, but I'm gonna have some shirts made for that pair. Something else. Look at this."

He opened a sliding door in his credenza. He took out a leather box and carried it back to the table where he and Columbo were eating. "Open that," he said.

Columbo put aside the last of his sandwich and opened the leather box. "I've seen these before," he said, unfolding the handles and uncovering the blade of the knife.

"I bet you never saw one like that before," said Willsberger. "The town is full, unfortunately, of knives with folding handles. But that one there is something else. That's a Bali-Song. Look at the workmanship! You want to pay, like, two hundred dollars for a knife? And probably more? A street thug doesn't. But Joe Khoury did. Why? Why would he want a thing like that? Because it's the *best*, the best of its kind; and in its way, it's a beautiful thing. Joe gave me that. He gave several of them to his friends. What can you do with it? Nothing. It's a trophy, a treasure. I keep that one in the office. My wife wouldn't want it in the house."

"Well . . ." said Columbo. "I'll keep what you told me in mind. And I'll keep it confidential, like you said. I thank ya for the lunch."

"No after-lunch cigar?"

"I'm afraid not. Y' see, I've got a lot of things to check. So I gotta be moving on."

"Actually, I do too," said Willsberger. "We'll be shooting again this afternoon."

Columbo retrieved his raincoat from the closet.

"It's hot and dry outside," said Willsberger. "You don't need a coat today."

"Well, I know I don't," said Columbo. "But it's sort of like an office away from the office. I carry a lot of stuff in the pockets. Including a cigar, which I'll smoke in the car. You happen to have a match handy?"

The receptionist handed Willsberger a book of paper matches, which he gave to Columbo.

"So, uh . . . So thank ya again, for lunch. I wish you luck with that picture you're shooting. It looks interesting."

"If you'd like to see some more of the shooting, stop around any time."

"Maybe I will," said Columbo. "I'd like to. I—Oh, say, there is one more little thing I'd like to ask you." He ran his hands down over his eyes. "That dinner and dance you mentioned. A very fancy affair, was it? I mean formal?"

"Oh, sure. Black tie."

"Jewels?"

"Absolutely. The gals wore their jewels, if they had any."

"What jewels was Mrs. Khoury wearing?"

Willsberger shook his head. "I don't remember."

"In July Mr. Khoury bought Mrs. Khoury a forty-eight-thousand-dollar jeweled choker. Gold and diamonds and emeralds. Wasn't she wearing it that night?"

"Are you sure it has emeralds on it?" Willsberger asked.

"I'm sure. It was stolen the night of the murder and recovered this morning. I personally carried it to headquarters to be locked up as evidence. Emeralds. Green stones, right?"

"Right," said Willsberger. "So why wasn't she wearing it with her green dress?"

"I wonder about that," said Columbo.

NINETEEN

1

"How could you have done it, Kim? How *could* you? We had *agreed* the choker was to go in the Pacific."

Still concerned that no one should see him with Kim in public, Joe Khoury had again arranged to meet her at Le Cirque in Pasadena, and once again he had driven his Toyota, not the gull-wing Mercedes. Again, she waited for him, casually sipping a Bombay gin martini and nibbling a sesame breadstick. She was wearing the purple-and-white denim shorts she had worn on the pier and after the beach volleyball game, with the rib-knit cotton T-shirt. It was one of his favorites among her outfits.

"You might have said, 'Hello, how are you?' first," she remarked. "So, hello, how are *you*? Less gloomy than last night?"

"The choker! It's not in a mayonnaise jar off San Luis Rio," he said. "It's at police head-quarters, locked up in a property-room safe for evidence!"

Kim nodded. "Where it's doing us some good. Since you know about it, you know where it was found. Evidence. It's doing us some good."

"For god's sake! The damned thing doesn't have Arlene's fingerprints on it!"

"No, and it doesn't have mine, either," said Kim. "Or yours. Or anybody else's. Before I put it in the mail, I cleaned it of every fingerprint. I spent half an hour rubbing it with a cloth, handling it with gloves."

"Suspicious in itself!" he whispered hoarsely. "Columbo will wonder why it's clean of finger-prints."

She smiled. "If you were Puss Dogood and had the choker and were going to mail it, what would you have done? Cleaned your own fingerprints off. Well . . ."

"It couldn't have been mailed by Cathy—by Puss Dogood, for god's sake! She was in jail!"

Kim smiled. "The postmark shows she mailed it Tuesday night."

"How . . . ?"

"Simplest thing in the world," she said. "When you mail a package at a post office, they run a little white tape through a meter and stick that little tape on your package. When we mail something from the store, the postage is put on the same way, by the meter. And you set the date on the meter. I mailed the package Friday. But I set the store postage meter back to show it was mailed Tuesday. Set it to Tuesday, ran it once, set it back to the correct date. The store meter doesn't add a logo or message, thank god. It looks exactly like the tape from a post-office meter."

"Well . . . It sounds okay. I can only hope you didn't some way outsmart yourself."

Kim shook her head. "I thought it all through. Puss Dogood snatched the choker off the dresser, wiped it off, and stuck it in the mail. She figured they'd have to let her go within forty-eight hours, for lack of evidence, and the choker would be waiting for her in Arlene's office at the store."

"Lack of evidence . . ." Joe mused. "We went to some trouble to set up enough evidence."

"Not enough evidence," said Kim. "As it turned out. Columbo didn't buy it. Puss stays in jail, but that son of a bitch is investigating *us*. Everything he does, so far as I can figure out, is against *us*."

"The man's not bright," said Joe. "If I have to be investigated by a homicide detective, give me Lieutenant Columbo." He smiled nervously. "Right?"

"I'm not so sure," said Kim. "That's why I decided to reinforce the case against Puss Dogood."

"Right. Yes. But one thing, my lover. Let's agree we don't do things this important all by ourselves, not without talking it over together. From now on, everything's a partnership between us. Isn't it?"

"It's been that for a long time, Joe. And it always will be. It was just that—You had so much on your mind. I thought throwing forty-eight thousand dollars in the Pacific . . . Hey! Not when it could do us some good. Major good! They've got to charge Puss Dogood with the murders now. The choker may close the case! Besides, think of something else. We get it back!"

2

"You still don't buy it," said Captain Sczciegel. "You don't think Puss Dogood did it."

Columbo shook his head.

Sczciegel sighed. "We're getting heat," he said. "The murders were committed a week ago tomorrow night. The chief wants to know—"

"Remind him how long it took to crack the Tate-LaBianca case," said Columbo.

"But this one seems so simple."

"It's not simple. There's a lot of things not simple," said Columbo.

"Ted Jackson thinks it's simple. He thinks that finding the choker where it was closes the case."

Columbo turned down the corners of his mouth and nodded. "Whose fingerprints were on the choker?" he asked.

"No one's."

"On the wrapping paper? On any part of the package?"

Sczciegel shook his head.

"None in the house," said Columbo. "That is, none of Puss Dogood's and none of Bum Rapp's or Kid's. What evidence places them at the scene?"

Captain Sczciegel lifted himself from his chair, stepped to the window, and looked down on the streets of Los Angeles. "Tell me something, Columbo," he said. "You kinda like Puss Dogood, don't you?"

Columbo shook his head. "I'm not old enough to have a daughter her age. But I have a daughter. When I look at Puss, I hafta think about what a crazy world she grew up in and what it made of her. Hey, I'm not one of those guys that thinks the world is responsible for every dumb thing somebody does. But I hafta wonder what my daughter would be if *she'd* met Charlie Manson."

"Or if she played with chemicals," said Sczciegel.

"Yeah, that too."

"You met the *real* Manson girls. And Charlie Manson, too. Didn't you? I didn't. I was on The Job, but not assigned to that case."

Columbo took a half-burned cigar from his pocket, stared at it for a moment, decided enough was left to light it again, and began patting his pockets, looking for matches. "Yeah, I'd been out here from New York for ten years or so when the Tate-LaBianca murders happened. Uh . . . Gotta match? I was already a homicide detective when the Helter Skelter case came along. I met Manson, too. I talked to him. You know what he was, Captain? He was a scuzzball. A *nothin'.*"

"How'd he ever get so much power over all those young people?" the captain asked.

It was a rhetorical question. He didn't expect an answer, and he didn't get one. Columbo only shook his head.

"Maybe you'd like to look at this," said Captain

Sczciegel, handing a file to Columbo. "That's the Cathy Murphy file. It finally came down from Fontera. Read the personal statement she gave the prison psychologist."

Columbo flipped through the pages: the usual stuff, the record of her arrests, her convictions, her sentences; then, the personal statement she had voluntarily given.

I was born in Lancaster, Ohio. My father was an insurance agent. My parents were very strict. They wouldn't let me date. I had to go to church and Sunday school. I wanted to be a cheerleader or a majorette, but they wouldn't let me. The majorettes' skirts were too short, and the cheerleaders' skirts flipped up when they jumped. Anyway, I'd be showing my legs. I started seeing a boy. It had to be a secret. When they found out, they just went ape!

I left home when I was seventeen years old. My boyfriend helped me, but he wasn't willing to take off with me. He drove me to Columbus, and I caught a bus there for California. I'd stolen something like four hundred dollars out of the house, so I had enough money to get to California.

I came to L.A. first, but later I went up to San Francisco because I heard it was more fun up there. That's where I met Charlie. I heard him sing. At first I just thought of him as a wonderful singer who wrote great songs. Then I found out who he is and what he is. Since then, Charlie has been my whole life. I'd do anything for him. I mean, I'd do anything for Charlie.

"Columbo," said Captain Sczciegel, "the newspeople saw us recover the choker this morning. They're gonna say it closes the case. We've going to have to charge Puss Dogood with murder. We're gonna have heat."

"We've had heat before," said Columbo. "How many cases we have, we *don't* get heat?"

3

"Hi-ya, Mike."

Columbo walked up to the desk of Detective Sergeant Miguel Lopez. Lopez, who was younger than Columbo but had gray hair, stood up to shake hands.

"How's it goin', Columbo?"

"Tough," said Columbo. "Always somethin' tough. Maybe you can help me out a little."

"Sure."

"I got here a tape I'd like you to listen to," said Columbo. He dug into his raincoat pocket and pulled out a Sony Walkman with the tape cartridge in place. "Tell me if Spanish is that person's native language."

Columbo started the tape, and Lopez leaned forward and listened intently. When he heard the words "Strange peoples there. Running around house. Not kind peoples Khourys invite their house," he began to shake his head.

"That's not a Spanish accent," said Lopez.

"That's not Spanish grammar transplanted to English. That's an English-speaker faking an accent."

"Hey, that's just what I figured," said Columbo. "I appreciate it, Mike."

TWENTY

Columbo arrived at the Khoury house about four. He had expected to find Mrs. Takeshi there and Yussef Khoury not yet home, and that was how it was.

She met him in the kitchen and invited him to sit down and have a cup of coffee.

"I have been hoping, Lieutenant, to hear that you have solved the mystery of the murder of Mrs. Khoury. It will be so much easier for Mr. Khoury when the case is closed."

"I was hopin' I could say that by now, too, ma'am. The more time goes by, the tougher it gets."

"Isn't it clear that the Manson types broke into this house and duplicated the Tate-LaBianca murders?" she asked, innocently and yet a little indignantly.

"Well, that looks clear enough until you try to put together the evidence to prove it," Columbo said.

"I should have supposed that wouldn't have been too very difficult."

Columbo ran his hand through his hair. "So did I," he said. "I wanted to ask you about that young woman, Melissa Mead. Just how did it happen she came to work here?"

"Mr. Khoury hired her. He told me she needed work and he felt sorry for her. From the day she arrived here, it was plain she would be worthless as a housemaid."

"A graduate of Radcliffe," said Columbo. "She's a graduate of a girls' prep school, then of Radcliffe. Housemaid work is not exactly what she was educated to do."

"Oh, indeed? That explains a good deal," said Mrs. Takeshi. "She simply wasn't the type of person who does a job of work earnestly. I couldn't understand her exactly. She said she needed the job, but she obviously wasn't willing to do it."

"What did Mrs. Khoury think of her?"

"Mrs. Khoury made some comment about Mr. Khoury hiring misfits to work for him. She told the girl one day that if she ever caught her smoking marijuana on the premises, she'd not only fire her but would call the police."

Columbo sipped from his cup. In the Khoury household, even the coffee was exceptional. "How do you make good coffee like this, ma'am?"

"As Mr. Khoury prescribes," she said. "The beans are from Jamaica. I grind them freshly each time I make a pot of coffee. What's more, the measure must be exact. If I put in a teaspoon too much or too little, Mr. Khoury will taste the difference."

"Mrs. Khoury?"

Mrs. Takeshi shrugged. "She'd have been content with Maxwell House Instant."

Columbo smiled. "Mrs. Columbo makes pretty good coffee out of Eight O'Clock," he said. "I think I'll suggest she try grinding beans, though. Anyway, when this Mead girl came here to work, did you really need her?"

"No, not at all. Sergio was a good worker. We have a part-time gardener. I—I couldn't see that we needed additional personnel to run this house."

"She worked here about two weeks?" Columbo asked.

"That's right. About that. Then things began to turn up missing."

"Like what kind of things, ma'am?"

"Money, chiefly," said Mrs. Takeshi. "Mr. Khoury was careless about leaving money in his bedroom, frankly. I myself once suggested to him that he install a wall safe. He just laughed. He said he never had more than one or two hundred dollars in the house and that he trusted me and Sergio. Then . . . money began to disappear. Little amounts . . . but several times."

"How much money?" Columbo asked.

"Oh, I'd say not more than fifty or sixty dollars. Like . . . He would leave, say, a hundred fifty dollars in his bureau drawer, and the next day he'd find a hundred ten or a hundred twenty. That happened twice or three times."

"What else was stolen?"

"Well—" she said solemnly. "The big item was a

sterling silver sugar and creamer on a sterling silver tray. Those disappeared from a glass-front cabinet in the dining room. When I saw they were missing, I called the police. They came. They searched Miss Mead's car and found the items under the front seat. They arrested her and took her to jail. But Mr. Khoury did not want to press charges, and they were compelled to release her. Of course, she was not allowed to return here after that. Except—"

"Except?"

"I should think it is rather obvious she was here last Tuesday night. She had been in this house long enough to know the arrangement of rooms, the habits of the people who lived here, and how the alarm system worked."

Columbo nodded. "Makes sense," he said.

Mrs. Takeshi sighed. "Poor Mr. Khoury! He . . . authorized me to hire people to clean up the master-bedroom suite. Everything is being changed. The carpet has all been taken up and the drapes taken down. The walls are being repainted. All the furniture has been removed. I've bought, with his authority, all new furniture for both rooms." She shook her head. "And likely as not, it will all have to be done again."

"Oh? How come?" asked Columbo.

"Let's not be coy, Lieutenant Columbo. I expect Miss Dana will be moving into the house before very long. I would not be surprised if she becomes the second Mrs. Khoury. I can only hope to keep my job. Mr. Khoury has promised to keep me, even if he sells this house and buys another one. But— You know how it can be."

Columbo raised his eyebrows and nodded. "Has Miss Dana ever been in the house?" he asked.

Mrs. Takeshi shook her head. "Not to my knowledge. And I very much doubt it. Mr. Khoury has a pronounced sense of propriety." She paused and lifted her chin. "As Mrs. Khoury didn't, I'm afraid. As Mrs. Khoury didn't."

"Well, ma'am, I won't take any more of your time. I sure do appreciate the coffee. Jamaican beans . . . ground each time you make a pot. I'm gonna tell Mrs. Columbo about that."

Mrs. Takeshi nodded and smiled faintly. "Any time, Lieutenant," she said.

He rose and walked toward the back door, with the intention of walking around the house as he left. "Thanks again, and—Oh. There is one more little thing I meant to ask. Uh . . . You know, whoever killed Mrs. Khoury and Mr. Heck and Sergio Flores stole a gold choker set with diamonds and emeralds, that Mr. Khoury paid $48,350 for. Did you think that necklace was worth that much money?"

"Lieutenant Columbo," said Mrs. Takeshi, "Mr. Khoury has an excellent sense of values. If he paid that much for it, I'm sure it was worth every penny of it."

"Well, I mean, when you looked at it, could you see that much value in it? Was it obvious it was worth a fortune?"

She shook her head. "I never saw it."

"You never saw it?"

"There is nothing unusual in that. Mrs. Khoury kept her jewelry inside a special jewelry drawer. She was more careful of her jewelry than Mr. Khoury was of his cash. I never saw any of it."

"But this piece is supposed to have been snatched off the bureau top, layin' out in plain sight."

"I never saw it, Lieutenant. I never saw any of Mrs. Khoury's jewelry, except what she wore. When she had it on her, I saw it. Otherwise, I never saw it."

"I see. Well, thank ya again, ma'am. I appreciate the talk and the coffee. I—Uh . . . Sorry. One more question comes to mind. Is it possible Melissa had a key to the house? And kept it?"

"It wouldn't have made any difference. When the police came, they suggested we change the locks, and I had a locksmith come here to do it the same day."

2

Melissa Mead sat uncomfortably on a nubby green couch in the parlor of a motel suite. Though she was a thirty-four-year-old woman, she was dressed like a member of the girl's field-hockey team at a private girls' school in New England—that is, in a pleated plaid skirt and a white long-sleeved blouse with its collar fastened by a gold safety pin. She was smoking a cigarette, which did not look like something a member of a girl's field-hockey team would do. She smoked hungrily, drawing the smoke deep into her lungs and blowing it out through her nose.

Her mother, Martha Bonner Mead, sat on the couch, too: a lofty, thin woman with professionally coiffed hair obviously kept blonde by chemicals. Her complexion was completely covered with some kind of makeup that unfortunately was so smooth it was shiny. She wore a lavender cashmere dress. Her back and shoulders were rigidly straight and her lips primly compressed.

Boobs's father, Lloyd Mead, sat in a chair facing the couch. He was a square-faced man with steel-gray hair, looking something like The Businessman that used to appear in whisky ads.

The attorney, Earl Schob, sat in another chair. He puffed thoughtfully on his pipe.

Columbo sat on the straight chair behind a small table, wearing his raincoat.

Schob had left a message for him at headquarters that the Mead family would like to meet with him if at all possible. They wanted to take their daughter home and they wanted his assurance that he would not have her arrested again and held as a material witness.

"Whatever has given her the notion that she has any relationship whatsoever to Charles Manson is utterly beyond my comprehension," said Mrs. Mead. "Why, she's never met the man, never corresponded with him, never—"

"You don't have to meet him to love him," said Boobs defiantly. "You talk about loving Christ. Did you ever meet *Him?*"

"There is more *involved* than that," said Mrs. Mead coldly.

"The question is—" Schob interrupted. "The question is, can Melissa go home to Connecticut?"

"I want to ask her a few more questions," said Columbo.

"What are my options?" asked Boobs. "Do I just have two: go back to jail or go to Connecticut?"

"Where do you *want* to go?" asked Mrs. Mead.

"Home," said Boobs.

"To Connecticut—"

"No. *My* home. The little place I share with Squatty."

"Lieutenant—?" asked Schob.

"The girl is obviously deranged," said Mrs. Mead, not entirely successful in holding back her anger. "Can't we force her to come home to Connecticut, Mr. Schob?"

"Not with *my* help, you can't," said Schob. "I was retained to be Melissa's attorney. She's thirty-four years old. She's got some odd ideas, but I would resist on her behalf any effort to declare her incompetent. In any event, she's a resident of the State of California. If she's found incompetent, she'll be committed to a California medical facility, for treatment."

"This is outrageous . . ." the woman muttered. "It is simply outrageous."

"The only charge against her is possession of a small amount of marijuana. Isn't that right, Lieutenant Columbo?" asked Schob.

"That's right," said Columbo. "A misdemeanor."

"And the grand theft charge from June is—"

"Dead," said Columbo.

Boobs drew a deep breath. "Suppose I plead guilty to the possession, and suppose I can't pay any fine. How much time will I have to do?"

Columbo shrugged. "What would you guess, Earl?" he asked Schob.

Schob, too, shrugged. "Thirty days, at most," he said. "Probably not that."

"Then I won't owe anybody anything," said Boobs. She sighed. "I can do it." She turned to her mother and added, "I've been in jail before."

Lloyd Mead spoke for the first time. "I don't limit you to two options, Melissa," he said. "I retained Mr. Schob to get you as light a penalty as possible, and I will pay your fine."

"Thank you, Daddy," Boobs whispered.

"I do suggest one thing," Lloyd Mead went on. "I suggest you answer Lieutenant Columbo's questions. Honestly and completely. Then I propose we go to dinner. And if you want to go home, go home, to the place you share with . . . uh—"

"Squatty," said Boobs. "Patricia Finch. You remember her. She was at Country Day with me."

"Your mother and I will talk to you again tomorrow, before we leave," said Lloyd Mead.

"Obviously *I* have no influence," hissed Martha Mead.

"You haven't for many years," said Boobs. She turned toward Columbo. "What did you want to ask me?"

"You and Puss Dogood—"

"Puss Dogood!" interjected Martha Mead. "Who—or what—in the world is Puss Dogood?"

"Do you know what Melissa's nickname is?" asked Schob.

"Do I want to know?"

"I doubt it, ma'am," said Columbo. "Anyway, you and Puss contradict each other on one point," he said to Boobs. "You say she got you the job at Khoury's house. She says she doesn't know you."

"She thinks she's a princess, because she got pregnant by Charlie," said Boobs. "Kid and Bum think so, too. Charlie answers her letters. That makes her better than anybody else."

"Is she lying, then?"

Boobs hesitated, then nodded.

"Who interviewed you before you went to work for the Khourys?"

"Nobody. Puss told me I had the job and all I had to do was go up there."

Martha Mead swelled with indignation and asked, "Do you mean to say you went to work at these people's house without so much as an interview? Without references?"

Boobs shrugged. "I told Puss I needed money, and she said she'd see if she could get me a job with the Khourys. And she did. Pretty soon she told me it was all set."

"What day did you go to work?" Columbo asked.

"It was a Tuesday. I think it was probably May twenty-fourth."

"And you were fired on—?"

"I was *arrested* on June tenth. That was a Friday."

"Arrested!"

"And charged with theft," said Boobs to her mother. "Oh, yes. Taken from the house in handcuffs."

"All right," said Columbo. "Money was missing. That was the first thing. By the way, what did the Khourys pay you to work for them?"

"Three hundred dollars a week."

"According to Mrs. Takeshi, the amount stolen

probably didn't come to as much as a hundred dollars," said Columbo.

"The silver was worth a lot more," said Boobs. "If I'm any judge."

"And they found that under the front seat of your car," said Columbo.

"Right."

"Melissa!"

"How long were you in jail?" Columbo asked.

"Three or four hours. Mr. Khoury came and told the cops he wouldn't press charges, so they let me go."

"Okay, I guess that's about all I wanted to ask you about, Miss Mead. You'll still be here with Squatty, so I can find you if there's anything else?"

Boobs glanced at her father and mother, then nodded.

Columbo stood up. "I thank ya all," he said. "I hope you understand that in my line of work we have to ask some tough questions. It's nothing personal." He nodded and moved toward the door.

"Uh, Lieutenant Columbo . . ." said Lloyd Mead. "I said I'd take Melissa to dinner this evening. I'm afraid that has a potential for a somewhat tense evening. I'm going to ask Mr. Schob to join us. Could I interest you in coming, too? It's a little unusual, I suppose, but if Melissa is no longer charged with anything—at least anything more serious than possession of a little marijuana —then maybe it's not improper."

"Oh, sir, I—"

"I'd appreciate it, Lieutenant," said Boobs quietly. "I really would."

"Lieutenant Columbo probably has a family expecting him at home," said Martha Mead.

"As a matter of fact, it's my wife's night to go to her accounting class at the university," said Columbo. "But I—" He glanced down at his rumpled gray suit.

"Your choice of restaurants, Lieutenant. I bet you know good places in Los Angeles," said Lloyd Mead.

Columbo frowned. "As a matter of fact, there's a place I've been meaning to try," he said. "I understand they have good steaks and fish. It's in a motel called Piscina Linda. Might be kinda interesting. Nothing fancy, y' understand, but interesting."

3

"I guess I, uh . . . I guess I oughta apologize for suggesting this place," said Columbo. "Mr. Khoury eats here often, and he's supposed to have gourmet taste."

"Don't apologize," said Lloyd Mead. "It's really not bad. And, as you said, it's interesting. California . . . Wide open onto a swimming pool. Real California."

"If you like steaks and French fries, it's the perfect place," said Schob. "And I'm a man who likes steaks and fries."

"Well, the sole wasn't so good," said Columbo. "I guess you're right. They know how to grill steaks."

"What did you think of the wine?" Columbo asked Lloyd Mead.

"Very good, for a California red," said Mead.

"But can you imagine a connoisseur of good food and wine eating here?" asked Columbo.

"Really, Lieutenant," interjected Martha Mead. "The place is actually not so bad you need to keep apologizing for it."

"Thank ya, ma'am. I just thought I was recommending a place where a man with very distinguished tastes eats, and—If you're not unhappy, I'm not."

PART FOUR

Bringing in the sheaves,
Bringing IN the sheaves,
Here we go rejoicing,
B-RING-ING IN . . . the sheaves.

TWENTY-ONE

1

Tuesday morning. Columbo met with Yussef Khoury in his office above the store.

"Lieutenant, it has become obvious that you suspect *me* of killing my wife," said Yussef Khoury. "That's all you're doing, that I can find out about: questioning my friends, my housekeeper, and so on. You have Cathy Murphy in jail, but you're not focused on her."

"Not so, Mr. Khoury," said Columbo. "I am focused on her. I've questioned her several times, also her friends. I expect to talk to her again today."

They were in Khoury's opulently furnished office, Khoury seated behind the huge and elaborately carved Chinese ebony table that served as his desk. Columbo, in his raincoat, sat on the leather couch and had opened his notepad on the intricately carved ivory table.

Khoury had telephoned headquarters, spoken with Captain Sczciegel, and asked that Lieutenant Columbo come by to see him. Telling Columbo about the call, Sczciegel had warned him that Khoury was angry.

"Lieutenant, I don't like to talk to you this way, but I think I had better tell you I have many prominent and influential friends in this town."

"Yes, sir, you sure do," said Columbo. "And they think very highly of you, too."

"Please understand I don't mean to threaten you. I probably said too much just there. But the newspapers are asking what's holding up the investigation into my wife's death. Friends are calling me and asking the same thing. Cathy was arrested within hours after the death of Arlene, but she and her friends are being held on a marijuana charge. Everybody I know or talk to thinks it's obvious Cathy and her friends are the killers. If it's obvious to everybody else, why is it so mysterious to the police?"

"Well, ya see, sir, it's in the nature of our work. What we have to do is put together enough evidence to get a conviction. And when there are discrepancies, we've gotta resolve them. If we don't, you can bet the defense lawyers will use them."

"Give me an example of a discrepancy that's so great," said Khoury.

"Well, sir, here is something that bothers me. I saw the bodies of Sharon Tate and the others killed in the house at 10050 Cielo Drive. I wish I hadn't, but I did. The bodies of Mrs. Khoury and Mr. Heck were very different."

"In what respect, Lieutenant?"

"Miss Folger and Mr. Frykowski had tried hard to escape. Their killers ran them down and shot and clubbed and stabbed them. Miss Tate and Mr. Sebring had probably tried to run, too, from the looks of it. But in this case, only Sergio Flores tried to escape."

"I know what you're trying to suggest," said Khoury. "That Arlene and Steve knew their murderers and didn't suspect until it was too late that they were about to be killed. They had to be killed by somebody they knew. Well . . . Arlene knew Cathy Murphy very well, very damned well."

"Wouldn't she have been surprised to see her walk into her bedroom in the middle of the night?" Columbo asked.

Khoury shrugged. "Okay. That leaves me. *I* could have walked in on them and—"

"That doesn't make much sense either," said Columbo. "Mr. Heck was in bed with Mrs. Khoury. I'd think he would've jumped out of bed pretty fast when he saw *you* coming in. I mean . . . Well, you can see what I mean. Besides, it looks awfully unlikely that one person could have committed all three murders. So two people came in, maybe three."

Khoury sighed impatiently. "All of which leads us to what?" he asked.

"I just wanted to show you what I mean when I say the case is not as simple as it looks," said Columbo. "Believe me, sir, I lay awake nights, running the facts around in my head, trying to make sense of them."

"You can understand how I have to feel—"

"Oh, yes, sir. Absolutely."

"Is there anything else you need to ask me?"

"Actually, sir, there is," said Columbo. "I try to stay away from subjects like this, but the fact is it might be helpful if you told me just what kind of relationship you have, or had, with Cathy Murphy."

"You're asking if I had an affair with her," said Khoury. "The answer is yes. Puss is a very complaisant woman, Lieutenant. If she thinks you're doing something nice for her, she's happy to go to bed with you. It doesn't mean anything to her. She's just being friendly—reciprocating friendship. I wouldn't say she has the morals of an alley cat. The truth is, that sexual intimacy doesn't have the same significance for her as it has for you and me."

Columbo nodded. "I understand. How does this fit in, timewise, with your relationship with Miss Dana?"

"When Kim and I . . . fell in love, I stopped seeing Puss. Puss worked in the store for six or eight months, then I brought her up to the third floor as a secretary. That would have been last fall, maybe October. My relationship with Kim developed in March, February and March."

"And Mrs. Khoury's relationship with Mr. Heck? When did that start?"

"I don't know. For a while they tried to hide it. Maybe two years."

"You and Mrs. Khoury?"

"Not in the last five years."

Columbo nodded. "I hope you can forgive me

prying into your personal life this way, but—"

"Think nothing of it, as I've said before."

Columbo stood. "Well, sir, if you don't have anything more you want to say to me, I'll be on my way."

Khoury came out from behind his desk and shook Columbo's hand. "I hope you have good luck, Lieutenant. You can understand my emotions."

"I sure can, and thank ya for your time."

Khoury opened the door.

"Oh," said Columbo. "There is just one other little thing I'd like to try to clear up. Just how did you happen to hire Melissa Mead to work at your house?"

"Puss asked me to give her a job."

"Puss says she doesn't know her."

"Unfortunately, Lieutenant Columbo," said Khoury icily, "my friend Puss Dogood does not always tell the truth. Her sense of . . . morals, ethics, whatever . . . is unique."

"Then I suppose Melissa looked good when you or Mrs. Khoury interviewed her."

Khoury shook his head. "We didn't interview her. I took her on Puss's recommendation."

"But she proved to be a thief," said Columbo.

"Yes. Well . . . To tell you the truth, I was not convinced Melissa Mead actually was taking money. I could have been wrong about how much I'd left lying around. But when the silver service disappeared and the police found it in her car—who else could have taken it? I mean, if we want to wonder if maybe somebody else took it and put it in her car, we have to ask who? I trust Mrs. Takeshi implicitly. She's been with me for many years. And Sergio— You know, there is one possibility."

"What is that, sir?"

"That my wife did it. That Arlene put the silver in Melissa's car, to get rid of her."

"Why would she have wanted to get rid of her?"

"God knows what moved Arlene sometimes. She disliked Puss. Well . . . I guess she had reason. Or thought she did. She wasn't completely rational at all times, Lieutenant. She drank heavily. And you know she used crack from time to time."

Columbo frowned. "How do I know that?"

"You found crack in her handbag," said Khoury.

"Oh—Well, that's right, we did. A little."

"Maybe her dealer killed her. Have you checked out that possibility?"

"Uh . . . Yeah, right. We've been looking into that possibility."

"Sure," said Khoury. "Let's say he came to the house from time to time and sold her stuff. So he knew the place. And maybe she owed him money. Or maybe . . . Well, all that's speculation. But you see what I mean. I hope you're checking every possibility."

Columbo nodded. "Oh, sure. Every possibility, sir. You can count on it."

2

Columbo stared at the five balls that remained on the pool table, shaking his head in dissatisfaction at how they lay. He continued to shake his head as he chalked his cue generously, sprinkling blue chalk over his raincoat.

"If I didn't know better, I'd think you did that on purpose, Mulhaney," he said to the young detective sergeant from the Scientific Investigation Division.

"Well, position is half the game, isn't it, Lieutenant?" Mulhaney asked.

"Yeah, but now I've gotta do something like the same to poor Jackson," Columbo complained, "and probably he can't do it to you, which will leave you an open shot."

"Next game," said Jackson, "you two guys are gonna play, and I'm gonna watch. I'm not in your league."

"Y' gotta *think,* Ted," said Columbo. "That's all that's wrong with your game of pool. You make good shots, but you don't think ahead. You don't plan your game."

"How could anybody think while spooning this stuff down his throat?" Mulhaney asked.

The young detective sat on one of the stools at the foot of the table, cue propped against the wall behind him, bowl of Burt's chili in one hand, spoon in the other. Jackson rather enjoyed the chili, though not as much as Columbo did, and his bowl sat on a shelf on the wall, beside his can of Dr Pepper, and he stood and ate, pouring on a lot of salt.

"Let's see here, now," Columbo muttered as he bent over the table and took aim. He sent the cue ball into the right-hand cushion with a lot of right-hand English. The cue ball skidded along the cushion, glanced off the orange five ball, and crossed the table to the far cushion, where it came to a stop. It left Jackson an open shot on the five but not a shot he was likely to make—not a shot any player was likely to make.

Columbo picked up his spoon and bowl and ate chili as he watched.

Jackson, who shot skillfully but did not plan, as Columbo had said, did his best to sink the five but could not and left it in the middle of the foot cushion. He left Mulhaney much as Columbo had left him: with a very difficult shot on the five.

Mulhaney was of course required to hit the five ball. What he wanted to do was hit it, then send the cue ball behind some other balls, leaving Columbo no shot at all. He studied and studied, aimed and aimed, and shot. The cue ball retreated behind the seven and eight, as he wanted, but the five did not behave; it kissed off the nine ball and came to a rest in midtable, giving Columbo an open shot.

Columbo grinned. He put down his bowl and spoon, picked up his cue, and moved to the table.

He sang as he sank the five ball and drove the cue ball into position for the six.

> "Bringing in the sheaves,
> Bringing IN the sheaves,
> Here we go rejoicing,
> B-RING-ING IN . . . the sheaves."

He ran the table and picked up the one-dollar bets lying on the head rail.

"Don't play pool with him," said Jackson. "I tell ya. Don't play pool with him."

"Evidence of a wasted youth," said Columbo, picking up his bowl. "But it's worth it for you two guys to lose a dollar or three, to get to eat chili like this. However—I gotta change the subject."

"I'd like to do that," said Jackson.

Columbo lifted himself up on one of the high stools. "Business," he said. "The day when we were at the Khoury house, the three of us together, you told me, Tim, that you'd found four lumps of crack in Mrs. Khoury's handbag. I asked you not to mention it to anybody. You, too, Ted. Did either one of you mention it?"

"When I turned it in to be held for evidence, I gave Captain Sczciegel a confidential report on it," said Mulhaney. "Nobody else knows anything about it."

"I haven't said anything about it," said Jackson.

"They hadn't used it," said Columbo. "Mrs. Khoury and Heck. The autopsy showed it wasn't in their blood. They were drunk as lords, but they hadn't had anything else." He frowned and nodded. "Isn't that interestin'?"

Mulhaney picked up his cue. "Give me a chance to get even," he said.

"Like to," said Columbo, "and we will sometime, but right now I gotta go see a movie."

3

He telephoned Benjamin Willsberger's office and learned that the director was shooting that afternoon. Good. Columbo had enjoyed watching the shoot on the Culver soundstage and was glad for an opportunity to see more.

Once again, Brad Volney and Katherine Boyd were before the cameras. Last evening Columbo had asked his wife about the two stars, and she had given him a run-down on them. Katherine Boyd was best known for her roles as an earthy girl, a little too provocative and not quite modest enough for the innocent she really was: A quip around town was that Brad Volney could never play a cowboy. Anything but the rugged outdoor type, he was the archetypal urban male, never able—maybe never willing—entirely to shed his Brooklyn accent. He was conspicuously suited to the sidewalk, unsuited to the plains and mountains; and another joke about him was that he probably didn't know one end of a horse from the other.

As before, Willsberger's gofer handed Columbo a script, open to the scene being shot—

122   INT.   SCHMIDT   BEDROOM—NIGHT

Nancy lies on iron bed. She wears shiny satin slip. Kurt sits on bed talking with her. He wears ribbed vest undershirt and dark pants.

KURT

If I don't . . . It's the only chance I got. The only chance! What'm I supposed to tell the man?

NANCY

What do you want me to say?

KURT

How 'bout sayin' Go for it!

NANCY
(mournful, resigned)

Go for it.

KURT

I'll be back in a week.

NANCY

If everything goes okay. If it don't, you might not come back at all.

KURT

The man knows what he's doin'! Ya gotta have faith in somethin', in somebody.

That's the only way anything is ever gonna turn out right. Y' gotta believe!

The shoot stopped so the camera could be moved. Columbo sat through two more shots of the same scene, fascinated. "Boy," he said to Willsberger when they could talk, "I sure wish Mrs. Columbo could see this!"

"Well, bring her around," said Willsberger. "We'll be glad to have her watch us shoot."

"I'll do that," said Columbo.

"Okay. I guess you didn't come *just* to see us at work. What can I do for you, Lieutenant?"

"I guess you knew Mrs. Khoury pretty well," said Columbo. "Am I right?"

"Rather well," said Willsberger. "I could even say better than I wanted to know her."

"You didn't kindly overlook her faults, I imagine," said Columbo. "Am I right?"

"I was not at pains to find fault with Arlene," said Willsberger, "but she had faults, and I couldn't help but notice."

"Then, tell me if you ever suspected she meddled with cocaine or crack."

Willsberger frowned. "Lieutenant," he said, "Arlene may have done a lot of things I know nothing about, but it'd surprise me very much if she as much as *experimented* with cocaine, in any form."

"What's the basis of your judgment?" Columbo asked.

Willsberger hesitated, apparently searching for words. "In my business," he said, "I have to put up with a lot of people who use a variety of chemicals. In that unhappy experience, I have acquired some insight into the symptoms. I wasn't handcuffed to Arlene Khoury for the past ten years, so I can't testify as to what she may or may not have ingested, but I can tell you she was free of the usual symptoms of cocaine use."

"Did you ever know her to use crack?" Columbo asked.

"No, Lieutenant. That's what I'm saying. I never knew her to use anything like that."

Columbo nodded. "Okay. One more thing. You know that knife you showed me? The Bali-Song?"

"Yes."

"I wonder if I could borrow that for a day or so. I'll be careful with it and bring it back."

Willsberger lifted his eyebrows and for a moment hesitated. "Yes, of course," he said then. "I'll call my office and tell my secretary to get it out for you. I'm afraid to ask why you want it."

"Nothin', probably," said Columbo. "But I have to check all angles, y' understand. I have to check all angles."

4

Columbo arranged to see Puss Dogood in a room where both of them could smoke, and when they sat down to talk he lit a cigar and handed her a pack of Marlboros. She shook out a cigarette and dropped the pack into the big pocket on her gray uniform dress.

"For once, I gotta match," he said. "When I bought the smokes, I asked the man for a book of matches, and I stuck 'em in my coat pocket and managed not to lose 'em."

"Thanks, Columbo," she said. She lit her cigarette and drew deeply on it. She blew out smoke, then said, "You're an odd cop. What do you want, a confession?"

"To what?" he asked.

She smiled at him. "To the Khoury murders, of course. Incidentally, Kid's been talking with a public defender. He may ask a judge to let her out of here."

"What about you?"

Puss shook her head. "I'm a permanent resident."

"You just might be, if you don't start tellin' the truth," said Columbo.

"Have I lied to you?"

"Somebody has."

"About what?"

"Boobs is out. Out on bail. I wanta know the answer to somethin'. Do you know her? Or do you not know her?"

"What's the difference?"

"Well, let's put it this way. You may want to confess to the murder of Mrs. Khoury and the others. You may want to plead guilty. What I've gotta think about is, if you do and if you're not guilty, somebody who is walks. That means there'll be murderers loose on the streets."

"Lieutenant Columbo, there are always murderers loose on the streets," she said.

"Okay. Let me remind you of something else. You told me you're worried about Kid. Well, if you plead guilty to three murders, what happens to

Kid? Or to Bum, for that matter?"

"What do you want from me, Columbo?"

"I'm tryin' to clear up some little points in this investigation," he said. "So tell me, did you know Boobs or didn't you?"

Puss shrugged. "So I knew her."

"And you got her the job at the Khoury house. Right?"

"I got her the job. So what?"

"How'd you work it?" Columbo asked.

"I just told Joe Khoury that a friend of mine, a girl, needed a job in the worst way. He asked me if she was one of my family."

"By family he meant—"

"Charlie's family. I said she wasn't exactly but that she hung around with us. I told him she had a good education and if she got dressed up could make a good impression in the store."

"He didn't even interview her."

Puss shook her head. "He didn't interview her. At first he said have her come in so he could talk to her and see what qualifications she had. The next day, I think it was, he called me in his office and told me to have Boobs go up to the house and report to the housekeeper. It wasn't the kind of job Boobs wanted, but she was into a dealer for some money, and she'd take any job she could get. She'd tried turning tricks and didn't like that. She'd take any job. Really, she didn't make enough before they fired her to pay off her dealer, so she had to turn tricks for a couple of weeks."

"When I asked you about her before, you told me you didn't even know her," said Columbo.

"Being a friend of Puss Dogood is not the world's greatest thing to be right now. You had the Kid and Bum in the slammer. I wasn't going to help you put anybody else in."

Columbo stood up. He grinned and shook his head. "Don't do me any favors," he said. "You might want to do some for yourself, though. Like, by telling the truth when I ask you something."

Puss crushed her cigarette in an ashtray. "I'll think about it," she said.

"One more thing," said Columbo. "How do you suppose Khoury's silver got into Boobs's car?"

She returned his grin. "C'mon! How the hell would I know?" she asked.

5

Toward the end of the day, Columbo drove to the morgue to deliver Willsberger's Bali-Song to Dr. Harold Culp. They did not meet in the autopsy room, and Columbo was glad to be spared the sight of another cut-open corpse. They met instead in Dr. Culp's antiseptic little office.

"I brought you something to look at," said Columbo as he opened the box containing the folding knife.

"Ah. The weapon that killed Mrs. Khoury and the others," said Dr. Culp.

"Maybe," said Columbo. "Not this one. But one like it."

The doctor opened a drawer in his desk and took out a short measuring stick calibrated in metric units. He began to measure the knife. "Sixteen centimeters long. Two and a half centimeters wide. Those were the dimensions of many of the wounds." He rolled the Bali-Song over and over in his hands, extending the handles, closing them. "Yes. This could have been the knife. Or one just like it."

"That's interesting," said Columbo.

"Something else about it," said Dr. Culp. "You see the way you can grip it, with both handles extended at right angles to the blade? That gives a powerful thrust. It would also explain the broken rib and the large bruises around some of the stab wounds." He shook his head. "This thing is deadly."

Columbo nodded. "I'm gonna see if I can find another one," he said.

TWENTY-TWO

1

Dog loved to go for a walk, especially in the morning, especially on the beach. Columbo enjoyed taking him early in the morning, when the beach was all but deserted, when he could release Dog from his leash and the happy Basset hound could scamper after gulls and hermit crabs, could bark, could drop what he needed to drop—which Columbo could cover with a kick of sand or leave for an incoming tide. Dog would get thoroughly saltwater wet—to which of course sand clung and turned him into a dripping sand sculpture.

Columbo had surprised—astounded would have been a better word—his wife some years back by coming home from the pound with "the mutt with soulful eyes," as she called him. Amused friends had waited impatiently to hear what name Columbo would give his dog. He disappointed them. He had explained that he wanted to watch the dog for a while and see what habits he had, then to name him something like "Frisky," or "Snoopy," or "Scamp." But later the lieutenant had to explain, "All he does is sleep and drool, and I can't hardly name him. . . ."

So the dog became Dog. Aging, he slept more and drooled more, and he remained Dog.

King Canute could not make the incoming tide retreat, and neither could Dog, though he tried, charging at incoming waves, barking and snarling threats he seemed to think the waves might heed, or should, anyway.

Every gull on the Pacific coast knew him—or so Dog must have believed, since there was no gull who would let him cross the last three feet and pounce. They seemed to ignore him until he was that close, then flapped their wings and moved no more than ten feet and let him resume his stalking.

Crabs were not so clever. He could move to within *one* foot and sniff and growl. They knew he would not approach closer—not since the morning when one of them had fastened a pincher on his lip and hung there throughout a long gallop up and down the beach. Crabs would rise and glare at him, and Dog would frown and ponder, and would invariably decide to break off the confrontation.

Occasionally in the hour just after dawn, Dog would interrupt a pair of young lovers who should have gone home earlier. "It's a public beach, kids!" he seemed to say with his wide eyes and wagging tail, and he would scamper away exuberantly, as if their interrupted energies had been transferred to him.

Columbo enjoyed walking along the beach at sunrise, but it could be boring after a little while. With Dog to amuse him, he was never bored.

It was a time, too, when he could clear his mind of things that had intruded on his sleep. He would get up, let Dog out for his first morning necessities, make a pot of coffee, and eat a hard-boiled egg from the refrigerator, before setting out in the car for the beach. He couldn't do it often, only once a week at best, but when he did, he enjoyed it.

He was almost never interrupted and resented it when he was.

"Hey, Columbo!"

He looked up and saw Captain Sczciegel waving at him. He waved back, reluctantly, and the captain trotted across the sand toward him. He watched skeptically as the captain, who was older than he was, trotted a hundred yards over the sand.

"Mrs. Columbo told me where to find you," said the captain, only a little winded. "When I saw the car, I knew—"

"Some of these days I'm gonna have to get a new car," said Columbo.

Captain Sczciegel smiled. He understood the sarcasm, a rarity with Columbo. "Something odd has happened," he said. "I thought you'd wanta know."

Columbo nodded. "Sure. I wanta know."

"Guess who got bailed out of the slammer last night?"

Columbo closed his eyes. "Puss Dogood."

"Also the Kid and Bum. Three thousand bucks. They were being held on a thousand apiece, on the possession charge—"

"Four lids," said Columbo.

"Well . . . We'd never charged them with anything more serious."

"We didn't have evidence to back anything more serious," said Columbo.

"Anyway . . . The three thousand dollars was posted for them last night a little before midnight. By guess who?"

"Yussef Khoury," said Columbo.

The captain nodded. "Yussef Khoury."

Dog ran up and clamped his teeth on Columbo's trouser leg, which he shook gently.

"Wants my attention," said Columbo, reaching down to scratch Dog's ears. "It's *his* time, y' understand." He bent over and spoke. "Listen, pal. I need a bird. A gull. Go get me one, okay?"

Dog looked up with sorrowful eyes, as if he couldn't believe his master would assign him so impossible, so frustrating a task. But he seemed to resign himself to it, looked around for gulls, spotted a few working over something in the edge of the surf, and galloped off to give the assignment a valiant effort.

"Not all," said Sczciegel. "There's more. The night shift didn't understand the significance of the release of these people. By the time anybody put two and two together, Puss and her buddies had absquatulated. Gone without a trace. Those people have a way, you know."

"Like from Spahn Ranch to Barker Ranch," said

Columbo. "Check Death Valley. Also, there was a fourth Manson type, who was never arrested. Buddy Drake. He has a car."

"But why would Yussef Khoury put up the money?" Sczciegel asked.

"I can think of reasons," said Columbo. "I guess we'll have to ask."

Columbo walked toward where Dog was busily stalking gulls. The captain followed him.

"I've already had a call from the mayor," said Sczciegel. "And that's just the start. Why did we let these people go? What am I gonna say?"

"What did you say to the mayor?"

"I said we were almost ready to close the case."

Columbo nodded. "Right. Good enough. We're almost ready to close the case."

Sczciegel's chin jerked up. "You mean it? You know who killed Arlene Khoury, Steve Heck, and Sergio Flores?"

"I'm ninety percent sure," said Columbo. "Ninety-five."

"And it's not Puss Dogood?"

"No, sir. It's not Puss Dogood."

"You never did think it was."

"Not after five minutes looking at the case," said Columbo.

Dog gave up on the gulls and ran back toward his master and the stranger who had interrupted his time. He'd caught no gull, but he had charged into an incoming breaker, which had rolled him over and over, and he was soaking wet. Tail wagging, he ran up to Columbo and the captain and happily shook.

2

Columbo took Dog home, then drove to headquarters and signed in.

He greeted Elliott Carter, a black detective sergeant in the burglary division. "Hi-ya, Carter."

"I checked that file for you, Lieutenant," said Carter. "Actually, I've even got my notebook here. And look what it says."

Carter handed Columbo a spiral-bound steno pad. He had investigated the complaint, called in by Mrs. Takeshi, of the theft of silver at the Khoury house.

"See what I wrote down?" Carter asked.

Columbo nodded over the final entry.

Closed. Mr. Yussef Khoury declines to press charges. *Highly doubtful silver was stolen from house. More likely planted by somebody.*

"I asked if the girl's fingerprints were on the silver," said Columbo.

"*Nada* fingerprints," said Carter. "Wiped clean and handled without putting any more on."

"Well, thank ya, Carter. That's very helpful."

"You ever meet the young lady we arrested that afternoon?" asked Carter.

"I had a meeting with her and her family Monday night," said Columbo.

"Man! She deserves her nickname, doesn't she?"

"Twice over," said Columbo.

3

Columbo placed a call to Antonio Vado, the producer. Vado came on the line, greeting him enthusiastically.

"Hey! Lieutenant Columbo! Glad to hear from you."

"I'd like to stop by, sir," said Columbo. "I've got just one little question I'd like to ask you. Nothing very important. Just one of those little points I gotta clear up."

"Lieutenant, I am up to my you-know-what in alligators all morning. But, look—I'm having lunch at the Topanga Beach Club. Kind of an occasion. Something to celebrate. Love to have you join me."

"All I need to ask is—"

"You can ask it, pal! Over lunch. Hey, it's gonna be a fun occasion! C'mon. Unwind! We'll slip off to the side, so you can ask me in private, if you need to. About one?"

"Okay, Mr. Vado. About one."

It would give him time to stop by the main Los Angeles post office and talk with a postal inspector.

A little before one, he drove up to the valet-parking station at the Topanga Beach Club.

"Whatta ya want me to do with the car, sir?" the attendant asked him.

"Park it. Park it. And drive it very carefully. It's a French car, and it's got a lotta miles on it, which is the result of my treatin' it right. I mean . . . you don't see very many cars like this anymore."

"Yeah," said the attendant. "I don't remember ever seeing a car like this before."

The Topanga Beach Club was a country club without golf, having instead an Olympic-size pool with diving bay, tennis courts, squash courts, and a bowling green—all overlooking but separated by a wall from the public beach. Columbo had eaten lunch there before, notably with the Texan Charles Bell, one of the conspirators in the murder of television news personality Paul Drury. He remembered that the lunch tables had a view of the ocean.

He remembered too that he would draw stares if he did not check his raincoat, so he left it with a check girl who was surprised to see it on a hot, sunny August day.

The maître d' remembered Columbo. People tended not to forget even chance encounters with a homicide detective, particularly one who had sent a prominent member of the club to prison. "Mr. Vado's table?" he asked.

Columbo nodded, and the maître d' led him to a table set for six people, near the glass, with a spectacular view of the blue Pacific. Kimberly Dana sat there, sipping from a Bombay gin martini.

"Lieutenant Columbo! This is a surprise, though I suppose it shouldn't be; no one ever knows where you'll show up next."

She was wearing a skin-tight navy-blue unitard

—a term new to Columbo—and a loose navy-blue tunic with a neck designed to slip off either shoulder and show the strap of the unitard. The unitard clung to her legs and hips, shaping itself to them, while the thigh-length tunic hung loosely and casually.

"Mr. Valdo invited me, ma'am," said Columbo.

"Well, I guess it's not inappropriate to have you as a part of our celebration," she said.

"Celebration?"

"Celebration. Tony is giving me a contract to star in a picture. And if you start that 'ma'am' business again, I'm going to kick you under the table."

"Star in a picture! Congratulations. I guess that's something you've wanted for a long time."

"Yes. Tony Vado has always felt I have talent. Joe knows I do and is going to put some money in the picture. Ben Willsberger doesn't think I can act, but that's all right; he'll direct and teach me all I need to know as we go along."

"Wonderful," said Columbo.

"I know what you have to be thinking," she said. "You have to be thinking that Arlene's death changed Joe's financial situation enough to make it possible for him to buy a participation in the film. But that's immaterial. Tony would make the film anyway."

"I'm glad to hear it," said Columbo. "Uh . . . who's joining us, besides Mr. Vado?"

"Joe. And Ben. Maybe somebody else. I don't know."

"Kim . . . Did you know that Mr. Khoury posted bond for Puss Dogood and Kid and Bum last night?"

"I know."

"Why'd he do that? Do you know?"

"He *says* it's because he felt sorry for Puss. He said it was obvious you weren't really holding her on a possession charge but on suspicion of murdering Arlene, a charge you couldn't begin to prove. He said people's freedom is not something you should play games with. I'm sorry he used those terms, but that's his honest feeling."

"You say that what he *says.* I guess you think there was another reason?"

"I know he went to see her. What they talked about in private, I can only guess. My guess is she told him she'd make a public statement saying she used to sleep with him. That would be so contrary to the reputation of Yussef Khoury. He's very sensitive about things like that."

"Do you know she's disappeared?" Columbo asked.

"What?"

"Gone. The three of them."

"My god! Don't tell Joe until after the luncheon. Let's let him enjoy himself a little."

"Tell me about your movie," said Columbo.

"Well, it's not *Altarpiece,* not the picture I wanted to make. But it will give me a start. It's a true story about a girl who became a *Playboy* Playmate of the Month and then was paralyzed in an automobile accident and struggled her way back. Kitsch."

"Might be interesting," said Columbo.

"I'll have to shed a lot of tears and show a lot of gritty courage. Besides that, I'll have to show a lot of me, since I'm going to be a playmate. That's something else I always wanted: to be a *Playboy* playmate. I mean, for real. But I guess playing one in a film is even better. Wouldn't you say?"

The four people who were to fill the other chairs at the table now arrived—Yussef Khoury, Antonio Vado, Benjamin Willsberger, and a young woman Columbo did not recognize.

"That's Willa Wood," said Kim. "She'll be in the picture, too."

Columbo remembered that Willa Wood was the star of Khoury's first picture, *Joelle*. Writers had described her as a sex kitten, which was her specialty role, and her appearance confirmed it. Blonde and voluptuous, wearing a white silk dress filled to bursting, she was in character as she crossed the club dining room, drawing a variety of stares, from the appreciative to the indignant.

"Hello, Lieutenant Columbo," said Khoury. "I suppose you know I bailed Puss and her friends out of jail last night."

"I got that word this morning," said Columbo.

"I hope I haven't interfered with anything," said Khoury, "but my conscience just wouldn't let me allow that misguided young woman to remain behind bars when it was obvious you could not charge her with the murder of Arlene."

"No problem, sir," said Columbo, and he conformed to Kim's request that he not tell Khoury that Puss and her friends had disappeared.

"I have to ask you, Lieutenant Columbo, how long will you have to retain Arlene's choker as evidence?"

"Ordinarily, sir, we would hold on to that until a trial."

"I was wondering if it could be photographed, measured, appraised . . . and whatever, and the item returned to me. I should like—I hate having to say it, but I must acknowledge that I need the money. I'd like to sell it."

"I'll see if I can arrange for its release," said Columbo.

The luncheon was festive. Willa Wood, sex kitten though she might be, was a perceptive, witty young woman, playing the role of dumb blonde. Told that Columbo was a homicide detective, she purred breathlessly, "Oh, Lieutenant, I'm glad to meet you. If I ever need a homicide done, I'll know who to ask." Everyone laughed, but a few minutes later, when she had a private word with Columbo across the table, she asked, "Have you seen a case yet where DNA evidence solved the mystery?"

Vado made a little speech. He said he was happy they had agreed to make the film. Kimberly Dana, he said, bore a remarkable resemblance to the playmate who was injured and recovered and he was sure her performance would be as inspiring as the original story. He was glad that Willa Wood had agreed to play the role of another playmate, a young woman who in real life had pressed her friend to persevere and recover. He was glad that Ben Willsberger had agreed to direct. He was sorry that Steve Heck would not design the production—although, he added with weak and saturnine humor, that might mean the picture would come in under budget.

He welcomed Lieutenant Columbo of LAPD

homicide, who had come to know them all exceptionally well. "I am sure the lieutenant's professional efforts will soon take off our shoulders the burden of having to wonder who killed Arlene Khoury and Steve Heck." He stopped and pointed at Columbo, as if asking for a comment. Columbo smiled and held out his empty palms.

4

When they had finished their drinks and were eating lunch, Vado suggested to Columbo that the two of them go to the men's room, where they could speak for a moment out of the presence of the others. They went there and talked as they stood before a pair of urinals. Columbo looked around to see if any other man was in the room before he told Vado what he wanted to ask.

"Sir, what I need to know is, do you by any chance happen to own a Philippine folding knife called by the name Bali-Song?"

Vado turned his face toward Columbo. "Uh . . . As a matter of fact, I do. But . . . What does that have to do with anything, if you don't mind my asking."

"Maybe nothing," said Columbo. "It may not mean anything at all. But it just might, and I—"

"Do you want it? Do you want to see it?" Vado asked.

"Not necessarily. I'd like to know two things

about it. One you can tell me now. The other you can phone me and tell me."

"Shoot, Lieutenant."

"What you can phone and tell me," said Columbo, "is the dimensions of the blade. I'd appreciate it, sir, if you would measure it in centimeters."

"You got it. I'll call my secretary, have her measure it, and she'll call you this afternoon. And, of course, I know what the second question is. You don't even have to ask me."

Columbo nodded. "Where'd you get it?"

"Just where you think I got it. It was a gift from Joe Khoury. Hey . . . You don't suspect that Joe killed his wife, do you? Yeah. You do."

"No, Mr. Vado," said Columbo. "Don't jump to that conclusion. It's just that I gotta check out all the facts."

"There are probably tens of thousands of those knives," said Vado.

"Absolutely," said Columbo.

"Listen," said Vado. "There's going to be an announcement. Hey, I—The reason I wanted you here, I had hoped maybe you could make an announcement of your own: that you've cleared up the murders and will file charges against—But Joe bailed her out! Listen, if he gave me one of those knives, why couldn't he have given one to her? You know he . . . Maybe she stole one from him."

"Now, there's a thought," said Columbo, nodding slowly. "Maybe she did."

5

While Columbo and Vado were in the men's room, Khoury and Kim had stepped out on the deck.

"Should we do this?" she asked.

"Why not?" he asked. "It's not going to make Columbo any more suspicious, and it might just give him pause."

Kim gripped the deck railing with both hands and stared out to sea. "You know what? We didn't have to do it. If Tony Vado had told us he wanted to make this picture—"

"If the dog hadn't stopped to pee, he'd have caught the rabbit," said Joe Khoury. "Ifs don't count. You can't plan things on the basis of what *might* happen."

"Tell me again exactly what Puss Dogood said."

Khoury blew a loud sigh. "She said if I'd bail her out she'd run. She said Charlie had shown her a place in Nevada where she could hole up for a year and no one could find her. All these years, they've kept this place stocked with food and water—guns and ammunition, too—in anticipation of the day when Charlie would come back and they'd need a hideout for a while. She said if she could just get to that place, she could hide and wait for Charlie. When he found out she was missing, he'd know where she'd gone, and he'd come out and join her."

"There's something wrong about this, Joe," said Kim. "Why did LAPD let her get away on bail?"

Khoury glanced around. "Because the case we made against her wasn't strong enough to hold her for murder. Even when you let them have the choker, they didn't file a murder charge. I posted her bond in the middle of the night, to give her a head start before they figured out they didn't want her loose. She promised me she'd run. She was grateful to get the chance. She really believes Charles Manson will find out she's on the run and escape to come to Nevada and join her."

"Columbo—"

"When the story gets out that Lieutenant Columbo let the chief suspect in the Manson copy-cat murders get away on bail, because he neglected to file murder charges, we may have Columbo off our backs."

"I have to hope you're right, Joe."

Khoury turned away from the view of the Pacific Ocean and smiled at Kim. "When a couple of people like you and me can't outsmart a stupid career cop like Lieutenant Columbo, that's gonna be a cold day in hell."

She continued looking out to sea, shaking her head. "I can only hope you're right."

6

A young woman in white blouse and black skirt walked up to Columbo and Vado as they were on their way back to the table. "Excuse me, sir," she said. "Are you Lieutenant Columbo?"

"That's me."

"I have a telephone message for you."

Columbo took the pink slip and read it. "I have to call headquarters," he told Vado.

"Don't be too long," said Vado. "We are going to hear another announcement."

The young woman who had handed him the telephone slip had pointed out a row of little telephone rooms. Columbo went into one and sat down at a table. He punched in Captain Sczciegel's number.

"Living high on the hog, Columbo?"

"Not bad. Not bad at all."

"Okay. I have news for you. Your friend Puss Dogood and her pals are in the Esmerelda County jail in Goldfield, Nevada."

"What charge?" Columbo asked.

"Skipping bail. They weren't supposed to leave the county, much less the state."

"Nice work," said Columbo.

"Well, you said they'd go for Death Valley, because that's where the Manson family holed up twenty-five years ago. Buddy Drake was missing, so we figured he must be driving. We asked the California Highway Patrol to watch for his Toyota on the main highways in the Death Valley area. They spotted that car going toward the Nevada state line and not far from it, so they alerted the Esmerelda County sheriff, and two of his cars caught them. Thought you'd want to know."

"Yeah, thanks," said Columbo.

7

As soon as Columbo returned to the luncheon table, Tony Vado stood and said Joe Khoury had an announcement to make.

Khoury stood, glanced around the table, nodding at each person in turn, and then said, "I'm most happy to announce that I've asked Kim to marry me and she has accepted."

The others applauded politely and lifted their glasses in toast.

"Some may think it is a little soon," Khoury went on, "but I know you all understand that Kim and I have cared deeply for each another for a long time. We see no reason not to acknowledge that and no reason to postpone our marriage. It is a little odd that a homicide detective investigating the murder of my late wife is among our happy group, but I am glad he is and I welcome him. All of you have been kind and supportive of Kim and me, and we want you to know we cherish you all."

Everyone shook hands all around, and Willa Wood embraced Kim. They had finished lunch and so did not sit down again.

"Before you leave," said Willsberger, waving a hand. "I'm going back to the soundstage to shoot the final scene of the picture. You're all welcome. We'll celebrate with champagne when it's finished."

They left the dining room and walked toward the parking lot.

As Columbo was retrieving his raincoat from the check room, Kim came up to him and spoke quietly.

"I'm grateful to you for not mentioning that Puss and her crowd skipped bail," she said.

"It doesn't make any difference," he said. "They were picked up in Nevada. They're in jail over there. We'll have them back by tomorrow."

"Now are you going to file a murder charge?" she asked.

"I'm probably going to file murder charges before the afternoon is over," said Columbo.

TWENTY-THREE

1

Benjamin Willsberger strode off the soundstage, where the rest of the luncheon crowd were gathered, with his hand out to shake Columbo's hand, but he faltered and stopped when he saw that Columbo was not alone. Two other men, probably detectives, and two uniformed officers, one of them a woman, were with him.

"This . . . is not a social call," he muttered, shaking his head.

"No, sir, afraid not," said Columbo. "This is official business."

They had switched off the big lights above and around the soundstage. A carpenter was hammering at something behind one of the walls of the set—a set that ironically represented the detective squad room in a New York precinct house.

Willsberger pointed at the uniformed officers. Each carried a short length of chain. "My god! You . . ."

"I've got two arrest warrants," said Columbo.

Kimberly Dana understood instantly that she was about to be arrested. She guessed that the chain the woman officer was carrying was for her. She covered her face with her hands and moaned.

Yussef Khoury understood, too, after a moment. He walked toward Columbo, the color draining from his face as he came. "What is this, Lieutenant?" he asked belligerently. "Why are you here?"

"We have a warrant for your arrest, and one for the arrest of Miss Dana, on charges of murder in the deaths of Mrs. Arlene Khoury, Mr. Stephen Heck, and Mr. Sergio Flores."

Yussef Khoury shook his head and sneered. "From the moment I met you, Columbo, I knew you were an incompetent ass."

"Yes, sir, that may be," said Columbo.

"Surely, Lieutenant Columbo," said Willsberger. "Surely there's a mistake here."

Columbo turned down the corners of his mouth and tipped his head to one side. "No, sir, I don't think so. But . . . A court will decide. Miss Dana, would you come here, please?"

Kim came so hesitantly that Antonio Vado put his hand under her elbow to steady her and walked beside her. She was still wearing her navy unitard and loose tunic, but they looked different on a woman who seemed to have shrunk in the past two minutes.

"Mr. Khoury, Miss Dana," said Columbo, "you are under arrest. You have the right to remain silent. Any statements you make will be taken down and may be used in evidence against you. You have the right to be represented by an attorney. If you cannot afford an attorney, one will be appointed for you at the public expense. Do you understand your rights?"

"How could you *do* this?" asked Kimberly Dana.

"Do you understand your rights, Miss Dana?" Columbo persisted gently.

"Yes! But you *can't*—You sat and listened to us announce our engagement, all the while knowing . . ." She covered her face with her hands and sobbed.

"Mr. Khoury? Do you understand your rights?"

"I understand them," Khoury muttered. "And *you're* going to understand them before this is over."

Columbo nodded at the uniformed officers. One of them stepped up to Khoury, patted him down, and then with the assistance of Ted Jackson circled his middle with a belly chain, and passed a pair of handcuffs through a large link. With the handcuffs locked on his wrists, Khoury could not lift his hands more than a few inches above his waist. He jerked up on the chain as if to test it, and his eyes darted from one person to another.

The female officer patted Kim down and chained and handcuffed her the same way, with Mulhaney helping. Kim staggered and seemed about to fall. The officer helped her to sit down on a steel-and-vinyl chair. Kim clenched her fists and jerked against the handcuffs as if she could tear them apart. Her lips trembled, she gasped, and she began to weep loudly. She could not lift her hands to cover her face, but she dropped her chin to her chest and shook. The policewoman hovered over her and patted her shoulder.

Vado spoke quietly to Columbo. "Is it necessary to chain these two people?" he asked.

"The charge is murder, sir," said Columbo, shaking his head. "Multiple murder. There are certain specific regulations—"

Khoury was indignant—or pretended he was, to cover his fear. "You have jumped to the wrong conclusions," he said in a wavering voice. "And to the wrong conclusions. Even after Puss ran away you—"

"We'll have her back here tomorrow," said Columbo.

"But you won't charge *her* with murder, I suppose."

"We bring charges on the basis of the evidence, sir. That's all we can do."

"So what happens now? Do we go to jail?"

"Yes, sir. You go to jail."

Kim shrieked. Her face gleamed red and was wet with tears. Still more color faded from Khoury's face, leaving him quite pale.

Khoury shook his head. "What in the name of God could make you believe . . . what you believe?"

"Maybe we shouldn't talk about it," said Columbo. "You have a right to keep silent, you know. If I start telling you things, and you start denying things, you'll be making a statement. I doubt your lawyers would want you to do that."

"To hell with lawyers," said Khoury. "I can take care of myself."

"Well . . . We oughta sit down and—" He glanced around. There were not enough chairs for all of them.

"Sit in the set," said Willsberger. "Sort of bitterly appropriate, huh?"

They walked out onto the soundstage. The desks and chairs and the rest of the set were nostalgically familiar to Columbo. The set *was* like a Manhattan precinct station. He sat down behind an old scarred oak desk, in a wooden armchair. The others found chairs. Khoury and Kim sat in the center of the room, together.

Seeing cigarette butts and cigar ash in the ashtray on the desk, Columbo decided he could smoke there. He reached into his pocket and found a half-smoked cigar.

"Anybody got a match?" he asked.

Ted Jackson offered his lighter.

"Where to start?" asked Columbo rhetorically. "What I'd like to know is, which one of you first had the idea? The idea of killing Mrs. Khoury didn't come up on the spur of the moment. You hired Melissa Mead ten weeks ago."

"What's hiring Melissa Mead have to do with the murder of my wife?" Khoury asked. "Unless she was the one who knew the layout of the house and either guided the killers in or was one of them herself."

"Mrs. Takeshi says the house was fully staffed and you didn't need anybody, but you hired her anyway."

"Mrs. Takeshi works for *me*," said Khoury. "*I* decide when we need more household staff. The truth is, we didn't need her, but I was trying to help a girl in trouble," said Khoury. "Puss told me Melissa was desperate to earn some money."

"You hired her in a very peculiar way, then: on the word of Puss Dogood, a Manson follower with a long criminal record, without ever interviewing Melissa or asking for references. You put her to work in your house, and then you started to complain that money was disappearing. Then silver. You fired her, but you wouldn't press charges."

"I still felt sorry for her," said Khoury.

"I gotta read it another way," said Columbo. "You were planning on murdering your wife, and you wanted to hang that on Puss Dogood and her pals. But that would be hard to do if none of them had ever been in your house and didn't know the layout. You could have invited her up there for some reason, and I'd guess you were figuring on doing that, but when Puss asked you to give Melissa a job she handed you the perfect opportunity. You'd let Melissa work for you a while, long enough to learn the layout of the house and people's habits; then you'd accuse her of stealing and fire her— giving her reason to resent you and reason to help Puss murder Mrs. Khoury. Of course you wanted the larceny charges dropped. A Melissa in jail didn't fit the plan."

"We always wonder," said Ted Jackson, who by now was smoking, pinching his cigarette tight between his lips and drawing in the smoke as if it sustained life, "why someone who's the victim of a theft refuses to cooperate in prosecuting."

"You build inference on inference on inference," said Khoury scornfully. "All you're doing is guessing. Do you really expect to convince a jury that all your guesswork is correct?"

"Oh, no, sir. There's more. Somebody pried open the utility-room window but then didn't climb in through that window. The pry bar had splintered the wood of the sill, and those splinters were standing straight up. A person climbing in that window would have flattened those splinters. The window was pried open to make it *look* like somebody climbed in. Whoever entered the house, entered through a locked door, with a key."

"'Whoever,'" said Khoury. "That's the word: 'whoever.' None of this proves it was me."

"That's right, sir. It doesn't. But there are some other things—"

"Anyway, Kim and I were at Piscina Linda that night and didn't leave until well after the murders had been committed."

Columbo paused as he drew on his cigar. "You were at Piscina Linda," said Columbo, "but you weren't necessarily there all evening. You had been going there for some time and had established a pattern—dinner in the dining room, then privacy in your room until midnight, and midnight coffee brought up by a room-service waiter. You left big tips so people would remember you. But the room-service waiter never saw you when he came up to your suite, not that night or any other. He heard voices from your room, but those could have come from the television set. You could have checked the TV schedules to be sure a quiet program with voices—no western with shooting—would be on at midnight."

"I am a little relieved," Khoury said to Kim. "I was worried that they had something."

"I'm covering the circumstantial stuff first," said Columbo. "I'm telling you some of the things that made me suspicious, that made me focus the investigation on you and not on Puss Dogood. I've gotta tell you, I'm curious about why you ate so many dinners at Piscina Linda. You're a man with a taste for the best, and that restaurant is anything but. The only explanation I can think of is, you were busy establishing your pattern."

Khoury sneered. Kim blinked out her tears and began to look a bit defiant. She lifted her chin and stared at Columbo.

"I can be a little more concrete," said Columbo. "The murders of Mrs. Khoury, Mr. Heck, and Mr. Flores were exceptionally bloody. Knives make bloody deaths. One of the perpetrators stepped in blood and tracked it across the carpet. Of course the Scientific Investigation Division took a tracing of the most complete footprint. The shoe was not a running shoe, in fact not a rubber-sole shoe of any kind. A shoe with a leather sole. Interesting. The tracing of that footprint makes that shoe a Gucci loafer, a very elegant and expensive shoe that you yourself wear, Mr. Khoury."

"How many thousands of those shoes do you suppose there are in Los Angeles, Lieutenant Columbo?" Khoury asked.

"You got a point. But it builds up little by little, y' see." He gestured with his cigar and with his left hand. "One little thing and then another, building up toward a proved case."

"You'll have to do better than that," snapped

Kim, speaking for the first time since she had entered the room. With her fists clenched, she tugged at her chain, angrily frustrated at being unable to move her hands more than a few inches.

Two of the actors who had been working in this set appeared at the edge of the soundstage and stared in amazement at what must have looked to them like a new cast preparing a different scene—until they recognized the two characters in handcuffs.

"We can do better than that, Miss Dana," said Columbo. "Let's look at the way the two bodies in bed were lying. They hadn't jumped up or rolled over or tried to escape. Some of the bodies in the Tate-LaBianca murders had knife wounds on their arms, because they'd tried to shield themselves against the attacks. But these bodies didn't. That means these two people didn't suspect until the very last second that the people who came into that bedroom were there to kill them. If they'd looked up and seen Puss Dogood, Kid, and Bum Rapp coming into their bedroom, they'd have . . . Well. What would they have done? Not just lay there and waited for people with knives to stab them. They'd been found in an embarrassing situation, but obviously they didn't think their lives were threatened."

"Which doesn't prove Kim and I were there," grunted Khoury indignantly. "Other people could have embarrassed them and not terrified them."

"Friends? Social friends?" asked Columbo. "Walking into the bedroom and interrupting what they were doing. How many of your friends had keys to the house, Mr. Khoury? How many knew the alarm was not on yet?"

"I have no idea who Arlene may have trusted with keys," said Khoury.

"I can tell you something else that doesn't conclusively prove it but still goes to build the case," said Columbo. "The three people were killed with the same knife, or with two identical knives. The blades were sixteen centimeters long and two and a half centimeters wide. Not only that, the murderers drove the knives into the bodies with great force, making big bruises where the guard hit the flesh, and even breaking one of Mr. Heck's ribs. It looks like the killers used both hands to drive the knives in. There's a kind of knife that has a handle that folds out into two grips, which makes it possible for a person to stab with two hands. Mr. Willsberger has one of those knives. Mr. Vado has one, too. And where do you suppose they got them?"

Kim flexed her shoulders and rubbed her manacles against her stomach, to slip them into a different position on her wrists. "What about Puss Dogood?" she demanded. "It looks to me like you've ignored her completely."

"Oh, not at all, Miss Dana," said Columbo. "But, y' see, the facts just don't fit for her. Why would she and her friends pry open a back window and then not climb in that window? If she didn't climb in that window, how'd she get in?"

"Maybe Melissa gave her a key," suggested Kim.

"I thought of that, too. But Mrs. Takeshi had the locks changed within a few hours after she had Melissa arrested."

Khoury shot a hard glance at Kim. His frown darkened.

"There were no complete fingerprints on the

front door knob," Columbo went on. *"No* finger-prints. Why would that be? Because somebody wearing gloves turned the knob."

"Which could have been anybody," said Kim.

"Could have been," Columbo agreed. "So maybe it's time to move on to something still more concrete."

"I think that would be a good idea," said Khoury.

"Okay," said Columbo. "Let's talk about the choker. What would make me think Mrs. Khoury never saw the choker?"

"Stupidity," grumbled Khoury.

"A possible explanation," said Columbo, nodding. He paused to puff on his cigar. "But what else do we know? The murderers stole nothing else, according to Mrs. Takeshi and according to you, Mr. Khoury. Mrs. Khoury had other jewelry, but the killers took only a jeweled choker worth $48,350. Why? Your explanation, sir, was that Mrs. Khoury had left the choker out on her dresser. All her other jewelry was inside her jewelry drawer. Just one item, worth more than all her other jewelry put together probably, was lying out in plain sight."

"Arlene could be careless, particularly when she was drinking," said Khoury. "And she was always drinking."

"You told me you bought it for her in June," said Columbo. "Isn't that right? When you come to trial, Mr. Khoury, produce a witness who saw her wearing it. Produce a witness who heard her speak of it. On—" He stopped to check a note. "On Monday night, August first, you took Mrs. Khoury to a dress dinner and ball, where all the women wore their jewelry. Mrs. Khoury didn't wear the choker. She wore a green dress, and the green emeralds of the choker would have looked great on it, but she didn't wear it."

"Do you expect to send me to prison on the evidence that my wife didn't wear a particular piece of jewelry on a particular night?" Khoury asked.

"No, sir. On the basis of something else about the choker," said Columbo.

"Oh, let's do hear it."

"The package with the choker in it arrived in your office on Saturday morning. Because the store was closed Saturday and Sunday out of respect to Mrs. Khoury, no one opened it until Monday morning. The postmark on it was Tuesday, August ninth. Now, we're supposed to believe that package was mailed on Tuesday, August ninth, by Puss Dogood. But of course it wasn't. It couldn't have been. Mr. Heck was alive at eleven-forty when he took delivery of a pizza."

"Pizza?" asked Kim. "What's a pizza got to do with anything?"

"Well, ya see, ma'am, Mr. Heck accepted delivery of a pizza, and paid for it, at eleven-forty or even a little after. For the choker to have been mailed on Tuesday, the murderers had to arrive at the house, kill three people, snatch the choker, escape from the house, wipe the fingerprints off the choker and pack it in a box, and get to a post office open that late at night . . . all in twenty minutes. The nearest post office that has windows open in the middle of the night is at least thirty minutes away."

"Then how did the mailing carry a postmark of Tuesday, August ninth?" asked Kim.

"That's very easy, ma'am. When you have a postage meter, you set the date. You can set it forward or back. That's why the courts won't accept postage-meter imprints as evidence of the date something was mailed. The box could have been mailed Wednesday, Thursday, or Friday. Of course it couldn't have been mailed by Puss Dogood, because she was in jail."

"Anybody with access to a postage meter could have set the date back and mailed the package," said Khoury.

"Only somebody who had access to the postage meter at Khoury's," said Columbo. "A microscopic comparison of the meter imprints on the choker box and on packages mailed from Khoury's proves the package was mailed from the store. *You* did it, Miss Dana. You set the meter back to Tuesday, imprinted the little white tape you put on the package, and reset the meter to the correct date. It wasn't a bad trick, but you outsmarted yourself. If you'd set it to Wednesday, August tenth, you'd have left open a possibility."

"You still don't have a case, Columbo," said Khoury. "Even if a jury believed all that, it's a long way from convicting two people of murder."

"The nine-one-one call that came into headquarters at twelve-thirty-six A.M. was recorded," said Columbo. "All nine-one-one calls are. The voice was a woman faking a Spanish accent. The police lab has made a voice print off that tape. We served a search warrant at the store this morning and got a tape of Miss Dana's voice, one of those tapes she uses to announce the lunchtime fashion show at Hammond's. The lab made a voice print off that tape, too. The prints match."

Kim began to cry again, but Khoury turned down the corners of his mouth and shook his head. "A smart lawyer can beat this," he said to her.

"Mr. Khoury," said Columbo. "Do you mind if I ask you one question?"

Khoury shrugged.

"You said we found crack in Mrs. Khoury's handbag. How'd you know about that?"

"You told me," said Khoury. "Even if you hadn't, it would have been easy enough to guess. She used the stuff."

"She hadn't used any that evening," said Columbo. "And not for quite some time. Neither had Mr. Heck. The autopsy didn't find a trace of it in either of them, and not a symptom of its use. People who knew her say they never saw a symptom of it. Of course . . . she might have been just a minor user. She only had a tiny little bit of it."

"I hadn't supposed four rocks is a 'tiny little bit,'" said Khoury sarcastically.

"What makes you think she had four rocks?" Columbo asked.

"You told me."

"No, sir. I didn't tell you we found crack in her handbag, and I sure didn't tell you there were four rocks. There *were* four rocks, but I was very careful not to tell you."

"Well, one of your men told me."

"No, sir. Sergeant Mulhaney found the four rocks. He showed them to Sergeant Jackson and to me. I ordered them not to mention the crack to anybody but Captain Sczciegel, and they didn't."

Khoury glared at Columbo, his face turning red.

"You know there were four rocks, sir, because you put them in Mrs. Khoury's handbag. You put them there after she was dead. That handbag was the one she had carried that day; it had her billfold and car keys in it. If you had put the four rocks of crack, wrapped in a handkerchief, in her handbag while she was alive, she would have found it when she opened the bag for her car keys or for some money."

"Fanciful . . ." Khoury muttered uncertainly.

"An investigative technique," said Columbo. "Sometimes we withhold a piece of information, to see if somebody will mention it. We didn't tell the news media or anyone else about the four rocks of crack. You knew about them because you put them there. It's the only way you could have known."

Kim dropped her chin to her chest and groaned. She began to shake with sobs.

Khoury watched. "She'll break," he said quietly. "She'll confess."

"And you?" asked Columbo.

Yussef Khoury shrugged. He stared down disconsolately at his handcuffs and chain. "What's the difference?" he whispered. "I might as well."

Ben Willsberger looked confused, as if he were unsure if he should offer his sympathy to Khoury, or should condemn and shun him, or should applaud Columbo for having solved the mystery. He did none of these. Instead, he said to Columbo, "It is really unbelievable."

"What?" Columbo asked. "You mean unbelievable that those two could have murdered three people?"

"Well, that, yes. But it's unbelievable too that they could have been so stupid. With all due respect to you, Lieutenant, Joe and Kim weren't very smart."

"Well, sir, I look at it different. I'd say they were *too* smart. If they hadn't been so clever making false clues and giving false leads, they might've got away with it. If they wanted the police to believe Puss Dogood did it, they should have left *us* a little work to do to figure it out."

A guilty plea is not allowed when the charge is murder in the first degree. Yussef Khoury and Kimberly Dana were tried as they requested—without a jury, before a judge, in the Superior Court of the State of California in and for the County of Los Angeles. They offered only a perfunctory defense and pleaded for mercy.

Khoury claimed that he had never wanted to murder his wife but had been bewitched by Kim, who was so beguilingly beautiful that he had loved her to the point of insanity. She claimed that he had been planning for months to kill his wife because the threat of divorce would have been financially disastrous for him and that she had helped him commit the crime only because she was deeply in love with him. Both claimed they had never intended to kill Heck but had felt compelled to do it, because he was there and was a witness. Similarly they had never dreamed of harming Sergio Flores.

The judge found both guilty of murder in the first degree and sentenced them to imprisonment for twenty-five years to life on each of the three counts. Under California law, they will be eligible for their first parole hearing in the year 2001. Considering the circumstances of the crimes, they are likely to be "flopped," as convict terminology is, and to remain in prison at least until 2019.

Cathy Murphy/Puss Dogood and her two friends were released from jail ten days after state police returned them from Nevada. Jenny Schmidt—Kid—disappeared and is believed to have gone back to Wisconsin, her original home. Bum Rapp is in prison again, serving a long sentence for wounding the attendant while robbing a gas station. Puss Dogood remained free for eighteen weeks after she was released and was then arrested while burglarizing a home in Santa Monica. She is back in Fontera, serving what will likely be for her a life term.

In the women's prison, Puss is shunned by the other Manson girls who are still there. They want no identification with her. She could care less. She believes she is just about the only one of Charlie's followers who remains wholly loyal and will be freed by him when he chooses the time. She is confident and patient.

Puss Dogood and Kim Dana have become close friends. Kim has made a difficult, painful adjustment to prison life. When Puss arrived, the staff psychologist asked her if she didn't know Kimberly Dana. Puss said she did, and the psychologist asked her if she would be willing to be housed with Kim, to see if she could help her. After all, the psychologist said, you've had a lot of experience with confinement. Puss—smiling inwardly at the irony—agreed to try to help Kim, so they are housed together, and Puss has been able to help Kim cope. Kim still weeps often, but Puss's sympathy has helped her.

Puss works on the groundskeeping crew, mowing

grass, working in flower beds, trimming shrubbery. Kim works on the interior maintenance crew, cleaning, sweeping, mopping, and so on, and plays first base on the prison softball team.

Yussef Khoury sorts laundry at Folsom Prison. He remains listless and spends much of his time just lying on his cot staring at the ceiling. He has never met Charles Manson, though he is aware that Manson is in the same prison. Manson is kept in a special unit for difficult cases, where Khoury can hope he will never go.

He is aware that his children have sold Khoury's to a department-store chain, which has already radically changed the nature of the store.

Melissa Mead and Patricia Finch—Boobs and Squatty—have opened a boutique, with assistance from their Connecticut families, where they sell herbs and spices, health foods and juices, and such items as handwoven sweaters and skirts and hand-made shoes. Openly lovers, they also stock and distribute pamphlets and booklets on the gay and lesbian lifestyle and on their rights.

The film Kim was to have starred in, about the *Playboy* playmate who was disabled in an accident, is being produced, starring Willa Wood.

Having served the police apprenticeship required by the federal program that made him a detective, Tim Mulhaney could have opted out and returned to school to study law, his first career choice. He chose to stay with the Department and study law at night.

Asked if he would ever retire, Columbo frowned and asked why a man would ever give up the work he loved.

THE BEST OF FORGE

☐ 53441-7   CAT ON A BLUE MONDAY $4.99
            Carole Nelson Douglas   Canada $5.99

☐ 53538-3   CITY OF WIDOWS $4.99
            Loren Estleman   Canada $5.99

☐ 51092-5   THE CUTTING HOURS $4.99
            Julia Grice   Canada $5.99

☐ 55043-9   FALSE PROMISES $5.99
            Ralph Arnote   Canada $6.99

☐ 52074-2   GRASS KINGDOM $5.99
            Jory Sherman   Canada $6.99

☐ 51703-2   IRENE'S LAST WALTZ $4.99
            Carole Nelson Douglas   Canada $5.99

Buy them at your local bookstore or use this handy coupon:
Clip and mail this page with your order.

Publishers Book and Audio Mailing Service
P.O. Box 120159, Staten Island, NY 10312-0004

Please send me the book(s) I have checked above. I am enclosing $ _____
(Please add $1.50 for the first book, and $.50 for each additional book to cover postage and
handling. Send check or money order only — no CODs.)

Name _____

Address _____

City _____ State / Zip _____

Please allow six weeks for delivery. Prices subject to change without notice.

THE BEST OF FORGE

☐ 55052-8   **LITERARY REFLECTIONS** $5.99
               James Michener   Canada $6.99

☐ 52046-7   **A MEMBER OF THE FAMILY** $5.99
               Nick Vasile   Canada $6.99

☐ 55056-0   **MY UNFORGETTABLE** $4.99
               SEASON—1970
               Red Holzman   Canada $5.99

☐ 58193-8   **PATH OF THE SUN** $4.99
               Al Dempsey   Canada $5.99

☐ 51380-0   **WHEN SHE WAS BAD** $5.99
               Ron Faust   Canada $6.99

☐ 52145-5   **ZERO COUPON** $5.99
               Paul Erdman   Canada $6.99

Buy them at your local bookstore or use this handy coupon:
Clip and mail this page with your order.

Publishers Book and Audio Mailing Service
P.O. Box 120159, Staten Island, NY 10312-0004

Please send me the book(s) I have checked above. I am enclosing $ _____
(Please add $1.50 for the first book, and $.50 for each additional book to cover postage and handling. Send check or money order only— no CODs.)

Name _____

Address _____

City _____ State / Zip _____

Please allow six weeks for delivery. Prices subject to change without notice.